About the Author

Shelby has enjoyed a career teaching art and English in the public schools. Working in the classroom has allowed her to help students acquire her love for English and art, while building lifelong relationships and memories with the kids shuffling in and out of her room, not to mention her heart. Her students' spontaneity and innate creativity made each day a once-in-a-lifetime experience. She lives on a small lake in Southern Minnesota. When she's not writing, she's traveling with her husband; on the tennis court; or playing pickleball.

Trail of Evidence
A Sam Rogers Mystery

Shelby E. Phillips

Trail of Evidence
A Sam Rogers Mystery

Vanguard Press

VANGUARD PAPERBACK

© Copyright 2024
Shelby E. Phillips

The right of Shelby E. Phillips to be identified as author of this work has been asserted by her in accordance with the Copyright, Designs and Patents Act 1988.

All Rights Reserved

No reproduction, copy or transmission of this publication may be made without written permission.
No paragraph of this publication may be reproduced, copied or transmitted save with the written permission of the publisher, or in accordance with the provisions of the Copyright Act 1956 (as amended).

Any person who commits any unauthorised act in relation to this publication may be liable to criminal prosecution and civil claims for damages.

A CIP catalogue record for this title is available from the British Library.

ISBN 978 1 83794 098 1

This is a work of fiction. Names, characters, businesses, places, events and incidents are either the product of the author's imagination or are used in a fictitious manner. Any resemblance to actual persons, living or dead, or actual events is purely coincidental.

Vanguard Press is an imprint of
Pegasus Elliot Mackenzie Publishers Ltd.
www.pegasuspublishers.com

First Published in 2024

Vanguard Press
Sheraton House Castle Park
Cambridge England

Printed & Bound in Great Britain

To Ron.
You are by far my biggest fan, my best friend, and of course, the love of my life. Thank you for all the reads and re-reads of this book. It is unfortunate that every fiction writer doesn't have a 'plotmaster' like you! Your love and support are immeasurable.

And Scott.
Thank you for allowing me to call upon your expertise in basketball. You helped make the kids' pickup game come alive and allowed Paige to exemplify today's female athletes. You are a great brother and friend!

Cover design based on the artwork provided by Shelby E. Phillips

Contents

CHAPTER ONE 13
Somethin' Evil's Goin' Down ....
CHAPTER TWO 20
The Big House ....
CHAPTER THREE 24
It's Going to be a Long Year ....
CHAPTER FOUR 32
Living on Borrowed Time ....
CHAPTER FIVE 39
Like a Bug Under a Microscope ....
CHAPTER SIX 44
The Guy in the Mirror ....
CHAPTER SEVEN 48
Rejected by a Girl ....
CHAPTER EIGHT 55
Thirty-seven Dollars and Ninety-five Cents ....
CHAPTER NINE 61
The Stats Man ....
CHAPTER TEN 69
A Circus on Wheels ....
CHAPTER ELEVEN 76
A Planned Escape ....
CHAPTER TWELVE 85
Time's Up ....
CHAPTER THIRTEEN 91

Safe at Last ....
CHAPTER FOURTEEN 99
Chef Pierre...
CHAPTER FIFTEEN 103
Ajoey ....
CHAPTER SIXTEEN 112
An Unfinished Cup of Coffee....................................
CHAPTER SEVENTEEN... 122
Gertrude Rockelstadt..
CHAPTER EIGHTEEN 131
The Zipper...
CHAPTER NINETEEN 140
Another Double Eagle ....
CHAPTER TWENTY 149
A Gold 'Demallion'...
CHAPTER TWENTY-ONE 153
Cracked Goggles ....
CHAPTER TWENTY-TWO 162
Black Waters..
CHAPTER TWENTY-THREE 172
File That Under Never..
CHAPTER TWENTY-FOUR 180
When Your Life Goes Up In Smoke..........................
CHAPTER TWENTY-FIVE 191
The Crystal Ball ....
CHAPTER TWENTY-SIX.. 199
It's Not Easy Catching an Elephant...........................
CHAPTER TWENTY-SEVEN 205
From Bad to Worse..

CHAPTER TWENTY-EIGHT 215
Not Again ....
CHAPTER TWENTY-NINE 221
Copy That ....
CHAPTER THIRTY 225
A Step into the Unknown ....
CHAPTER THIRTY-ONE 232
The Click of a Safety ....
CHAPTER THIRTY-TWO 238
The Closet Door ....
CHAPTER THIRTY-THREE 244
A Loose Screw ....
CHAPTER THIRTY-FOUR 250
Eyes of a Monster ....
CHAPTER THIRTY-FIVE 256
A Cheap Fiddle ....
CHAPTER THIRTY-SIX 263
The Big Dipper ....
CHAPTER THIRTY-SEVEN 267
Over and Out ....
CHAPTER THIRTY-EIGHT 270
S-S-S-T-T-T-O-O-O-P-P-P ....
CHAPTER THIRTY-NINE 278
They Always Come Back ....
CHAPTER FORTY 282
A Lifeline to Safety ....
CHAPTER FORTY-ONE 290
A Shifty Devil's Double-cross ....

CHAPTER ONE

Somethin' Evil's Goin' Down

His head was pounding, and the constant drip, drip, drip from the kitchen faucet was grinding on his nerves. Each drop grew louder until it sounded like one bomb exploding after another.

"I gotta get a cigarette." Victor pushed the table away with more effort than he intended. It flipped on its side and slid in front of the door. He kicked the table out of his way and left the abandoned house.

He knew he couldn't take the van into town. There had been articles online and dozens more in the local paper about a dark van parked outside the bakery when the Decker kid went missing. It was too risky. That left two choices: walk or hitchhike. Considering the three-mile hike into town, the first choice wasn't even a possibility.

He stuck out his thumb, hoping some compassionate do-gooder would give him a ride. A blue 1998 Chevy pickup finally slowed to a stop. There was more rust on it than paint, and the gruff, gray-haired man driving was having trouble rolling down the passenger window. "Need a ride, son?" he finally asked after opening the passenger door.

Victor climbed in the cab with no response.

The old man put the truck back in gear and headed down the road. "Where you from?"

"Here and there. How 'bout you?" Victor had become the master of the unanswered question. He enjoyed answering one question with another, hoping to see if he could get through an entire conversation without revealing anything about himself.

The driver smiled. "Lived here my whole life, and wouldn't live anywhere else. Just finished up thirty years with the Esterville police department. My final stop was chief of police. Finally have some time to spend with the family now. You have relatives around here?" the retired police chief asked.

"Nah…" Victor choked on his own words. Someone finally gives him a ride into town, and the guy ends up being a thirty-year veteran with the Esterville police. The Chief of Police no less. He cleared his throat and tried to finish his sentence. "Just passin' through." Victor needed some air. He cranked on the window. It rolled down with ease for Victor. The fresh air felt good.

"Haven't been able to get that window down for months. You must have the magic touch."

Oh yeah, that's me, he thought, *I'm the guy with the magic touch.* Victor tried to think of something to say, but he couldn't. He was too busy covering up the eight ball he had tattooed on his left forearm. It was the last thing the cop needed to see. He tugged on his sleeve, hoping the driver hadn't noticed.

He had it etched into his arm the week he landed in prison for his third drunk-driving arrest, thinking it might break his streak of bad luck. A con drew it with the same blue ink all the inmates used.

During his six months in prison, the tattoo helped him fit in with the rest of the prisoners. And adding a teardrop to the eight ball was a nice touch, but now, only two days after his release from prison, he knew it was a mistake. Victor shook his head. Any cop with half a brain would recognize a prison tattoo.

The driver was a huge man. Slouched over the steering wheel, his head still brushed the top of the cab. The old man's legs were spread to either side to keep them from hitting the steering wheel. His massive hands covered the top third of the wheel and were easily twice the size of his passenger's.

The gray-haired man turned on the radio to a Country station and waited to see if his passenger had more to say. He didn't. Turning up the volume, the driver started singing to 'Somethin' Evil's Goin' Down'. It was one of his favorites.

Victor rolled his eyes at the sticker on the glove compartment: 'If you don't like Country, you don't like music!' *Really? I'm sitting in a truck with some old cop, and the voice blaring from the radio is warning me that somethin' evil's goin' down. You've got to be kidding.* He rubbed his face and stared out the window, hoping to see anything that would take his mind off the situation.

The truck finally pulled into town and came to a halt at the first stop sign. "Here we are: the thriving little metropolis of Esterville. The drive into town is pretty quick when the traffic is light," the chief commented with a grin.

"I'll get out here, Mister. Thanks." Victor slid off the seat and closed the door. He started walking to the side of the road, but he could still feel the old coot staring at him.

He stepped up on the sidewalk, pretending not to notice that the truck was still sitting at the stop sign. *What's a guy gotta do to be left alone around here?*

Victor looked over his shoulder to see why the gray-haired man hadn't driven away. "Need directions, son?" the driver asked with a smile.

Victor's shoulders slumped with relief. "No thanks, I'll be okay."

The man turned up the Country music and waved goodbye.

Might as well be one of the prison guards stalking me, Victor thought as he watched the truck roll down the street.

The sign hanging over the store where he was standing read: Decker's Groceries.

"Huh. Now there's a coincidence. That was the punk's name who stole my coins," Victor muttered. "How many people named Decker can there be in this so-called 'thriving metropolis' anyway?" Victor grinned as he moseyed through the front door.

The cigarettes were stacked behind the checkout counter. Victor groaned. There was already a lady in line with an overflowing cart of groceries. And worse yet, the little kid with her couldn't sit still.

Victor definitely had issues with little kids. If he never saw another one, it would have been all right by him. Victor looked the other way, trying to ignore the commotion. *Is this really necessary? Can't a guy get a pack of cigarettes without suffering through all this chaos?*

Just then, the little boy pulled his hand out of his jacket pocket clutching a 1933 Double Eagle, twenty-dollar gold coin. Lady Liberty holding an olive branch and torch backed by the rays of the sun along with the date on the coin were as clear as the nose on the little kid's face. Victor gasped. *It's one of the coins from my stolen collection!*

As Victor grabbed for the coin, the little boy pulled it back and slipped it into his pocket.

"How'd you get one of my coins? Let me see," he snarled under his breath, still much louder than he had intended it to be.

The little boy's mother turned around. "Excuse me. Did you say something?"

Victor tried to smile, but his lips stuck to his teeth. Instead, he cleared his throat and coughed, until he finally thought of something to say. "It's a beautiful day. Don't you agree?"

"Oh yes it is. My boys and I just moved back to Esterville. We were lucky to have such good weather for our move."

Victor could hardly breathe. Could this be the woman who bought Decker's old house? He recalled a newspaper article he read while in prison about a woman doctor and her two sons. They had come back to Esterville to take over some retired doctor's medical practice. She and her family had bought Alex Decker's family home. This had to be her. Where else could that little kid have gotten a Double Eagle, twenty-dollar gold coin?

He seized the opportunity. "Did you and your family move close by?"

The lady was waiting for the last of her groceries to be bagged. "Actually, we bought Mr. Decker's house out on the edge of town."

As John Decker turned around to put the last of the grocery bags into the customer's cart, Victor steadied himself against the counter. The father's resemblance to his son was haunting. For a brief second he was looking into the face of the dying boy. He rubbed his forehead and closed his eyes, trying to make the image of the kid's face go away.

The man pushed the cart to the front door for his new customer. "There you go, Rose. Glad to hear your move went okay, and everything seems to be working. The wife and I loved that house, but the memories just became too much after Alex died. You let me know if anything needs fixing."

"Thank you, Mr. Decker. We will, but we are already enjoying our new home."

So this is Mister Decker, Victor thought. *A lot older than I expected. Can't believe he had a kid that young. Too bad for me he sold the house. I could have broken into that house, got my coins, and taken him with one hand tied behind my back. Oh well, a woman and a couple of kids shouldn't be any problem either.* The pain in his head began to fade. He paid for the cigarettes and left the store whistling; the three-mile hike to the abandoned house didn't seem so bad after all.

CHAPTER TWO

The Big House

Sam sat on the back porch of his new house, thinking about how quickly his life changed. It had been less than six months since his dad died, and his mom had already moved their family from Minneapolis to this tiny, little town of Esterville.

He thought about how he looked forward to shooting hoops with his dad every night after dinner, and how being coached by his dad helped him prepare for team tryouts. Sam hung his head, remembering that it was not long after his first game as starting guard that his dad got sick, and things were never the same again. Nothing would ever replace his dad's love and encouragement.

He missed his friends, his teammates, and the way things used to be. Now he had to start seventh grade in a brand-new school, with brand-new kids, and brand-new teachers, and he wished his dad was here to talk with him about all the challenges he was about to face. He knew there would be big changes when he started junior high. Each subject would have a different teacher and a different room, and trying to get to each of those rooms with only five minutes of passing time sounded almost impossible.

"How's a kid supposed to make new friends in a small-town school like this? My grade school in Minneapolis was three times that size," he grumbled as he thought about the pint-sized building. Its gloomy, gray brick exterior made it look more like a prison than a school. Every window was the same shape: long thin rectangles that prevented even the skinniest student's escape. The only things missing were the guard towers. Although he was about to enter junior high school, the challenges awaiting him didn't seem very 'junior' to him.

Sam had heard stories about how the eighth graders picked on the seventh graders all year long as part of their 'welcoming' to the big house. *Some welcome*, Sam thought. But that was his old school. Maybe these kids will be different.

As he sat trying to picture what the kids in his new school would be like, his mom pulled into the driveway. Sam walked over to the car and unbuckled Tommy's car seat. His five-year-old brother jumped out of the lime green VW jabbering about a gold coin and some kid named Alex Decker. But Sam couldn't make any sense of what he was saying.

"What's he talking about, Mom? Who is Alex Decker?"

"When I was deciding if we should buy this house, the realtor was telling me about the Decker family who lived here. They decided to sell it and move to the country after their son Alex died. Tommy must have overheard the realtor talking to me about their son's untimely death."

"How come I never heard about Alex Decker?"

Rose shrugged her shoulders and handed Sam another bag of groceries. "From what I understand, Alex went missing last spring. His friend had to run an errand to the bakery for his mom and asked Alex to go with him. Alex waited outside the bakery, and when his friend came out, Alex was gone. His bike was lying in front of the bakery, but there was no sign of Alex. He was missing three days before they found his body outside of town at the bottom of the lake."

"Wow. That's scary, and I thought Esterville was going to be a safe place to live. So they never found out what happened to Alex?"

"No. That was the last case your Grandpa Hank worked on before he retired as Chief of Police. He never did solve the case. Now here it is, six months later, and they still don't have any leads. The police have a curfew in place, Sam. They want all kids sixteen and under home every night by six-thirty."

Sam groaned. "That's even earlier than my curfew in Minneapolis, Mom."

"It's just until they find who's responsible for Alex's death. I don't think it's going to cramp your style too much, big guy."

Sam rolled his eyes and smiled at his mom.

"Maybe we should finish this conversation later, Sam, so you can get ready for your first day of school tomorrow."

Sam nodded. "I guess so. Looks like the big day is finally here."

As Sam turned to head for his room, he ran right into Tommy lying on the kitchen floor, playing with a large round medallion.

"Hey, Squirt, did you get another Super Medal from the Pizza Villa last night?" Sam asked.

"No. Alex Decker gave this one to me," Tommy replied.

But Sam didn't hear a word Tommy said. He was already halfway up the stairs, thinking about what a new kid should wear on the first day of school.

CHAPTER THREE

It's Going to be a Long Year

Sam overslept and was late to his first hour class. He hoped school had started late, so he could sneak into class unnoticed and find a seat near the door. No such luck.

The door was in the front of the classroom, the teacher was in mid-sentence, and the only available seats were in the far side of the room by the window. Sam brushed his wavy, brown hair off his face as he made his way to an empty desk and sat down. Right away, two boys in the back of the room started razzing the late student.

"Did you get lost in the big house, Newbie?"

"Were those big eighth graders picking on you?"

Snickering soon turned to laughter when his new English teacher, Miss Thompson, addressed him by his full name, "Samuel Rogers, is that you?"

Sam's face turned beet red as he sank into his chair. Much to his surprise, the laughter abruptly quieted to a murmur as Miss Thompson slowly walked down the middle aisle of students with her whiteboard pointer in hand and a take-no-prisoners look on her face.

Addressing the loudest laughers more clearly than she had Sam, Miss Thompson asked, "Baxter Johnson and Marco Garcia, is there something you would like to share with the rest of the class? I'm sure we would all like to know what you think is so funny."

Sam turned around to give both of them 'the look', only to find each of their faces more red than his own. Baxter's short, blue, Jell-O-stained hair was cemented into perfect little spikes and only emphasized the temporary neon color of his round face. Already too big for the desk, Baxter had slouched down in his seat until his legs were tangled around the chair in front of him.

The cute red-haired girl sitting in front of Baxter watched as he pushed her books stacked neatly under her chair into the aisle with his super-sized feet. Pursing her lips and scowling, she laid into Baxter. "Now look what you did, you big oaf! You better not do that again, or you'll be sorry." She abruptly turned around, flipping her long curly hair in his face as she tried to restack the books under her chair.

Baxter smirked.

DJ, who sat two seats away from Baxter took advantage of the interruption and made his move. He wadded up his gum wrapper, rolled it around in his mouth until it was good and slimy, and stuffed it inside the barrel of an empty ballpoint pen. Blowing through the barrel of the pen as hard as he could, DJ sent the wrapper flying through the air, hitting Baxter smack in the back of the head.

"Gotcha, fatso!" DJ chuckled. He had already been suspended three times in sixth grade and had no plans of changing his behavior just because he was in junior high.

Laughter spread across the room.

By now, Baxter was relying on his biceps to prevent himself from slipping completely under his desk. When Baxter slumped down in the little seventh grade desk, he looked like a gangly giant. His limbs spread out beyond his desk in every direction.

Baxter's size worked in his favor in the hall or on the basketball court. There he lorded over his classmates at six-foot-one and almost two hundred pounds. Every high school coach was already watching his progress, but squashed into a little junior high desk made it apparent to everyone how out of place he was.

Still locked in Miss Thompson's stare, Baxter didn't dare look to see who hit him. He was familiar with DJ's handiwork and there would be time to deal with him later.

Miss Thompson, on the other hand, wasn't so patient. She spun around, searching for the culprit. Zeroing in on DJ, she waited, hoping for a sign, but DJ had already slid the empty ballpoint pen into his thick, shoulder-length dreadlocks, preventing any chance of Miss Thompson finding the weapon. DJ resumed his strict military pose: eyes forward and shoulders back.

The rest of the class sat silently, trying to avoid Miss Thompson's stare as she walked to the front of the room. It was going to be a long year.

Baxter's head and shoulders went down. He hated Miss Thompson for picking on him the first day of school. He had been getting in trouble as long as he could remember. If teachers weren't watching him, kids were tattling on him. Using his size and physical strength as a defense had become his way to even the score. Intimidation and retaliation became second nature to him. *Looks like this year isn't going to be any different than the rest of them*, Baxter thought.

"All right, Class," Miss Thompson began, "let's take your grammar book out and turn to page twenty-four. I want you to review adverb clauses and have Exercise A completed for class tomorrow. I will be at my desk if you have any questions."

As Sam reached for his grammar book, his pencil fell to the floor. Before he could bend over and grab it, the boy sitting across the aisle from him picked it up and put it back on Sam's desk.

After opening his book, Sam turned to thank the boy for picking up his pencil, but the seat next to him where the boy sat was empty. No books, no pencils, and no boy. Sam's mouth dropped open. He turned to the girl sitting behind the empty desk. "Where did that boy sitting in front of you go?"

A look of bewilderment crossed her face. "No one was sitting there," she whispered.

"Yeah there was. He just picked up my pencil off the floor. A freckle-faced kid with a blond-haired butch, braces, and a big smile."

The little girl was speechless, and drew in a long breath of air before she spoke. "That sounds like you're describing Alex Decker… but…uh…you know..." She dropped her head before finishing her sentence. "He… well… he's not here this year."

Alex Decker! Sam stared at the empty desk. Even he knew that Alex Decker couldn't have been sitting in the seat next to him. He looked at the pencil lying on his desk and was certain it had fallen to the floor; and even more certain that he wasn't the one who picked it up.

Miss Thompson stood up from her desk as the bell rang dismissing class. "Don't forget to bring your grammar books tomorrow, Class, and Sam Rogers, I hope to see you here on time."

"Yes, Miss Thompson." Sam picked up his books and headed for the door.

As the kids filtered out of class, Sam waited for Baxter and Marco in the hall. He didn't appreciate the two of them making fun of him when he walked into class.

"What do you think you're looking at?" Baxter asked as he moved his chest to within inches of Sam's nose.

"You. Ya big hyena," Sam replied. "What's it to ya?"

No one had ever dared stand up to Baxter before. He was going to have to show this new kid who was boss.

Outweighing Sam by at least sixty pounds, Baxter shoved his fingers into Sam's shoulder, knocking him to the ground with little effort. Before Sam could recover, Baxter planted one of his new black, size thirteen Adidas squarely on Sam's chest, forcing the last breath of air from his lungs.

I thought Big Foot was just a myth, but now I'm beginning to wonder, Sam thought as he gulped for air. If this overgrown bully was going to level him, at least he would go down fighting. "You're just a bully who likes picking on everyone," Sam growled as he tried pushing Baxter's foot off his chest.

Baxter stopped and a change came over him. *Is that how kids see me? Just some bully who goes around picking on everyone*, Baxter thought. *Now here I am again. The first day of school and I already have some new kid I don't even know, pinned to the ground trying to humiliate him.*

He had taken more than his share of beatings, some he would never forget. That didn't mean he had to hurt someone else. *I have to stop bullying people.* Baxter fought back the tears; every gulp of air he took hit his stomach like a rock. His breathing became erratic. He couldn't speak.

Sam had seen that look before on the people's faces at his dad's funeral. The overgrown bully was crushing him, but Sam still felt sorry for him.

Marco had been quietly watching the whole situation. "Are you all right, Bax?"

"I'm just not doing this anymore," Baxter choked. "I'm done picking on people."

"Well then, let's go. You're hurting the poor kid. I don't think he's afraid of you anyway."

Marco and Baxter had been friends since second grade. No one ever stood up to Baxter before, even if this kid was standing up to him lying flat on his back. In the past, Baxter had successfully used his boisterous personality to remind his classmates of his size and physical strength. In this case he didn't think Sam had even noticed.

"Who asked your opinion, Marco?" Sam retorted from somewhere underneath Baxter's enormous foot.

Marco let out one of his big belly laughs. "I guess nobody, but it looks like you could use some help, Sam." Over the years Marco had watched Baxter get into dozens of scuffles. It had become difficult for Marco to take any of them too seriously, but watching this new kid in action was pretty funny.

"Yeah. Well, let's see you take on Sasquatch when he's grinding his foot into your chest," Sam snapped back.

At this point all three of them began to laugh. Baxter offered Sam a hand and pulled him to his feet, as if to say, 'Okay, tough guy, you talked your way out of this one. You're one of the guys now.'

Marco was impressed with the new kid. He had a lot of courage and wasn't afraid to take on anything. "How did you become so fearless, Sam? You must get into a lot of fights."

Brushing Baxter's footprint off his chest, Sam stood up as straight as possible, trying to find the extra inches that would stretch his medium build to Marco and Baxter's height. "I just moved to this hole-in-the-wall from

Minneapolis," using the lowest, deepest voice he could find.

His new arch-rivals didn't seem too impressed, so Sam straightened his shoulders even more and sneered. "The kids there call it 'Murder-apolis.'. And they are a lot nastier than you, Baxter. Anyway, you don't scare me."

Baxter patted him on the back. "Enough with the attitude, Sam. We won't pick on you anymore."

There is something special about this new kid, Marco thought. *He never gives up.* "What class do you have next, Sam?"

"I have math with Mr. Spellmore."

"We have him too, but the kids call him Mr. Smell More. I heard he gives you an hour of detention if you are even a second late to his class," announced Baxter.

"Yeah," Marco agreed. "The kids say that he has a sign hanging under his clock that says: 'Time passes. Will you?' He makes you read it out loud if he even catches you looking at the clock."

"My brother says he shuts the door and locks you out of the room if you don't get to class on time, and he doesn't open it till he's given a pop quiz with no makeups till after school."

The three of them started sprinting to their second hour math class. None of them wanted to get locked out or have detention on the first day of school.

CHAPTER FOUR

Living on Borrowed Time

Victor's van was about as much good as a horse with a broken leg. There were posters about Alex Decker hanging all over town asking if anyone had seen the black van reportedly used in the abduction.

An internet site was posted at the bottom of the poster and a phone number to call with any additional information. The death of Alex Decker had put Esterville on the map. Victor knew that driving the van around Esterville would be like having a bumper sticker that says: 'Here I am. I'm the guy who kidnapped Alex Decker.' So he walked everywhere.

But walking was getting old. No one picked him up hitchhiking this morning, and the three-mile hike into town felt like ten. His feet felt like lead weights.

He had spent hours trying to find the house where Alex Decker once lived. It wasn't until Victor noticed a phone booth outside the hardware store with a tattered phonebook hanging from a rusty chain inside the booth that his luck changed. Victor squeezed into the booth, opened up the phonebook to the letter D, and ran his finger down the page. Sure enough, there it was: 'John L. Decker, 413 Horace Avenue NE.' Looking back, it was an ingenious move on his part.

The new information gave him a glimmer of hope and a spring in his step. Before he knew it, he was three blocks from the hardware store, looking up at a blue street sign that read 'Horace Avenue'.

As he walked down Horace Avenue he grumbled, "Now, if I could just find 413, I could get the coins and rid myself of this hick town." He took off his boot and shook out another stone. "If that kid hadn't stolen my coins, I'd be in Vegas right now, living like royalty. I'd be driving a red Tesla, and I'd be King of the Road. Instead, all I've got is this king-size hole in the only pair of boots I own."

Out of sheer frustration, Victor threw the stone at a light post. It hit the post and ricocheted back at him. As he ducked out of the way, the stone flew by his head, hitting one of the black cast-iron numbers nailed to a white picket fence. The black numbers read 413. "Well, if Decker's old house was any closer, I guess it would jump out and bite me," Victor snickered. "Vegas, here I come!"

Even Victor could see Alex's death had taken a toll on the place. The number three was hanging by a single nail and would surely fall to the ground with the next gust of wind. The house itself was not in much better shape. Full-grown hemlock trees shaded the older, two-story home that was badly in need of a new coat of paint. A flower trellis attached to the side of the house stood barren, and the lilac bushes that grew in the unmowed yard were desperately in need of a trim.

Camouflaging himself behind one of the overgrown lilac bushes, Victor nodded his head and smiled. "Case this joint, break in, get my coins back, and blow this pop stand before anyone knows I was here." As Victor planned his move, Sam walked through the front door and onto the porch. Victor spread the limbs of the lilac bush apart and peered through the leaves.

"I'm shooting hoops with Marco and Baxter after school, Mom. I'll be home in time for dinner."

Rose stepped onto the porch. "Don't forget the curfew, Sam. I want you to abide by it until the Decker case is solved."

Sam slung his backpack over his shoulder before he began to speak. "Mom, I had a dream about Alex Decker last night, and it was so real. He was standing right next to my bed; like I could have reached out and touched him. He told me something bad was going to happen."

"How would you even know what Alex looked like, Sam?"

"Oh. I guess one of the girls at school was talking about him." Sam didn't dare say, "Because for a second I thought I saw him sitting right next to me in English class!"

Rose put her arm around her son's shoulder. "The Decker case has the whole town worked up; kids your age shouldn't have to worry about things like this. Hopefully, they will find who killed Alex, and life will get back to normal in Esterville." Rose brushed Sam's wavy, brown hair off his collar. "And maybe when things start to settle down around here, you will have time to get a haircut."

Sam laughed as he ran his fingers through his hair.

Rose studied her son's face. "You look so much like your father: his green eyes, and that mischievous grin of yours. I always knew he was up to something when he smiled like that. You're no little boy, Sam. Lifting those weights is paying off."

Sam flexed his bicep and they both began to laugh.

"Seriously, Mom, I miss Dad."

"I miss your father too, Sam. But I am thankful every day that I have you two boys."

Victor stiffened as he listened to their conversation. "Looks like that kid gets along just fine without a dad. As long as his mom is willing to take a few seconds from her own problems to focus on her kid," he mumbled to himself as he watched Rose give Sam a hug and kiss him on the forehead.

From the moment Victor's abusive father walked out on his family, his life only seemed to get worse. His mother had to get a job at the mill, working long hours for little pay. That left him in charge of his kid sister, and he missed countless days of school babysitting her.

The endless line of men his mother brought home was nauseating. None of them were ever interested in Victor. He moved out of the house when he was sixteen and never looked back. Seeing Sam and his mom together painfully reminded Victor one more time that his childhood should have been better.

No sooner had Sam climbed on his bike and pedaled down the street, when the front screen door flew open again. The little boy he had seen at the grocery store with one of his 1933 Double Eagles was running into the front yard and straight toward Victor.

Victor dropped to his knees, hoping his cover wasn't blown. He spread the branches apart to watch the boy kick a soccer ball that had been lying about ten feet in front of Victor to an imaginary teammate across the yard. The kid ran after the ball, stopped it with his foot, and kicked it between two hemlock trees for a goal. Tommy jumped up and down, cheering.

Victor's shoulders slumped with relief. But the kid was on the move again, using short, controlled taps, dribbling the ball right toward Victor. Trapping the ball with his left foot, he shot the ball straight into the lilac bush only inches above Victor's head.

When Tommy ran to get the ball, there was Victor crawling to his feet. The little boy stopped dead in his tracks; his eyes locked with Victor's. "You're the man at the gro-cer-y store," Tommy gulped. "The one who tried to take my coin." His words were barely audible.

Victor took a deep breath. He smiled until all of his smoke-stained teeth and most of his gums were showing. "Well, little guy, that's why I'm here. I'm looking for those coins."

Tommy backed away from Victor, getting ready to make a run for the house. "Alex told me some guy would come looing for them."

It was obvious the kid had trouble pronouncing his words, but Victor swore he heard him say something about Alex. Victor bent over and leaned closer to the kid. He stunk like cigarettes. "Who told you someone would be back looking for them?"

Tommy cringed and held his breath, trying to escape the smell. He finally spoke. "You know, Mis-ter. Alex Decker. He knew you'd be back for the coins."

A shiver ran through Victor's body. Alex Decker was dead, and nobody knew that better than Victor. "I don't think Alex Decker told you anything, sonny. Now where can I find those coins?"

Tommy took another step back and grabbed onto a branch of the lilac bush, pulling it between himself and Victor. The soccer ball fell from the bush and hit the ground. "Sorry, Mis-ter. Alex wouldn't tell me where he put them."

A woman's voice echoed from the back porch. "Tommy, where are you? It's time for us to go."

Tommy looked over his shoulder at his mother. "My mom's call-ing me. I gotta go."

"You tell anyone you saw me here..." Victor started coughing mid-sentence until he thought his lungs were going to burst. Still choking, Victor tried to finish his sentence. "And you're going to be... dead meat... kid."

As Victor reached out to grab him, the little boy took off, running toward the house.

"There you are, Tommy. I've been calling you. Let's get in the car and buckle up." His mother reached down and took the little boy's hand.

Victor froze, waiting to see if the kid was going to tell his mother about the man standing in the lilac bushes. He let out a long, slow breath as the engine of the lime green Volkswagen turned over and the car backed out of the driveway. "Well, isn't that perfect timing? Looks like the house is empty. Guess I'll go inside and check things out; maybe I'll get lucky and find those coins." Victor kicked the soccer ball out of his way and headed for the back door.

CHAPTER FIVE

Like a Bug Under a Microscope

Baxter froze. *Not again,* he thought. *That old bag's always watchin' me. You'd think after a whole week she would have found someone new to pick on.* Baxter hated this small, crowded classroom. Thirty-five kids crammed into a hot, stuffy room. He couldn't even see out the window. Trying to stretch his legs, Baxter pushed his chair back. Unfortunately, he pushed the desk behind him back, too.

The kid sitting behind him was Nick Bronson, the school loner. He had been held back in school a few times and was at least two years older than the rest of his class. Even the teachers left him alone. Nick could see Miss Thompson staring at him from across the room, so retaliation was out of the question right now, but Baxter was going to pay.

Nick's greasy hair hung in his face as he leaned forward, acting like he was looking over his assignment, but really he was making sure Baxter would hear what he was about to say. Every word. Loud and clear. "Don't think you got away with anything, Baxter. There will be time for your teachable moment later."

Baxter rolled his eyes. *Looks like not fighting anymore is going to be harder than I thought.*

Now Miss Thompson was on his case. "Baxter, I hope you and Nick have finished your assignment, or the two of you will be working on it with me at three o'clock today."

Nick Bronson was breathing down his neck to the rear and Miss Thompson was on the attack out in front. Baxter was cornered.

Without warning, Marco came to Baxter's rescue. "Kids are still talking about Alex Decker's kidnapping and death, Miss Thompson. When are they going to find out what happened to him?"

Miss Thompson was now standing right next to Baxter. Tapping her whiteboard pointer in the palm of her hand, she asked, "Is Marco right, Baxter? Were you and Nick talking about Alex Decker?"

Trying to escape the old maid's question, Baxter slumped farther down in his chair and began fiddling with his pencil. Baxter could feel the whole class staring at him; beads of sweat were forming on his forehead.

Sam turned around to watch Miss Thompson interrogate his friends. While Baxter looked like he was going to be physically sick, Marco appeared unfazed. Sam laughed to himself as he watched Marco smile at Miss Thompson. *I bet he thinks he has Miss Thompson wrapped around his finger.* He marveled at Marco's charisma and his ability to stay cool in any situation. *Nothing ever bothers that guy,* Sam thought.

Just as Miss Thompson turned to walk back to her desk, Baxter broke his silence. "It's just so weird that Alex isn't here this year. And I'm not the only one who thinks that. Kids talk about Alex all the time. He would have been one of the starting forwards on our basketball team this year."

The rest of the class was chaotically agreeing with Baxter.

"The worst part is we don't know what happened to him," someone blurted from across the room.

"It's not possible to find his bike in front of the bakery downtown and his body at the bottom of the lake out by the old railroad bridge!" someone else hollered.

"And without a clue of how he got there!"

Their pent-up fear exploded. Everyone was talking at once about the kidnapping and death of Alex Decker.

"Alex was supposedly waiting for Nate to come out of the bakery."

"Yeah! Why would he just up and leave without his bike?"

"And walk out to the lake by himself? It makes no sense!"

"What if the person who kidnapped Alex is still around here?"

"This town just isn't safe anymore!"

"Any one of us could be next!"

The long summer had only made the tragedy worse. Losing Alex was just the beginning. Every kid in Esterville was being watched like a bug under a microscope. They couldn't make a move without their parents asking them where they were going, who they were going with, and what time they would be home. And even after all that, they were lucky if their parents let them go. A kid's social life in Esterville was pretty grim.

Miss Thompson tapped her trusty whiteboard pointer on her desk to quiet them down.

"Settle down, class! It's not easy for any of us to lose someone. We all miss Alex. I am confident that they will find out what happened to him, and the person who did it will be caught. In the meantime, I am also confident that you are going to learn the difference between adjectives and adverbs."

The class groaned.

At that moment, Esterville's Junior High School Principal Mr. Nordinsky walked into their classroom with a new student. "Class, this is Penelope Paigenot. She comes to Esterville all the way from Arizona. I understand her last name is pronounced 'Paj-a-know'."

Sam studied every detail of the new student as Mr. Nordinsky spoke. Penelope's blonde ponytail hung down to the middle of her Phoenix Suns hoodie which was cropped at the waist. Her camouflaged pants were ripped at the knee, and most amazingly of all, she was wearing the black and white Nike high tops that Sam had been bugging his mother to buy him since summer began.

The Phoenix Suns had been Sam's favorite basketball team since he was a little kid. He wondered if Penelope had actually gone to a Phoenix Suns game, or was she just another girl who didn't have a clue about basketball? It didn't matter. What were the chances he'd ever get to know the new girl anyway?

Penelope smiled at Sam as she walked to her seat, but he never noticed. At least, he didn't want her to think he had noticed. Sam never really had time for girls, and he wasn't ready to make any exceptions for this one, at least not yet.

CHAPTER SIX

The Guy in the Mirror

Victor had to hurry. He figured the older kid was at school, but there was no way of knowing when his mom and the younger boy would be back.

"Those coins could be anywhere in this house. Where am I supposed to start?" Deciding on the kids' bedrooms, he rounded the banister, taking the stairs two at a time.

The first bedroom on the right was decorated in pink and gray. Frilly pillows covered the bed and a white nightgown lay at the foot. Lace curtains hung from the windows. In the center of the dresser was a silver tray filled with perfume and makeup. This had to be the mother's room, and no kid would be dumb enough to hide a million dollars' worth of coins in there.

Victor continued down the hall. The second room was filled with sports equipment. A state-of-the-art computer was sitting on the desk. Victor leaned against the doorframe and marveled at all the kid's stuff. He knew he should have gotten over his own pathetic childhood years ago, but it never took much for the painful memories to resurface.

Victor began digging through Sam's room. He looked under the bed, in the closet, and rummaged through each dresser drawer, but a gold basketball medal hanging on a red, white, and blue ribbon was as close as he came to finding his Double Eagle coins.

Victor sat down at the desk, dropped his head into his hands, and rubbed his eyes. He couldn't remember the last time he had gotten a decent night's sleep. For that matter, he couldn't remember the last time he had slept in a decent bed.

Victor looked at his reflection in the mirror. His hair was a mess, and his eyes were sunken. He hadn't shaved in a week, and the growth on his face made him look at least ten years older than a man in his early thirties. He hardly recognized himself.

He picked up the photograph from Sam's desk. It was a picture of the kid he saw on the porch that morning. He was standing on a dock with a fishing pole. Some guy, probably his dad, had his arm around him. He laid the picture face down on the desk.

The sullen image he saw in the mirror was leering at him. He raised his eyebrow and sneered back. "Let's see if the little puke has something about the Double Eagles on his computer."

The word 'illiterate' didn't begin to describe Victor's computer skills. Six months in prison was the only reason he even had a clue about how to use a computer. He tapped the screen and a half-finished game of Planet Coaster appeared. "So you think you can play Planet Coaster, do ya? No one is gonna coast through this planet like I am. I'm gonna be one of the richest guys on Earth."

He clicked the X in the upper right-hand corner of the screen and then the box labeled 'Yes' when the computer asked if he was sure he wanted to end the game. "I've been sure I wanted to end this game for the last six months. It's time to get on with it."

The Planet Coaster game closed and the kid's e-mail screen appeared:

Sam,
Isn't Emily Hanson hot? I think she likes u:)
g2g
ttyl
Marco

Victor rolled his eyes. "Like I have time for Emily Hanson." He closed down the e-mail and clicked the web browser. "Wouldn't that be something if he's trying to sell my coins on E-Bay?" Before the server connected, the sound of a car engine broke his concentration. He ran to the window in time to see the lime green Volkswagen pulling into the driveway.

Victor hit the wall with his fist. "They can't be home already. I just got started. What am I supposed to do now?"

Victor looked around the room. He thought about the closet. "No. I can't be hiding in the kid's closet. I gotta get out of here." He ran from the room and down the stairs. As he turned toward the kitchen, he heard the back door swing shut.

"Mom, can I have another donut?"

"Not till you clean up your room, Tommy."

"But Mom!"

Victor stopped dead in his tracks. Images of his prison cell flashed through his mind. "I'm not going back to prison. I'm not." He wiped the sweat from his forehead and turned toward the front door at the opposite end of the hall. It was his only chance.

He ran to the front door and turned the knob. His hand slipped. He wiped his sweaty hand off on his pants and tried again. It was locked. Through the kitchen door he could hear Tommy's mom telling him to go upstairs right now and clean his room; but the little brat was holding firm about having another donut. Victor had only seconds left to escape. He fumbled with the lock again. It had to open.

He finally heard a click. Slipping through the screen door, he closed it quietly behind him. The sweat from his eyebrows dripped into his eyes as he darted to the closest lilac bush. He controlled every inch of his body, trying to remain calm and fighting the urge to look back at the house. He could only hope no one was watching him, no one was running after him, and no one was calling the police.

His first steps turned into a block, and the first block into a mile. Without warning, the three-mile trek was over, and the abandoned house, his current refuge, was a welcoming sight.

CHAPTER SEVEN

Rejected by a Girl

Marco went in for a layup. He clenched his jaw and gritted his teeth as he watched the ball bounce off the backboard onto the front of the rim. Marco swerved his hips and tilted his head, as if his trademark body English would will the ball through the hoop. The basketball was now circling the outside of the rim. His body was nearly perpendicular to the ground when the ball finally dropped through the net into Sam's hands.

"Muy bueno, Marco," Baxter yelled when he saw the ball go through the hoop.

Hearing Baxter speak Spanish still made Marco smile after all these years. He tried teaching Baxter Spanish when he moved to Esterville from Mexico in second grade. The two of them became friends right away, and Baxter wanted to learn how to speak Spanish.

It only took a few days before Marco knew teaching Baxter any foreign language was a lost cause. At first, he tried correcting Baxter's mistakes, but he soon realized there was no hope. Baxter massacred even the easiest

Spanish words. But somehow 'muy bueno' stuck with Baxter, and now all of their friends said it, too.

"Thanks, Baxter," Marco said as he re-bounded the ball. "Try that shot again, Sam. We gotta keep practicing, or we're never going to make the school team."

Esterville's basketball tryouts were less than a month away, and making the team was on the top of almost every kid's list. Sam, Marco, and Baxter were on the courts every chance they got, but the competition was never easy. There was so little to do in Esterville that basketball had become every kid's main source of entertainment. Boys and girls of all ages played, and the adults were always there to cheer them on or help coach.

Esterville was so small that each team was made up of two grades. This year, Sam and his friends would be competing for their positions against the eighth graders: Randy Bartlett and the Brainless Wonders, as Baxter called them. Randy's gang was practicing on the other end of the court, taunting Baxter about his layups. Baxter was working on shooting from his left side when his shot ricocheted off the backboard and bounced into the weeds.

"My third grade brother can shoot a layup better than that, B-a-a-a-a-xter," chided Randy as he and the other three 'Brainless Wonders' finished their game of two-on-two.

Randy had been hassling Baxter for so many years that he knew exactly how to push his buttons. He would use a flawless imitation of a baaing sheep to say 'B-a-a-a-a-xter', and it made Baxter's blood boil every time he heard it.

Marco dug the ball out of the weeds and threw it to Baxter. "Just ignore him, Baxter. It's not worth getting mad over him."

Another year older, Randy was the only kid trying out for the school team who was bigger than Baxter, and Randy never let him forget it. They had competed against each other since Baxter was in second grade. The first time they met was at Esterville's Annual Free Throw Contest.

The competition lasted all morning, one free throw swooshing the net after another. Each round brought more disappointment as classmates dropped from the contest. But it was Baxter and Randy who made it to the final round.

Baxter watched Randy's ball swoosh through the net. "Let's see if you can do that, B-a-a-a-a-xter."

Baxter stepped up to the line, bounced the ball three times, and sucked in a long breath of air. He shot. The ball spiraled through the air in a perfect arc, with perfect backspin, finally hitting the rim and the backboard before ricocheting into the stands.

Randy had won the contest.

From then on they competed against each other in everything: football, baseball, Cub Scouts, even who would be first in the lunch line. Baxter thought the competition between the two of them had been pretty even over the years, but basketball had become the true test.

Baxter couldn't ignore Randy Bartlett any longer. "Your little brother will be wearing a school uniform this year before you do, Randy."

"And my little brother is gonna look good in that uniform 'cause it's going to be yours," Bartlett shot back.

As Baxter watched Randy go in for another layup, he heard himself saying, "Check it out, Bartlett. You're way too slow for basketball. You ought to think about wrestling this winter; if they have a weight class big enough for you."

Randy wasn't going to be intimidated. "You're the one who'll end up on the wrestling team this year, B-a-a-a-a-d A-a-a-a-x! You'll be their water boy."

By now Baxter was so mad he thought he could actually feel steam coming out of his ears. "Now he's calling me Bad Ax! If I hear him do that sheep imitation one more time, I'm gonna level the jerk."

"You know he lives to see you get mad. Don't even look at him, Baxter," Marco urged.

No one was going to call Baxter off at this point. He was very proud that he still hadn't picked on anyone since he confronted Sam the first day of school. But basketball was different. On the court everyone was fair game, especially Randy Bartlett.

"Okay, Bartlett," Baxter chided, "why don't you put your money where your mouth is? Let's have a little scrimmage. First team to twenty-one will tell who's going to be wearing the school uniforms this fall." Baxter had been working out ever since his run-in with Sam. A little scrimmage would be a good way to see if his hard work was paying off. He was ready to take on Randy and the rest of the Brainless Wonders.

Upon hearing Baxter's reply, Sam and Marco's eyes locked. Randy's team was in the junior state finals last year, and if it weren't for a questionable call in the last minute of the game, they probably would have won the championship.

"In case you haven't noticed, B-a-a-a-a-x, there's four of us, and only three of you."

Things were getting so heated up that no one noticed the new girl Penelope Paigenot on the side of the court watching them.

"I'll be the fourth," Penelope said.

Silence fell on the court. Sam and Marco's eyes re-locked. Their mouths fell open. They knew this could be an embarrassment of colossal proportions. Challenging the eighth graders was about all they could handle, and now the new girl wanted to be on their team.

If there was ever a chance that Sam could disappear, this would have been the time. Yet he stood his ground between the Brainless Wonders and the new girl in school who wanted to help take them on.

"Oh, this is perfect. It can be the shirts against the skirts, or aren't you girls up for it, B-a-a-a-xter?" Randy taunted.

"We could beat you, Bartlett, no matter who was on our team," Baxter said. "And yeah, Penelope's with us."

Marco nudged Baxter. "Penelope definitely needs a nickname," he whispered under his breath. "Bartlett will have made two layups by the time I get her name out of my mouth."

"Yeah, I can hardly say Penelope," Baxter agreed as he turned to the new girl. "Okay. But we're calling you Paige. Let's go. Let's kick some butt."

Penelope had never been called 'Paige' before. But she thought it was the coolest thing ever. The only nicknames she could think of were 'Penny' or 'Nell', but those names were still too feminine. 'Paige' was perfect.

"Bring it on, girls," yelled one of the Brainless Wonders, and the game began with a flourish.

Randy threw a pass to Jimmy Smith, last year's starting point guard, who seemed to effortlessly roll around Marco and drive to the hoop for their first two points. Sam took the ball out and passed it in to Baxter. There was no one in his class faster than Marco, who was already down at the other end of the court.

Baxter threw the ball down the court, trying to hit his teammate with a pass. Randy was about to intercept it when Marco ran in front of him and caught the ball. Making a fast break around Randy, Marco shot a fifteen-footer. Two points.

Sam knew who the 'go-to' guy was now. Marco looked like he had been playing varsity for years. "I saw that move in the playoffs last year," Sam yelled.

The Brainless Wonders had the ball again, and Randy was dribbling down the court. Everyone was trying to ignore the fact that Paige was even on the court, but she was there step-for-step guarding Luke Oswald. Randy passed the ball to Luke, who went up for a jump shot, but Paige went up too, and blocked it, tipping the ball to Marco.

"Eeeyowww!" Baxter howled. "Rejected by a girl. But I'm sure your team is used to that."

Marco cackled.

Shots continued to swoosh the net, and Randy's team was now up eighteen to sixteen. Jimmy Smith had the ball, but Marco was crouched in front of him, shuffling his feet from side to side, his arms spread wide, ready to deflect any passes. Dribbling with his left hand, Jimmy tried a pick and roll with Randy. In that instant, Marco stole the ball, threw a chest pass to Sam, who landed the tying basket.

Jimmy took the ball out and passed it to Jack Porter, the forward on the state team. Jack started down the court with Sam mirroring him defensively. Jack stopped, looking for someone open on his team. Sam reached in and the ball went rolling. The scramble was on.

Baxter moved toward the ball, but it ricocheted off his foot toward Jimmy. Just as Jimmy was ready to grab it, Paige came out of nowhere, snatched the ball, and tossed it to Sam who was still outside the arc. Sam's jump shot hit the back of the rim and bounded two feet in the air. Marco and Baxter, were already celebrating as Sam's three-pointer swooshed through the net. They won the game.

CHAPTER EIGHT

Thirty-seven Dollars and Ninety-five Cents

"Hate this stinkin' town," Victor mumbled to himself. "Been here seven days and I still don't have those coins. Nothin' ever goes my way around here." Sweat broke out on his face just thinking about his narrow escape from the kid's house. "That was way too close. I was lucky to get out of there."

Victor thought for sure he would have the treasure and be long gone by now. He tried waiting for the right moment to sneak back into the house, but it never came. He staked out Sam's family twenty-four/seven, but there was always someone home. How long could he hang around Esterville before he and the van were recognized? He had to make his move.

"One thing's for sure: I'm not dragging my sorry butt three miles into town anymore," Victor grumbled. No one had picked him up hitchhiking the past two days, and the blister on his left heel was the size of a quarter. "And when I do get a ride, it ends up being the stinkin' cop in charge of the Decker case."

Victor sat down on a park bench in the Esterville Town Square and rubbed his feet, but the pain wouldn't go away. "I definitely need a set of wheels. Maybe there's something I can do to change the looks of that van."

He pulled all the money out of his pocket and counted it. "Thirty-seven dollars and ninety-five cents. How pathetic." It was every last cent he had. He shook his head in disgust. "There are kids in this town who get more than that for a weekly allowance. I've gotta find those coins."

The words 'Guse Hardware' hung in red neon lights over the building across the street from where he sat. The letter G was burnt out, making the sign read: 'USE HARDWARE'. Victor raised his eyebrow. "Use hardware. Huh. Actually, that's not bad advice when you think about it. There must be something in that store I can use to change the looks of that van." Victor put the money back in his pocket and strolled across the street and into the hardware store.

The place was hotter than a sauna. It was packed from floor to ceiling with every gadget a guy could want. There was barely room for him to walk. He squeezed around the bird houses displayed in the center aisle and carefully maneuvered his way through the lawn and garden section. After bumping into the shovels and knocking a rake off the wall, he finally arrived in the paint department near the back of the store. A hand-made sign was hanging with fish line above the cans of spray paint:

Weekly Special

Rust-Away
Choose from six colors
$1.79 a can

Victor picked up a can of Bright White Rust-Away. *I wonder how many cans of this stuff it would take to paint the van. Let's see, thirty-seven ninety-five divided by $1.79... add a little tax... I could buy almost twenty-one cans. That oughta be enough to cover the beast.* He turned the can over and began reading the label: Dries in less than an hour. *I could have that van painted by tomorrow morning. Then maybe this stinkin' blister on my foot would go away.*

He began loading his arms with cans of Bright White Rust-Away. By the tenth can, he started wondering if twenty cans were going to be enough to cover the whole van. *Who says I can only take what I can pay for?* He lifted his shirt up and stuffed one can in the waistband of his jeans and one in each pocket. *I guess that prison diet paid off after all. Three extra cans ought to finish off the job.*

By the time he reached the front of the store, the can lodged in his waistband had fallen down his pant leg. He gently dragged his leg as he walked, hoping to keep the can from falling out of his pant leg and onto the floor.

He was standing at the front counter before the owner even noticed he was in his store. "Need some help there, sir?"

Victor rolled his eyes in disbelief. *Do I need some help? What's he think? I'm in here trying to make new friends?* He dropped the twenty cans in front of the register, and instantly stretched his arms across the counter to stop them from rolling onto the floor.

The can in his pant leg was barely resting on the top of his boot.

"No. I think I've got it," Victor said in his most accommodating voice.

"Looks like you've got quite the project ahead of you." The man methodically scanned each can of spray paint and placed them in a box as he talked. "What are ya gonna do with all of this paint?"

"Just one of those last-minute projects a guy likes to get done before the snow flies."

"And don't we know about snow around here. People are still talking about the big storm last spring. It was the worst one we've seen in years." Arnold Guse pressed the key in the bottom right hand corner of the register and waited for the total to appear. "Twenty cans of Rust-Away at one dollar and seventy-nine cents apiece comes to thirty-five eighty. And when we add a little tax for Uncle Sam…" The hardware store owner touched another box on the screen. "Your grand total becomes exactly thirty-seven, ninety-five." He stuck out his hand, smiled at Victor, and waited to be paid.

Exactly thirty-seven, ninety-five! If he only had a clue how exact that was, Victor thought, as he reached into his pocket. Hoping he had counted correctly, he dug every last cent out of his pocket and begrudgingly dumped it into the man's hand. *I guess that's why they say, 'Ya gotta spend money to make money'*, Victor thought. *Let's hope spending every last cent I got doesn't come back to bite me.*

While the man counted the money, Victor bent over and shoved the paint can that was slipping down his pant leg into his tube sock.

"Everything all right down there, sir?"

"Just fixing my boot. Don't want to trip." By the time Victor stood up, his face was as red as the sale stickers on the spray paint.

"You ain't lookin' so good. You want to sit down for a minute?"

"Just a little hot. You could use some air conditioning in here."

Victor took the box of paint cans and left the store, trying not to jar the can of spray paint stuffed in his sock. He had taken only a few steps when he accidentally bumped against the bench in front of the hardware store. The impact knocked the lid off the can of paint stored in his sock. The lid rolled down Victor's pant leg and onto the sidewalk. He looked the other way as the lid rolled into the street.

The nozzle of the open can in his tube sock was now pressed permanently on and paint was running down his leg. A trail of Bright White paint followed behind him.

By the time he reached the middle of the block, the paint had saturated his boot. His foot sloshed as he walked. His toes oozed with every step he took. He waited until he passed the last store on the block before leaning over to remove the half-empty paint can from his sock. His pant leg was Bright White, his sock was Bright White, his entire boot was Bright White, and now his hand was Bright White.

Victor looked at his clothes and groaned. "My bad luck never ends! I'm swimmin' in paint." Victor wiped his hand off on his pants. "That stolen can of paint is gonna cost me a lot more than $1.79. Now I need a new pair of boots, new socks, new pants. Worst yet, Mr. 'Use' Hardware is going to know exactly who left these Bright White footprints all the way down the sidewalk."

He finally reached the park bench and sat down. He put the three stolen cans of paint in the box and poured what paint he could out of his boot. Victor picked up his purchase and began the three-mile Death March back to the abandoned house. Hopefully for the last time.

CHAPTER NINE

The Stats Man

"That was the luckiest shot I've ever seen," Randy yelled. He hated to lose, and when he got mad he scrunched up his face until his eyes almost disappeared. "We're not done with you guys, B-a-a-d A-x-x-x. We're going to take you down at tryouts next month."

Sam knew his shot was lucky, but he was still in shock over Paige's steal and assist. She had never said one word the whole game. She had been everywhere she needed to be, doing exactly what her team needed her to do.

"Where did you learn to play ball like that?" Marco asked her.

"My three older brothers have been dragging me out on the court since I've been old enough to walk," Paige answered. "That was a close game. Thanks for letting me play. I'll see you guys tomorrow."

As she hopped on her bike, Sam heard himself saying, "Hey, Paige, we're going home, too. Wait a minute and we'll go with you."

Paige smiled at Sam. "I told Maxwell I'd ride home with him today, but thanks anyway."

Marching his motorized scooter straight toward the court was Maxwell Vanderbilt, who had been analyzing the game from a distance. It was well known that he was the smartest kid in school, never took a book home, and still got straight A's. Maxwell Vanderbilt was the newly elected captain of the junior high debate team and president of the math club. He sat in the front row of every class, raised his hand for every question, and was loved by every teacher.

Sam's eyebrows shot halfway up his forehead when he saw Maxwell. *How did Paige hook up with a guy like this? The dried ketchup spilled on the front of his shirt would totally embarrass most kids, but he wears it like a gold medal*, Sam thought. *And that black electrical tape holding the bridge of his glasses together! Where is his pride?* Sam shook his head. *Maybe if his pants were just long enough to cover his socks, or he'd get a haircut.* Sam remembered kids saying Maxwell wore his hair in that six-inch Afro to make himself look taller. *But let's face it: we're in seventh grade now. He just needs a whole new makeover.* Sam bit his lip and kept his thoughts to himself.

Maxwell was within feet of the court when he started wheezing. *Oh, not now,* he thought. Maxwell hated having to use his inhaler in front of other kids. He had suffered from asthma for as long as he could remember, but his attacks always seemed to come at the most inopportune moments. He tried to catch his breath, but no such luck. He finally pulled the inhaler out of his pocket.

"Well, Maxwell, what did you think of the game?" Marco asked.

After taking one last shot on his inhaler, he stuffed it back in his pocket and pulled out his new Apple iPad to review his notes from the game. "Marco, if you were to study the patterns and variables of the game, you would be able to see that your team could have done better. The percentage of shots your team made decreased considerably as the game wore on. You need to be in better shape. And I'm not just talking about Baxter. He is actually in pretty good shape after factoring in his girth."

Baxter grinned.

"I'm talking about you, Marco. You made three out of five shots, giving you a sixty percent field goal average, which isn't bad. But you made those shots in the first ten minutes. In the last part of the game, you were one for seven, making you four for twelve the whole game. Baseball is the only sport in which a thirty-three percent success ratio is considered acceptable. While it is obvious that you are by far the fastest player on your team, your endurance is lacking. Start running hills.

"Then there's your game, Baxter." Maxwell pulled the stylus out of his Afro and quickly worked several calculations on the left side of the screen. He stopped to make sure his breathing was steady before he continued.

Baxter shifted from foot to foot, waiting for Maxwell to speak.

"Baxter, you only made two of the five baskets you attempted, but both were from inside the paint. You have little trouble shooting over your opponent. If you work harder on your outside shots, you could easily convert them to three-pointers, and thus increase your team's scoring. Keep in mind if you hit two three-pointers, the other team must make three two-point baskets to stay even."

Baxter had been gloating over the fact that someone actually considered him in 'good shape after factoring in his girth'. His workouts were making a difference. By the time Maxwell was done analyzing the rest of his game, Baxter was already talking to Marco about lining up another practice session to work on his outside shots.

Scrolling to the next page on his iPad, Maxwell tapped his stylus on the screen and continued.

"Sam, you shot sixty-six percent. Your jump shot is excellent and you are very difficult to guard when you're driving to the hoop. You could be more of a weapon if you occasionally went to your left. You favor your right hand. Work on dribbling with your left hand. If you keep going to your right, teams will play you to your right. You'll become predictable, and thus less effective. You guard your assigned player pretty well, too. But you need to play better weak-side defense. If you see the opponent has beaten your teammate to the basket, you need to help out. Learn to keep your head up and your eyes open."

Maxwell, who had been hunched over, looking down at his notes during his extended analysis, looked up, straightened his shoulders, and carefully maneuvered his glasses to the top of his nose. With the stylus in one hand

and his iPad in the other, he announced, "Paige, you, of course, were wonderful."

Paige smiled at Maxwell and looked over at the other three boys, whose mouths were hanging wide open. They were speechless. Sam finally looked at Baxter, who was already nodding at Marco. Maxwell Vanderbilt was the stats man they had been looking for. The three of them couldn't have done the math and game analysis that Maxwell did so effortlessly in his head if they had a room full of computers and calculators.

"Max, how about riding home with us?" Marco asked. "If you're going to manage our team this winter, we need to start hanging out together."

"Marco, I prefer that people call me Maxwell."

Marco's shoulders shook up and down as he let out one of his contagious belly laughs. After hanging out with Baxter all these years, he never took anything people said too seriously. "Okay, Maxwell, but we're not just people; we're your friends. You're awesome with that math stuff, Maxwell. You've gotta be the stats man for our basketball team. What do you say? You riding home with us?"

Marco seemed so sincere. Even with all of his accomplishments, no one had ever called Maxwell their friend before. Maxwell couldn't believe his ears.

"Well, Maxwell, are we riding home with these guys?" Paige prodded.

"If we leave right now, I would be home by curfew and still have time to watch the last fifteen minutes of the CNBC Market Report. I think that would be a fine idea."

Baxter bounced the basketball and threw a chest pass to Maxwell. "If you're going to be a part of our team, Maxwell, we better start teaching you a few basketball moves. We spend a lot of time on the court."

Maxwell bobbled the ball before finally catching it. He readjusted his glasses and smiled as he held the ball up in the air like a trophy. "I suppose if I am going to be a part of this team, I better learn how to do this." He placed the ball on his index finger and gave it a spin. His finger bent and the ball spiraled to the ground.

Marco reached out and caught it, patting Maxwell on the back. "Don't worry, Maxwell, there will be plenty of time to work on spinning the ball."

Sam didn't notice Maxwell's performance. He was thinking about the boy he saw watching the game, and how much he looked like the kid who picked up his pencil in English class. "Who was that guy standing over there by the court?" Sam asked. "He looked like he wanted to get in on the action."

Marco shook his head. "I didn't see anybody, Sam."

"Yeah, he was standing right over there by the bleachers. He was about my size and had blond hair: a butch. Freckles… braces and a big smile."

By now Baxter turned away from Maxwell, so he could listen more carefully to Sam's description. "That's not funny, Sam."

"What? I'm not trying to be funny. I just want to know who that kid was," Sam retorted.

Baxter was starting to get a little agitated with Sam. "I didn't see any kids here except the ones on the court, until Maxwell showed up. And it sounds like you're describing Alex Decker."

Marco nodded his head. "Baxter's right. He was our friend. Have a little respect, Sam."

Sam took a minute to think about what his friends were saying. *The guy I saw by the basketball court looked just like the kid who picked up my pencil in English class, but no one seems to have seen that kid either. And the girl who sat behind the empty desk in English thought I was describing Alex Decker, too. But I've never met him, so how can I describe Alex Decker unless I actually did see him?* Sam shook his head at the thought. *But how could I have seen him? Alex Decker is dead!* Shivers ran down Sam's spine. *I better keep my mouth shut.* "Sorry, you guys. I thought I saw someone. I sure didn't think it was Alex Decker."

Paige turned away from her conversation with Maxwell. "We better get going if we want to make it home before curfew."

Maxwell agreed. "I'll miss the CNBC Market Report if we don't leave right now."

Marco and Baxter jumped on their bikes and the conversation about Alex Decker came to an abrupt end. Sam was already thinking that Paige was no ordinary girl. He would have liked to think that she was one of the guys, but he knew better. Paige was someone special.

"Sam, are you coming or not?" Marco yelled.

Sam looked up to see the rest of them riding across the field.

"Hey, you guys, wait for me." Sam jumped on his bike and started pedaling. There would be plenty of time to think about Paige later.

CHAPTER TEN

A Circus on Wheels

Victor revved up his Bright White van and headed back into town. The whole thing stunk like wet paint; but he didn't care. Anything beat walking, even a smelly old van. He shrugged his shoulders as he looked down at the paint stains all over his pants and boots. *I'll get me some new duds when I hit Vegas.* He rolled down the window and honked the horn. There was nothing to honk at, but it felt great to be driving again.

He had barely merged onto the highway before he realized his luck still hadn't changed. He put his foot on the brake and hit the horn again. "Hardly get on this road, and I'm already stuck behind some road hog going thirty. Doesn't anyone in this state know how to drive?"

There was a huge circus truck filled with animals in front of him, and it dropped at least ten miles an hour below the speed limit every time it went up a hill. The stench from the animals was making him gag. Worse yet, the winding mountain roads made it impossible for Victor to pass.

This time he laid on the horn. "Let's go, man. I don't have all day," Victor screamed.

He still didn't have his treasured coins, and time was running out. How much longer could he hang out in Esterville before the mystery of Alex Decker's death started to unfold? The kid's face was flashing through his mind. *If he had just given me the coins in the first place*, Victor thought, *the little punk would still be alive, and I'd be lounging by a pool drinking margaritas.*

Now he had pulled within inches of the truck's bumper. He swore the animals inside the truck were staring at him. Rolling his window halfway down, Victor stuck his fist outside and was shaking it at the driver of the truck. "Get this circus-on-wheels moving, will ya? If I wanna see a monkey, I'll go to the zoo."

An SUV roared by him in the opposite northbound lane, almost taking off Victor's arm. As Victor yanked his arm back in the van, his watch caught on the edge of the window. The band broke, and his watch fell on the road.

Victor blew the horn. "The only valuable thing I had," Victor growled, "and a SUV rips it off my arm." He watched the speedometer drop again as he headed up another winding hill. He was barely going thirty. He had pulled so close to the truck's bumper, it was impossible for him to see if there was any traffic approaching.

He'd had enough. It was time to pass. As Victor pulled out into the oncoming lane of traffic, a school bus was speeding toward him. At the last second, Victor swerved back into his own lane, avoiding a head-on collision.

"Get those animals moving," Victor roared. He reached over and flicked on the radio. Some guy was giving the Midday Traffic Report.

"The Traffic Report! What do you know about traffic?" he yelled at the voice on the radio. "I'll tell you about the stinkin' traffic. I'm sittin' here doin' thirty in a sixty. How 'bout that for a traffic report?" Instantly, he changed the channel. A Country tune was playing.

Victor groaned. "Anything but Country!"

He pushed a third button, totally ignoring the static that was now blaring at him through the speaker. Victor looked in the rearview mirror at his unshaven face. His eyes were bloodshot. The circles under them were blacker than coal from lack of sleep. He couldn't remember combing his hair that day. From the looks of it, he hadn't.

Slamming his hand on the dashboard, Victor started screaming at the top of his voice, "Are you ev-v-v-ver going to get those animals to the top of the hill? Some of us have a life, ya kn-o-o-o-o-w!"

Once again, Victor looked in his rearview mirror. He couldn't believe the long line of traffic that was developing. The silver Lincoln MKZ behind him had turned on its blinker. It was getting ready to pass him. "Oh no, you're not passing me! I'm not the problem," Victor raged at the MKZ. "You can waste your time smelling these stinkin' animals. I'm outta here!"

Victor cranked on the steering wheel and pulled out in front of the MKZ and into the oncoming lane. The road was clear. He punched the accelerator. "Looks like the old van still has some pick-up left." Victor was grinning. "Hasta la vista, Bay-bee!"

He was almost halfway past the circus truck before he saw it. A huge semi appeared on the top of the hill, and was coming straight at him. The truck filled with animals was only inches to his right. On his left side was a guardrail and beyond that a drop-off of at least two hundred feet.

Victor's heart was pounding so hard he thought his chest would explode. Sweat covered his face. The MKZ had filled in the gap behind the circus truck. There was no place for him to go.

Victor was trapped in the lane of oncoming traffic.

He pressed down on the gas pedal until he was no longer sitting on the seat. The back of his neck was braced against the top of the driver's seat. His arms were fully extended, and his back was arched. "Come on, you stupid van! Come on," Victor bellowed.

The oncoming rig was blowing its horn and trying to stop. The sound of the semi's screeching brakes filled the van. The circus truck next to him was also braking, trying to make room for Victor to pull in front of him. The space still looked too small for him to squeeze the van back into the right lane.

But it was now or never. Victor pushed down on the accelerator until he thought his foot would go through the floor. The clambering noises from his engine were deafening. He lunged back against the seat as the van surged ahead. Cranking the steering wheel to the right,

Victor squeezed the van in front of the circus truck. But the back part of the van was still hanging out in the left lane.

Trying to avoid a head-on collision with Victor, the eighteen-wheeler swerved to its right. It jack-knifed, and was sliding sideways down the two-lane highway, and straight toward Victor.

Victor leaned hard to the right as he pulled on the steering wheel, forcing the rest of the van into the lane in front of the circus truck and escaping collision with the oncoming semi. But he still didn't have the van under control. He had over-corrected the steering wheel and was now veering off onto the side of the road. A cloud of dirt exploded behind him as his tires hit the gravel on the berm, making it impossible for the driver of the circus truck to see anything.

In his rearview mirror Victor saw the truck filled with animals still on the road, but the loose gravel was too much for the weight of its cargo. The circus truck started to fishtail. The back end spun to the left, crashing into the jack-knifed semi. Upon impact, the circus truck rolled on its side and slammed into the MKZ.

Steering clear of the pileup, the next car in line bailed into the ditch, flipped onto its side and slid into a tree. The semi was still coming, taking out one vehicle after another.

Approaching traffic that was once miles in front of Victor was now careening out of control. Car after car was heading straight for Victor. Every time one swerved around him, another one skidded toward him.

An oncoming Jeep screeched within inches of the semi. In a last-ditch effort to save himself, the driver yanked on the steering wheel and sent the Jeep spinning in Victor's direction. Without thinking, Victor drove into the ditch. The van was flying over one bump after another. Victor's knuckles were white, trying to hold onto the wheel.

"Don't fail me now, baby," Victor shrieked.

Barely scraping by the Jeep, Victor was now at the top of the hill. He pulled out of the ditch and back onto the blacktop. He had survived. The last sight Victor had of the carnage was the semi crashing through the guardrail. Its cab was hanging over the edge of the mountain, and its twisted trailer was lying on its side in the middle of dozens of smashed vehicles.

Victor was trembling. His foot shook uncontrollably as he tried to maintain pressure on the gas pedal. He reached for his pack of cigarettes. "One left," he sighed.

He lit the cigarette and inhaled until his lungs couldn't hold another drop of smoke. "That was a close one," he mumbled. Victor coughed, trying to clear his lungs. "Hope I don't have to paint the van again."

The line of oncoming traffic had come to a complete halt. It went on for as long as he could see. *I knew the minute I saw that truck filled with animals, it was going to be trouble,* Victor thought. *Who drives around with a whole circus in the back of their truck on a dangerous road like this one?*

"Doesn't a driver's license mean anything in this state?" Victor mumbled without a trace of remorse. He took another drag of his cigarette and turned up the radio. It was a Country tune.

"I guess Country isn't so bad," Victor decided. Still trying to catch his breath, he recalled the old joke: Play Country songs backwards and you get your girl back, your dog back, your truck back… How had he gotten himself into this mess? For just a moment he wanted his old life back.

Off in the distance there was a green sign: 'Esterville 2 miles'. He barely noticed it. For a second he thought he saw the dead boy's face in the rearview mirror laughing at him. Victor whipped his head around and looked in the back seat, but the boy was gone. "Stupid kid. What did ya do with my coins?" Victor stomped on the gas pedal. "I'm done messing around. I better find those coins, or Esterville is going to wonder what hit it."

CHAPTER ELEVEN

A Planned Escape

Esterville was a small town nestled in the rolling hills of western Pennsylvania. Division Street was the town's main drag. The fire station and police department were located on the south end of the street.

The Esterville Railroad Station sat in the middle of town, with its cornerstone proudly bearing the date of 1898. From the moment the last tie was laid, the railroad line brought growth and prosperity to the town.

The Esterville line was only seventy-two miles in length, but it traveled one of the wildest mountain wildernesses in the country. The route had four tunnels plus seven bridges and trestles, but it was the old wooden bridge that continued to give Esterville its *Brigadoon* charm. John Miller was the tycoon in charge of building the railroad, and both the town and the railroad proudly bore the name of his wife Ester.

After the railroad line closed, Esterville never really changed much. Small shops still abutted a boardwalk on both sides of the street. The planks were faded. Some were crooked and loose. Others creaked and sank as the people walked on them.

Most of the buildings were still painted white with dark brown trim to match the railroad station. All were at least eighty years old and had long since shown their age. Awnings hung from each establishment, giving residents cover from the rain or shade from the sun. The people of Esterville liked spending Saturday mornings window-shopping on the boardwalk, even though the merchandise never really changed from week to week or from year to year.

Henley Ruffin's corner café, called Ruffin's Muffins, was one of the town's oldest establishments. Henley's great-grandfather Clyde Ruffin proudly opened the restaurant on November 11, 1918, the same day World War I ended, and Henley never let anyone forget it.

Henley Ruffin's pet Schnauzer Patton had been sleeping on the same plank outside the café for forty years. Actually, it was Henley's sixth Schnauzer named Patton, and this one had only been sleeping outside the café for three years. But Patton Number Six looked exactly like his five salt-and-pepper predecessors, and no one ever seemed to notice the changing of the guard.

Sam's mom Rose considered the lack of change part of Esterville's strong character, and that was the main reason she brought her sons back home to live after her husband died. It was a real family town. People still sat on their front porch in the evening reading the newspaper, and

Downtown still had the same bingo parlor that her parents had frequented.

Since bringing the family back to town, Rose found herself spending many evenings on her front porch perusing the *Esterville Gazette*. Come to think of it, she had even accepted an invitation to play bingo with Margaret John, who lived next door.

The town's favorite hangout was a man-made lake people referred to as 'The Pit'. A few years back, residents had grown bored with their lives and passed a measure to 'build' a lake. The only problem was there was no place to build one. So Town Hall doubled property taxes for three years straight and used the money to build a dam across Stony Creek, creating a natural reservoir, and a place for the community to swim in the summer.

With melting snow and heavy rains, nature still took its course in the spring, turning Stony Creek into a torrent river. The waters crested high above the dam and flooded into surrounding areas. So the town waited until late May when the water level returned to normal before opening the beach.

People had questioned putting the swimming area so close to Esterville's abandoned railroad bridge, but the bridge was Esterville's claim to fame, and Town Hall thought a historical landmark would enhance the new beach's ambience.

Once the dam was built and the reservoir filled with water, it still wasn't much to look at. From downstream the dam looked like an overgrown mound of rubble, but it didn't matter. The people of Esterville now had a place to cool off, picnic, and gossip in the hot, humid Pennsylvania summers.

Rumors of Sam's team winning the scrimmage against the eighth graders spread through school, making Sam and his new friends a frequent topic among the gossips. People never saw one of them without the other four nearby since that day on the basketball court, and they had made plans together again today.

The carnies were in town setting up the annual Esterville Carnival on Stony Creek Road, and Sam and his friends didn't want to miss a second of it. Their plan was to meet at Old Man Guse's Hardware Store and take off for the carnival from there. That was the plan, at least until Sam's mom walked into his room.

"Sam, the hospital called, and there's been a terrible accident out on Stony Creek Road. The emergency room is packed, and they need all the help they can get. I have to go. Grandpa is coming over to stay with you and Tommy. I want you to stay home and help Grandpa till I get back."

Sam couldn't believe his ears. It was like an atomic bomb hit! "But Mom…"

"Sam, I don't want any arguments. You know the hospital is under-staffed right now. People's lives are at stake."

Sam's life was the one at stake. He had finally made some friends, and now his mom wanted him to stay home and babysit! What would those guys say if he didn't show up at Old Man Guse's? "But Mom, Marco and Baxter and…"

"Sam, enough is enough. You can see your friends when I get home. Besides, this would be a good chance for you to spend some time with Tommy. You know how he looks up to you." And without another word, Sam's mom kissed him on the cheek and left his room.

Sam knew he wasn't going to win that argument. Things had changed since Sam's dad died. It had only been six months since he lost his dad, and he was taking on more responsibility all the time. Without Sam's help, it would be almost impossible for his mom to work. Without her job, their family couldn't survive. Sam knew his mom relied on him, but sometimes he just wanted to be a kid.

Sam had always been proud that his mom was a doctor. When he was little, Rose had started a small clinic in downtown Minneapolis. It had taken most of her professional life to build the clientele. She was just ready to move the clinic to a new building in the suburbs when Sam's dad passed away. Long commutes, over-crowded schools, and the increasing violence made it difficult for Rose to raise her family alone in such a big city. She finally decided to move her family home to the small town where she grew up.

Rose took over Dr Bunken's family practice when he retired. She moved into his office on Division Street and carried on his schedule. Rose knew almost every patient that came to see her. She had grown up with most of them. In the short time she had been home, she saved Old Man

Guse from a near-fatal heart attack, removed Miss Thompson's appendix, and delivered Marco's baby sister. The move home was a perfect fit. Rose felt like she had never left Esterville.

Sam's life, on the other hand, wasn't quite so perfect. He still had to let his friends know he wasn't going to meet them at Guse's. Sam reached for his phone and froze. His mom had his phone! She confiscated it Wednesday night when she found him still texting Baxter at two o' clock in the morning. "We've talked about staying up all night texting before, Sam; not on a school night. Kids your age need their sleep. This time I'm taking your phone away for a week; it will give you a little time to think about doing what I ask you to do."

The worst part was his phone was in her purse, and her purse was with his mom on the way to the hospital. Now what was he supposed to do? His friends were probably waiting for him at Guse's right now, and he wasn't coming. He flopped on his bed and stared at the ceiling.

Tommy bound into the room wearing a red winter jacket, yellow goggles on his face, a blue stocking hat on his head, and a pair of black boots. "I am Su-prem-o Grande, the King of all Robots. Watch and I will turn into an army tank!"

His little brother looked ridiculous. Sam usually got a good laugh out of Tommy's antics, but right now Sam wasn't in a laughing mood. "Get lost, Squirt! I don't have time for Supremo Grande!"

Tommy kept tugging at his goggles. The crack on the left side of the glass was making it difficult for him to see. "Mom said you had to play with me."

"I'm supposed to be meeting the gang right now, and mom won't let me go. And worse yet, she has my phone. I gotta figure out how to let them know I won't be there. So, like I said, Tommy, I don't have time for you right now." He looked at the picture of his father face-down on his desk and shook his head. "And I wish you'd leave my stuff alone."

"Grrrr-and-pa's downstairs; and Mom said you have to stay home with me till she gets back."

"I'm going downtown. I can't let them wait for me any longer, and you're not telling mom. Got that, Squirt?"

Sam looked down at Tommy, who was still yanking on his goggles, trying to see around the crack in the glass.

"If you leave, Sam, you are going to be in big tee-rub-le."

Sam adjusted Tommy's goggles so he could see his little brother's eyes. "The word is 'trou-ble', Squirt. Just two syllables. Not tee-rub-le."

"Well, that's what you're going to be in if you leave after mom told you to stay home with Grrrr-and-pa and me."

Sam looked at Tommy and shook his head. Five years old was so young. The eight-year span between the two brothers created quite a communication gap. *It's not easy explaining to a five-year-old why it's more important to meet my friends than it is to hang out with him*, Sam thought.

He still felt a strong bond between them, and tried one more time to explain his problem to his little brother. "Tommy, I'm just going downtown to tell those guys I can't go to the carnival with them, and then I'm coming right back home. If you don't tell mom I left, we'll play soccer when I get back."

"O-kee-doe-kee, Sam." Tommy left the bedroom tugging at his yellow goggles, giving his older brother a chance to plan his escape.

Sam started down the hall behind Tommy, but stopped in his tracks. The kitchen radio was playing a song on CMEP, Esterville's only Country radio station and his grandfather's favorite. Sam smiled. *I'm surprised Grandpa's not singing along.*

He knew his mom had given his grandfather strict instructions for Sam to stay home with Tommy. There was no way Sam would be leaving through the kitchen door, but there was still one more possibility.

Returning to his room, Sam opened the bedroom window and looked down at the barren flower trellis against the side of the house. *Well, here goes nothing*, he thought. He crawled over the window ledge and down the trellis, each board more wobbly than the last. Finally hitting the ground, he still had to maneuver between the house and the rose bush without getting stabbed by its prickly thorns. He carefully moved the thorny branch away from him and peered around the corner of the house: no sign of Grandpa.

Sam ran to the closest hemlock tree in the front yard and ducked behind it. He continued darting from tree to tree, finally reaching his bike leaning against the picket fence. Sam looked around one last time to see if his grandfather was anywhere to be found. The coast was clear.

He jumped on his bike, pedaled down the sidewalk, and onto Horace Avenue. In no time he was racing toward Division Street, hoping he would find his friends still waiting for him. If all went as planned, he would be home before his grandfather ever knew he left.

CHAPTER TWELVE

Time's Up

Victor's leg was still shaking when he drove by Sam's house. For that matter, so were his hands. He needed to park the van and get a grip on himself. The disaster on the highway had taken more out of him than he realized.

He drove onto Horace Avenue and pulled over to the side of the street. He still had to back up so he could get a better look at Decker's old house. As the van rolled backwards, a kid riding a black mountain bike streaked past him.

Victor slammed on the brakes. The kid swerved, missing the bumper by mere inches.

Victor rolled down his window. "Watch where you're going, ya stupid kid." He fell back against the seat, and blew out a long breath of air. "When did driving get to be such a problem? This state needs to work on some traffic regulations."

He finished backing up, and parked just close enough to keep his eye on the house. He turned off the radio, hoping the silence would calm his nerves and give him a chance to think. *Seems like I've seen that kid on the bike before. I haven't been in Esterville that long, so there's only a couple of places I could have seen him.* Then it came to him: the image of the lady hugging the kid goodbye on the porch this morning. "He's the big brother who lives in the Deckers' old house." Victor smiled. "Well, that's one less person I have to worry about. After that near-death fiasco on the highway, I could use a break."

Gloating about his good fortune came to an abrupt halt when he noticed a pickup parked in the driveway of Sam's house. *Must have some company*, Victor thought. He looked at the truck again. *Seems like I've seen that truck before, too.* He checked the license plate, but it was just a standard Pennsylvania number. *I guess I'm gonna need a closer look.*

He jumped the picket fence and strategically moved from tree to tree and bush to bush, checking at each stop to make sure no one was watching. When he reached the overgrown lilac bush, he stopped to catch his breath.

The yard was empty; there was no sight of the lime green Volkswagen; and no one was inside the truck. *The driver must be in the house. I need a better look at that truck, and now is as good a time as any*, Victor thought. He crouched as he ran from the lilac bush to the passenger side of the truck. He looked inside the vehicle and slid helplessly to the ground. "You have got to be kidding me!"

The decal on the glove compartment was a dead giveaway: 'If you don't like Country, you don't like music!' Victor knew of only one rusty blue truck in the whole town with that sticker on the glove box. The whole state, for that matter.

This is the ex-cop's truck... the guy who picked me up hitchhiking. He pulled his knees to his head and groaned. "Is anything ever gonna go my way? I'm surprised I don't hear the old coot belting out another Country tune."

Victor rubbed his face. "What's he doing here? He can't still be investigating the Decker case. He's retired. When's he going to give it up? If he's in there looking for those coins, I'm screwed."

The back door slammed shut. He crawled to his feet and peered through the truck windows. The gray-haired man who had given him a ride into town was walking toward the garage at the far end of the yard. Victor scrambled to the rear of the truck and out of sight. As the old man went into the garage, the little boy pushed the front screen door open with his foot so he could continue tossing his soccer ball from one hand to another. He threw the ball to the ground and dribbled it toward the street.

The ex-cop soon appeared with a pair of pruning shears in his hand. It was only minutes after he started clipping the hedge in the back yard when a blonde lady from the house next door appeared with a plate full of cookies. The old man gladly took a cookie as the neighbor began talking and pointing at an overgrown walkway that had once connected the two yards.

Victor watched as they continued to walk farther away from the house, examining the hedge as they went. "Looks like she's gonna keep that poor guy busy for quite a while.

The pendulum of good fortune may have just swung my way." His shoulders shook as he laughed. The sound caught in his throat, making his reaction more of a growl. "Here's my chance."

As the old man bent over to trim some branches from the hedge, Victor ran after Tommy, who was still dribbling the ball across the front yard. Coming up alongside Tommy, Victor brought the ball to a dead stop with his foot. "Another game of soccer, huh, kid? Can I play?"

Tommy froze.

Victor raised his eyebrows and tried to smile. "How 'bout if I'm the goalie?" Victor propositioned, gritting his yellowed teeth as he grinned.

Tommy took a step back and shook his head.

"Well, if you don't want to play soccer, maybe we can just talk about where you're finding these coins you have. You know they do actually belong to me."

Tommy continued nervously shaking his head back and forth.

Victor was taking his chances even talking to this kid. The driver of the blue truck was in the backyard and well within earshot of his conversation. One wrong move or one loud scream and that old guy would be all over him. Victor gave the ball a short tap to his left foot and then back to his right. "Maybe we can just kick the ball around until you feel like talking."

As Tommy watched Victor maneuver the ball back and forth with his feet, Victor kept his eye on the old man who had finished picking up the cut branches and was carrying them back to the garage. *I can't keep coming back here*, Victor thought. *This guy's a cop. Eventually, I'm going to get caught.* Victor looked from Tommy to the old man and shook his head. *I have to make my move. I need answers from this kid right now.*

Without another thought, Victor kicked the ball toward the van. Pure instinct made Tommy run after it; Victor followed closely behind the little boy. As the ball rolled to a stop, Victor picked it up and threw it in the van. "We can play more when we're done talking."

Tommy turned to run, but Victor grabbed him by the arm and pulled him behind a lilac bush, the only bit of cover between Victor and the old man who was now walking toward the back door of the house. "Just tell me where the coins are, kid, and I'll let you go."

Tears fell down Tommy's cheek. "I... don't... know... where they... are."

Victor's heart beat faster with every step the old man took. His time was up. Victor jumped in the side van door, pulling the little boy with him. Tommy crumbled to the floor. Victor shut the door, jumped into the driver's seat and drove away.

The old man walked into the house and the screen door banged shut behind him.

The sound of Tommy's sobbing was only broken by the little boy's short, involuntary gasps for air. Victor flipped the rearview mirror toward the ceiling, so he didn't have to look at the kid, but the image of him curled into a ball on the floor of the van was hard to shake. *I'm just going to get this kid to tell me where the coins are and drop him off right back here. I'll get the coins and disappear.*

He struggled to think what his next move should be. *Even once I have the coins, I still have to find someone to buy them.* He thought about his six months in prison and his cellmate Pete Peterson. Victor smiled. Good old Pete used to brag about some guy he knew in upstate New York that would pay top dollar for Double Eagles. Victor rubbed his forehead as if his fingers could tell him what to do. *And didn't I hear Pete landed a job as a cook in a carnival? Wouldn't that be something if Pete was working the carnival right here in town?*

Victor pulled the rearview mirror back into place. "Okay, kid. If this doesn't make you stop crying, nothing will. How 'bout we go to the carnival?" He felt his confidence returning.

Tommy watched the reflection of Victor's lifeless eyes come alive in the mirror and shuddered as the man's high-pitched laughter ricocheted off the walls of the van.

CHAPTER THIRTEEN

Safe at Last

Within a block of Guse's Hardware, Sam could see his friends were already waiting for him. Marco and Baxter were on their bikes, leaning against the hardware store window. Paige was sitting on the boardwalk with her bike propped against the lamp post, talking to some kid Sam didn't recognize.

As he pulled up to the store, he realized Paige was talking to Maxwell!

Paige stood up and patted Maxwell on the back. "What do you think of Maxwell's new look, Sam? I took him down to the Barber Shop this morning and then we went shopping," Paige exclaimed as a big smile crossed her face.

Maxwell's hair was cut into the new Afro fade, shaved two inches above his ears, leaving a quarter inch of growth on the rest of his scalp. The barber had shaved a part into the left side of Maxwell's head and artistically sculpted a 'V' for 'Vanderbilt' above his forehead and to the right of his part. The black T-shirt and baggy knee-length shorts finished off his updated look. The new Maxwell Vanderbilt looked more like the lead singer of a rap group than president of the school math club.

Sam couldn't believe his eyes. "Wow, Paige! He even got his glasses fixed. Maxwell, you're da GOAT!"

Maxwell raised his little finger, index finger, and thumb; tried adding a slight shake to his hand like he'd seen one of his favorite rappers do on YouTube; and went back to reading his book. He had made himself at home on the bench outside Guse's and was studying his already-worn copy of *Parabolas and Algorithms for Serious Students of Professional Basketball*. The book had been in his back pocket since the day it came in the mail. Sam was sure Maxwell had it memorized. The margins were saturated with equations, graphs, and notations. How Maxwell could find even the slightest connection between those calculations and winning a basketball game was a mystery to the rest of the group, but everything he said always made extraordinary sense.

Then Sam saw Baxter tapping the screen on his smartwatch and animatedly talking to Marco. His hands were flying in every direction, and he was furious. Marco and Baxter were always ten minutes early, and they hated to be kept waiting for anything. Paige was now trying to calm them down, but they weren't buying a word she said. Baxter had jumped off his bike and was now pacing back and forth, back and forth, twisting the blue spikes of hair that were sticking out of his visor until Paige thought he was going to break one of the spikes right off.

Baxter's visor consisted of a two-inch elastic band that went around his head and attached to a short brim. He liked to wear the brim of the hat upside down and backwards, placing the strap across his forehead and the visor in a cup-like position on the back of his head.

The open top of the visor let everyone see what flavor Jell-O he had used to color his hair that week without flattening the perfectly preserved spikes. Today he had pulled the elastic band too tight, and the neon color of his face was turning a brighter shade of red by the minute.

"Hey, guys," Sam stammered.

"Where ya been, Sam? We've been sitting in front of Old Man Guse's for almost twenty minutes," Baxter yelled before Sam could finish his sentence.

"My mom got called into the hospital; there was some big accident on the highway outside of Esterville. The emergency room is packed with people. She's making me stay home with my grandfather and watch Tommy."

"Ever heard of texting, Sam?" Baxter chided.

"My mom took my phone away after she caught me talking to you at two o' clock Wednesday morning, so I couldn't text. I had to come down here to let you know I can't go to the carnival today."

"You are such a momma's boy, Sam. Don't you think your grandfather can handle your five-year-old brother?"

"Back off, Baxter. I just snuck out of the house so you guys weren't sitting around all afternoon waiting for me. If my mom knew I was here, she'd kill me."

Sam's plea fell on deaf ears with Baxter, who really laid into him. "Didn't want us waiting for you! Old Man Guse's been out here twice already yelling at us to move along."

"Oh, tell me something new," Sam groaned. "You and Marco have been at war with Old Man Guse since he accused you of stealing those basketball cards in fourth grade."

Baxter remembered that day as if it was yesterday. They had only been looking at the new display of basketball cards a couple of minutes, when Old Man Guse accused them both of shoplifting. He said he had been watching from the storage room and wanted them to empty their pockets immediately. Even as fourth graders, they were outraged over his accusation, and refused to comply with Guse's demand.

Guse held his ground and threatened to call the Esterville police if they didn't empty their pockets. Both Baxter and Marco knew it wouldn't matter if they were innocent. They would be grounded until they graduated high school if their parents had to pick them up at the police station.

Both of the boys turned their pockets inside out, and much to his dismay, Guse found absolutely nothing. He tried to make amends, but Marco and Baxter would have no part of it.

From that day forward, they harassed Old Man Guse every chance they got, and over the years Guse did the same in return. Now Sam, Paige, and Maxwell were a part of Marco and Baxter's feud whether they liked it or not.

Just then, sixty-two-year-old Arnold Guse emerged from inside the hardware store, wildly waving one of this week's specials: the all-new magnetized and adjustable Monson's Floor Mop.

"If I have to tell you kids to move along one more time, I'm calling the police," Guse yelled.

Baxter let Guse have it. "Your threats don't scare us anymore. This sidewalk is public property, Guse. We can hang out here as long as we want."

"That's what you think, Sonny. Ever heard of 'gang loitering'? Well, gang loitering is a crime. And it means hanging around on a street corner doing a whole lot of nothing. Ring any bells, boys?"

Paige welcomed Guse excluding her from the conversation. Her dad was the new chief of police, and she didn't need her name included in any police reports Mr. Guse was threatening to file.

Maxwell, however, had already thought through the situation and realized there was a real weakness in Mr. Guse's argument. "First of all, Mr. Guse, Esterville has no 'gang loitering' ordinance to back up your demands. And secondly, even if they did, the Supreme Court has found such laws violate the freedom of association and assembly secured by the First Amendment."

Maxwell straightened his shoulders and waggled his new glasses in the air, waiting for Mr. Guse's rebuttal.

Arnold Guse was furious. "I am not wasting my time debating you kids! Who's going to come into my store with you kids hanging around the front door? I want you out of here, and I want you gone right now!"

"We're not in fourth grade anymore, Guse," Baxter snarled under his breath. "You're going to have to do better than that."

And with that, Guse pressed the button to adjust the all-new magnetized Monson's Floor Mop. The handle extended another foot, flying within inches of Baxter's face.

The excitement was more than Mr. Ruffin's Schnauzer Patton could stand. He slept straight through the first outbreak between Guse and the boys. The Great Schnauzer still remained fairly relaxed the second time Guse came charging out of his store, but this new round of commotion was too much. Patton sprang to his feet, charging toward the flying broom which, magnetized or not, was not going to intimidate a Schnauzer!

Trying to get out of the way of the adjustable mop, Baxter took a step back, tripping over Patton and falling backwards into Paige's lap. Patton instantly leaped on Baxter's chest, his wet nose in Baxter's face, his tongue drooling on Baxter's shirt.

"Now get on your bikes and get moving!" Old Man Guse said as he shook the magnetized Monson at Baxter one more time before retreating into his store.

Baxter was out of Paige's lap and chasing after Guse when Sam barely caught him by the back of his pants. "Let it go, Baxter. He's mad enough already. I have to get home before my mom finds out I was down here, or I'll never see the outside of my house again."

Baxter had almost forgotten why he was there before Guse had attacked him with the mop. "This would never have happened, Sam, if you had been on time. And now you're not even going to the carnival!"

Baxter was really worked up after his run-in with Old Man Guse. Sam's lame excuse was only driving Baxter closer to the edge. It was time for Marco to step in and calm things down. "Look, Baxter, we'll go down to the carnival and check out the hot spots. When Sam's mom gets home, we'll all go down there together."

Maxwell looked at his watch. He was still thinking about Guse's threat to call the police. "If we don't all get out of here pretty soon, Guse will make sure that none of us go anywhere except straight to the police station."

Paige pulled Baxter's bike up off the boardwalk and rolled it toward him. "The carnival doesn't open till tonight anyway, Baxter. All we can do right now is look around."

Baxter started to calm down when he saw there was no way all five of them would be going to the carnival together. "Yeah, Sam, I guess you better get home, or your mom won't ever let you go to the carnival. We'll stop by your house on our way home and figure out a time we can all go."

"I gotta get going before Grandpa realizes I'm gone. Make sure you guys stop by my house on your way home from the carnival."

Baxter can really lose it sometimes, Sam thought, *but he always comes to his senses.* Sam spun his bike around and took off down Division Street.

The move to Esterville had been a good one. Sam had friends he could count on. As he pedaled down Division Street, he laughed, thinking about Ruffin's Schnauzer Patton standing on Baxter's chest, sticking his wet nose in his face. Baxter tries so hard to be cool.

Sam pedaled faster and faster, trying to get home before his grandfather realized he was gone. He turned off Division Street and raced down Horace Avenue. His house was now in sight. His grandfather's Chevy truck was still sitting in the driveway. Sam searched the yard for signs of him.

The coast was clear. He rolled into the driveway and dropped his bike against the fence. Retracing his steps, he darted from tree to tree, finally working his way around the rose bush and out of sight.

Climbing his way back up the rickety trellis and into his room was always the biggest challenge. Feeling the boards wobble beneath his feet, Sam knew if he grew much bigger, his additional size and weight would close this route of escape permanently. Gradually, he reached the top of the trellis. Hoisting himself over the windowsill, he fell to the bedroom floor. Safe at last.

CHAPTER FOURTEEN

Chef Pierre

Kidnapping a hysterical kid and bringing him to a carnival was not one of Victor's better moves, but what could he do? He knew his idea was a long shot; still, he had to give it a try. As he pulled the white van up to the information booth by the front gate of the carnival, a heavy-set woman stood up and brushed her pink bangs back into her bleached blonde hair and out of her eyes. "What can I do for ya, honey?"

"I have a delivery for a chef here at the fair. His name is Pete Peterson. My boss said the information booth would have a list of people working here and a map showing their location."

The blonde reached under the counter and pulled out a couple sheets of paper. "Pete Peterson, huh?" She mumbled as she ran her finger down a long list of names. "Here's a Chef Pierre. That's as close as I get to anyone named Pete. Any chance that's who you're looking for?"

Wait a minute, Victor thought. *Pete lay in their prison cell at night talking about France... and hoping he could go to Paris someday. With any luck, maybe that is him.*

"Let's give Chef Pierre a try," Victor replied. "Where can I find him?"

She ran her finger across the page. "Looks like he's working at 14B." Adjusting her turquoise glasses and double-checking the map, she added, "That's the small white building next to the big top. It says here that deliveries should be taken to the front door."

"No problem with that." Victor nodded and drove ahead. "Hey, kid, was that a masterful job of problem-solving or what? If all goes well, you should be home in time for dinner." Realizing the sobbing had stopped, Victor's eyes darted to the rearview mirror to see the kid hanging out of the back window. The glass in that window had been missing since he bought the van. "Get back in the van right now and sit down," Victor snarled. "Or I'm comin' back there and strap you to that seat."

Tommy crumbled to the floor and began rocking himself back and forth, trying to stop trembling from the sound of Victor's raging voice. "My goggles... they fell out the window... I want my mom... I want to go home," Tommy whimpered. He bit his lip, trying to keep from crying again.

The blackened eyes in the rearview mirror fixated on the little boy. "After I talk to Pete about a coin dealer, and you show me where those coins are, then maybe I'll take you home," Victor growled. "But right now you better behave. I have had enough of your games."

Victor parked and tied Tommy's leg to the back seat of the van. "You sit there and don't you make a noise. Understand?"

Tommy hung his head and cried.

Victor climbed out of the van, walked through the front door of a small white diner, and into the kitchen.

"Pete Peterson! Did I hit the bullseye or what?" Victor laughed at the sight of his prison cellmate dressed in a white chef's jacket and hat, standing at the stove, stirring an oversized pot with a big wooden spoon.

Pete looked up and his mouth dropped open. "What are you doing here?"

"Is that any way to greet your cellmate, Pete?"

"It's Chef Pierre to you, Victor."

"I'm gonna make this short and sweet, Chef. I need the name of the fence you said would buy my Double Eagle coins. I got the kid in the van right now; he's gonna show me where those coins are, and I'll be ready to sell."

Chef Pierre shook his head. "Not now, Vic. The guy who owns this gig is going to be here any minute, and the last person I need the owner seeing me with is my cellmate from prison. So get out of here, Vic. And take that kid with you."

Just as Victor opened his mouth to respond, a short, round-faced man with an American flag tattooed on his left bicep walked through the kitchen door. "Hey, Chef. Thought I'd come by to make sure you have everything you need for the big opening night."

Before answering his boss's question, Chef Pierre strolled over to Victor, and wrapping his arm around Victor's shoulder, walked him directly to the emergency exit. "Thanks for stopping by, pal. We'll be open tonight at five. Bring the whole family with you. Our soup is delicious." And without waiting for Victor to respond, the Chef gently pushed him through the emergency exit and shut the door.

Victor spun around as the door closed behind him. "Not so fast, Pete. I'm not done with you." Victor tried to pull the door open, but the red and white sign hanging in front of him — 'Emergency Exit Only. Please Use Front Door' — made him realize he was done… for now.

CHAPTER FIFTEEN

Ajoey

Paige was soaring, propelling through space effortlessly like a meteor streaking through the sky. The wind swirled about her, tossing her hair and muffling sounds of the crisp fall day. She had dreams about flying, but this was better. As she opened her eyes, the trees flew past her, blending into a palette of muted greens and golds. Unwilling to control the speed of her bike, she watched the pavement melt away beneath her feet. And then it was over.

The wind subsided, the countryside was still, and the spinning wheels of her bike slowed to a less enrapturing pace. Her flight down Stony Creek Hill had ended. Paige wished the ride was longer, but her bike ride to the bottom of the hill only ever lasted a few minutes.

Now she could hear Baxter and Marco riding ahead of her, jabbering away. They were always arguing over who had the best team in the NBA. Growing up with three brothers, Paige was used to talking sports. If she had been younger, she would have thrown in her two cents. But now she knew better. Baxter and Marco knew she loved the Phoenix Suns, and that wasn't going to change.

Endless arguments over unanswerable questions. How pointless. Maybe it would improve their debating skills, Paige wondered. No, it hadn't improved her skills, or her brothers' for that matter. She laughed to herself. She actually liked hearing them banter back and forth, but she would never let them know. Baxter and Marco were a great form of entertainment, and she loved them for that.

From somewhere not too far behind was the quiet hum of Maxwell's silver, motorized scooter. She was amazed that he built it himself. It could easily go thirty to thirty-five miles an hour on any given straight away.

He was always saying, "Wait until I upgrade the motor on this thing, then it will really fly." But speed didn't seem to matter to Maxwell. He always coasted about ten feet behind Paige's back fender. She knew he could keep up with them on a bike, but she was glad he had the scooter. It made it easier on his asthma.

Above the purr of the scooter's motor was the sound of Maxwell's voice. He was saying something about free throw percentages. *He is by far the smartest kid I ever met. He can solve a math problem in his head before the rest of us even turn on our calculators*, Paige thought. *I can't wait for the kids at school to see Maxwell's new haircut and clothes*. She smiled. *Even Sam didn't recognize him!*

Paige and Maxwell clicked immediately. The two of them were always laughing about something. And he would listen to her smallest problems: the ones she would never tell anyone else. *I'm lucky to have a friend like Maxwell*, Paige thought.

"We have company, Paige," Maxwell yelled.

As Paige looked over her shoulder, she saw Mr. Ruffin's dog Patton running beside the back tire of Maxwell's scooter, barking wildly.

Maxwell picked up speed until he was riding next to Paige. "We better stop and take him back to Mr. Ruffin, Paige."

Paige shook her head. "Baxter's already mad because we got such a late start to the fairground. If we stop now, he'll lose it again for sure."

"If we don't stop now, Mr. Ruffin will accuse us of kidnapping Patton. Mr. Guse is already out to get us; we don't need any more problems."

As Paige slowed her bike to a stop, Patton took one leap and landed in the basket on Paige's bike. While firmly planting his hind legs in the basket, The Great Schnauzer hoisted his front paws onto the rim of the basket to see where he was going.

"Get out of my basket right now, Patton, and go home!" Paige firmly commanded in between her muffled laughs. Patton was having no part of Paige's orders and held tight to his strategic position.

"It doesn't look like he's going anywhere, Paige. You might be stuck riding to the carnival with a dog in your basket," Maxwell said. "He's as unyielding as the famous World War II general he was named after."

By this time Baxter and Marco had brought their basketball debate to an abrupt halt, so they could see what all the commotion was about. Neither of them could believe their eyes.

Marco groaned. "What does that dog think he's doing?"

"Paige, get that dog out of your basket and let's go. We've wasted enough time. We're going to miss all the action," Baxter shouted.

Paige stopped and put Patton on the ground, but the strong-willed animal jumped right back into Paige's basket, placing his front paws back on the rim and barking as if to say, "Forward March!"

"He won't stay down," Paige protested.

Marco shook his head at Paige's newfound friend. "Then I guess we're stuck with him, Paige. Let's get going."

Paige started pedaling as Patton held strong with his round black eyes focused on the road ahead, ready to lead his troops into battle at a moment's notice. "Patton, the least you could do is run alongside of my bike like normal dogs do," Paige teased. Patton wagged his stubby gray tail and barked, ordering his new troops to resume their mission.

As they pedaled faster and faster, the fairground was now in sight. Finally reaching the high wooden fence surrounding the carnival, they dropped their bikes near the long row of poplar trees.

"I bet that loose board we snuck through last year is still here," Baxter said.

He ran over to a knotty board in the middle of the fence and pushed on the top. The bottom of the board slowly rose up from the ground, creating enough space for them to crawl through. Maxwell held the board up, and Baxter began to squeeze his over-sized body through the narrow opening.

The three of them stood and waited their turn, but halfway through the fence Baxter came to a complete stop. He moved neither forward nor backwards.

"What's the problem, Baxter? Are you stuck?" Marco pressed his face against the narrow crack between the boards, trying to see what was happening, but the space was just too pencil-thin. "Come on, Baxter, will you move it? We want to see what's going on, too."

Baxter was too overwhelmed by the chaos surrounding him to move. Dozens of people were unloading trailers, carrying boxes, and setting up booths and tents. Voices echoed through the air, while the muddled clamor of countless work crews resounded in the background. Huge black electrical cables ran along the ground connecting one area to the next, breathing life into the jumbled mess. Baxter's eyes darted from place to place, not knowing where to look next.

Maxwell switched hands again as he let out a lamenting sigh. "I'm getting tired of holding this board. What do you think he's doing under there?"

Marco flipped his hands up into the air and shook his head. "He forgets how big he is; he must be stuck."

Maxwell shifted his weight to his back foot. "Marco, maybe you and Paige should try shoving him the rest of the way through the fence."

Paige cringed. "No way am I touching Baxter's butt."

Marco laughed. "I'll get him through that fence. Watch this." Picking up an old plank he saw lying on the ground, Marco marched over and slammed the board against the fence. The three of them jumped at the loud bang, but Baxter didn't flinch. "We are not going to stand out here one more minute and wait for you, Baxter. Now either get in there or get out, because the next time you hear that sound it will be you that…"

Before Marco could finish his sentence, the ground beneath them began to rumble. "It's an earthquake," Marco yelled. "We're going to die!"

"Settle down, Marco, we're not going to die," Paige responded as she walked over and began yanking on Baxter's shirt tail. "Make up your mind, Baxter, in or out, so we can see what's going on in there!"

The Great Schnauzer charged to Paige's assistance. Grabbing onto Baxter's pant leg, he clamped down and began tugging and pulling in all directions. Patton attacked with such force that Baxter's leg bounced up and down, making him speak in perfect staccato. "O-kay-ay-ay-ay. I'm go-ing-ing-ing through. Just get that stu-pid-pid-pid-mutt-off-off-off-me-me-me-me-me."

As Baxter began to crawl the rest of the way through the fence, a deafening, almost prehistoric cry trumpeted through the air. Circus elephants rumbled by, barely missing Baxter's head. Instinctively, he pulled out of their way, hitting the back of his head against the fence board and falling flat on his face.

When the last of the mammoth beasts had lumbered by, a strange voice from somewhere above him was asking, "Are you all right? That was a close one."

Baxter looked up to see someone about his own age standing over him. "A person could get killed around here." He rubbed the lump already starting to form on the back of his head, hoping for some sympathy.

"You know the carnival really doesn't open till tonight. It will be a lot safer then, and you could come in through the front gate."

"Well, yeah, ah," Baxter stammered, as he rose to his feet. Having just been caught sneaking into the carnival, he was trying to think of something good to say. Anything. "We just wanted to see if... ah... some of you guys needed some help." Baxter picked up his hat and tried smiling at the stranger as he dusted himself off. *The front gate sure would be easier than squeezing through the fence*, Baxter thought. *Now I see why Maxwell 'factors in my girth'. I'm no little kid anymore.*

Finally, Paige had room to crawl through the fence. As soon as she stood up, the stranger automatically turned his attention from Baxter to Paige. His eyes were glazed over, his mouth hung open. He had never seen anyone so beautiful. "Who is this?" he muttered, unable to take his eyes off of her.

Paige didn't wait for Baxter to answer. She was enjoying the attention. "I'm Paige. What's your name?"

"I work over there in the Big Top. I'm a joey and a Roma..."

Before he could finish his sentence, Baxter started laughing. "Ajoey Andaroma. That's a great name."

By now, Marco and Maxwell had made it through the fence and were listening to the conversation. Baxter's strange view of things never ceased to amaze Maxwell.

Dusting himself off and pushing his glasses against his face, Maxwell took it upon himself to clear up one more of life's mysteries for his good friend. "Ajoey Andaroma is not his name, Baxter. A joey is someone in the circus who is training to be a clown. A Roma is a member of a Gypsy tribe."

Maxwell's added information only seemed to confuse Baxter further. He couldn't decide if Ajoey was luckier to be a clown or a Gypsy. Totally ignoring Maxwell's explanation that Ajoey wasn't his name, Baxter continued his line of questioning. "You're really going to be a clown when you grow up, Ajoey?"

Baxter's constant string of questions took the Gypsy boy's mind off Paige for a moment. He was overwhelmed with her beauty and welcomed the break. "Your friend is right. My name is not Ajoey." He looked to Maxwell for help before he continued, but Maxwell just shrugged his shoulders and shook his head.

"My name is Marcel Myshka. I'm learning to be a clown with the circus. My grandmother is Madame

Myshka, the fortune-teller. Her booth is right over there across from the Big Top."

Baxter thought Ajoey was the coolest kid he ever met.

"Don't you have to go to school?"

"I'm supposed to go to school, but I don't. The carnival is the only life my grandmother has ever known. She says if it's good enough for her, then it's good enough for me, so I don't get to school very often."

There is actually a kid who doesn't have to go to school, Baxter thought. *This is the coolest thing I have ever heard.* "You don't go to school. You're going to be a clown, and you're a Gypsy. You rock! Do you think you could teach me to be a clown, Ajoey?"

Maxwell peered over his glasses at Marco and shook his head. "That's it. I can't listen to one more word of this ridiculous conversation."

Marco let out one of his contagious belly laughs, and the whole group joined in.

With a gleam in his eye, Marcel smiled at Paige one last time. "I gotta go help Butch with the elephants. Maybe I'll see you guys later." The Roma took off, running after the elephants, leaving his new friends standing in the midst of chaos and commotion, and Baxter wondering why his friends were laughing.

CHAPTER SIXTEEN

An Unfinished Cup of Coffee

Sam never realized guilt could weigh so heavily on his conscience. Come to think of it, until now he never realized he had a conscience. His mother's instructions were not to be taken lightly, and her orders were to be followed to the letter. *But I'm home now, and there was no harm done; not really*, he thought.

Didn't mom want me to start making more decisions on my own? Yeah, but this was a bad decision, definitely an error in judgement. Sam hated disobeying his mother. He stretched out on his back, now covering his anguished face with both hands. He closed his eyes and pictured his mom disciplining him. He could hear her pointed remarks. He felt the guilt move down his body into his back. The pain was so sharp he rolled over to see if something was actually poking him.

Sam smiled. It was Supremo Grande, Tommy's favorite robot: the only sign that his pesky little brother had ever been in his room. *That's weird. I thought for sure Tommy would be sitting right here waiting for me. It's time to follow through with my promise and kick the soccer ball around with Tommy*. Sam jumped to his feet and took off, looking for Tommy and his grandpa.

Sam marched down the hall, doing his best loudspeaker imitation: "Supremo Grande, report your location. Your leader demands to know your whereabouts."

Receiving no answer, Sam continued on his trek, sliding down the banister and landing in the front hallway. "Supremo, we cannot defeat the Aliens without you. Confirm your location."

He walked into the kitchen to find Paige's mom Mary Paigenot pacing back and forth, talking on her phone. She was speaking in a low, soft voice, her eyes focused on the floor as she walked. His grandfather stood up from the kitchen table, and Sam could see the stress on his face.

"Sam, where have you been? I've been looking all over for you and Tommy."

Sam's heart stopped. He didn't dare tell his grandfather that he had been downtown. If his grandfather knew that he had disobeyed his mother, he would be in huge trouble. "I was around the other side of the house working on my bike." Sam looked at the floor. He hated lying, but it was the only thing he could think of to say.

"Is Tommy with you?"

"No." Sam dropped his gaze again; his face was burning.

"We can't find him anywhere. I was hoping the two of you were together. I called Mrs. Paigenot, wondering if she had seen you two. She came over to help me look for you boys, but there is still no sign of Tommy. She's calling the neighbors to see if anyone has seen him."

How is this possible? Sam thought. He looked at the kitchen clock. It was only two-thirty. He had been gone for less than a half-hour. *How could Tommy have gone anywhere in such a short amount of time?*

Sam could feel his emotions welling up inside. He wanted to tell his grandfather the truth, but he couldn't. Not now. He slid into a chair at the kitchen table, hoping Mrs. Paigenot would have good news.

Mary Paigenot hung up the phone and shook her head. "No one has seen Tommy."

The Paigenots were also new to the neighborhood, and Sam's mom, Rose, couldn't have asked for a better friend and neighbor. From the first day they met, Mary Paigenot was there to help her new friend. Rose knew if she was called to the hospital unexpectedly, Sam was old enough to take care of Tommy, but it was still reassuring for Rose to have her new friend next door.

Now Tommy was missing, and Mary was determined to find him. "Sam, when did you see Tommy last?"

"He was in my room about forty minutes ago, dressed up like Supremo Grande. You know… his favorite robot. He had on a red winter jacket, yellow goggles, a blue stocking hat, and black boots. I don't know how he could have gone very far wearing all those clothes."

His grandfather shook his head. "Mary, we need to call Bill right now and let him know Tommy's missing."

When Rose and the boys moved back to Esterville, Hank decided it was time for him to walk away from the stress and politics that went along with being Esterville's police chief and get to know his family who had lived so far away.

Before he left the police force, Hank made sure Esterville found a good replacement for their chief of police. The search went on locally for months. It wasn't until the city council decided to expand the search that they found a twenty-year police veteran from Arizona, Captain Bill Paigenot, who was interested in the job. The new candidate came across as hard-working, detail-oriented, and very caring. Hank knew Esterville would be in good hands.

Overall, Hank considered his career with the Esterville police to be very successful, and thirty years was enough time for anyone to spend at one job. Hank knew the name of every family in town, who locked their doors at night, and who didn't. He was ready to take it easy and spend time with the grandkids.

Hank vowed he would lay down his badge and never look back, but that was easier said than done. Near the end of his career there was one case that continued to eat away at him. One mystery he never solved: the death of Alex Decker.

The week leading up to Alex's disappearance had been a slow one. The only crisis that week had been a call from Henley Ruffin. Someone had sprayed the letters EHS (Esterville High School) on his Schnauzer Patton with orange and blue paint, and Henley wanted Hank to find the culprit immediately. As Hank was driving away from the station to solve the mystery of the orange and blue Schnauzer, the police dispatcher came over his walkie-talkie with the hysterical voice of Mrs. Decker.

"Alex is gone. His bike is here, but Alex is nowhere to be found. We have looked everywhere for my son… my Alex… he's gone."

"Mrs. Decker, please calm down." Hank could hear the dispatcher trying to make sense of what Mrs. Decker was saying.

The frantic mother tried again. "Alex's friend, Nate Davison, had to pick up some bakery goods for his mother at Ruffin's Muffins. Alex rode his bike downtown with him and waited on his bike while Nate went into the bakery. When Nate returned, Alex's bike was there, but Alex was gone… gone… gone…" Mrs. Decker repeated the word over and over again until all the dispatcher could hear was her uncontrollable sobbing.

And so the search for Alex Decker began. There had been no sign of a struggle, and no one had seen or reported any abduction. Alex had disappeared without a trace. Hank ordered all police personnel on double shifts, and all other police business was placed on the back burner until the Decker boy was found. The police department worked twenty-four/seven following up a long list of calls and sightings of the boy, but they all resulted in the same dead end.

Three days passed, and Hank was working another twenty-four-hour shift when he decided to grab a quick cup of coffee at Cook's Café and think about his next move.

As Hank walked into the café, the usual people were sitting at the counter. He could hear them speculating about what happened to Alex Decker, and he didn't want any part of the conversation. He hoped sitting at the far end of the counter would help him avoid the gossip.

Oliver Cook was setting out the lunch menus when he saw Hank sit down.

"How about a cup of the strong stuff, Chief? Looks like you could use it."

"Thanks, Oliver."

The owner of the café set a mug of black coffee on the counter in front of Hank. "How's the Decker case going, Chief?"

"No conversation today, Oliver. I'll just drink my coffee."

"Hank, I think you should answer Oliver, and tell him what's happening with the Decker case," barked Arnold Guse from the far end of the counter. "When is this police department going to get their act together and find that little boy? Maybe it's time we bring in the FBI."

Hank took a sip of his coffee, trying to ignore Guse's remarks, but his taunting continued. "Arnold, you know every police department in Cambria County has been notified and we've sent out state-wide and national alerts.

Locally we are doing everything we can. Unfortunately, this is going to take time."

"We need to send a search party out to the swimming hole. That lake is the only area we haven't searched," Arnold Guse complained. "I tell you, if you want something done right around here, you have to do it yourself! And you're going to make us handle this one, too. Aren't you, Hank?"

Hank looked down the counter at a group of angry faces all nodding in agreement with Arnold Guse, waiting for Hank to answer. "Arnold, why don't you take care of the hardware store, and let me handle police business. I'll let you know when we've exhausted all possibilities." The gray-haired police chief picked up his coffee and took another sip.

"But have you dragged the lake?" Guse persisted. "No harm in searching that entire area. What do you have to lose, Hank? I bet these folks right here would be glad to help you."

Silence fell over the room as they saw Alex Decker's father John enter the café. Everyone could feel the sadness that weighed upon the poor man. They knew he still clung to hope that his son was alive. "I've been looking for you, Hank. What have you heard from the state patrol after issuing the missing person alert?"

Hank shook his head. "We keep checking that throughout the day, but no new leads yet, John."

John's temper flared at the news of Hank's dead-end report. "My son is out there somewhere, so why are you in here drinking coffee, Hank, when you should be searching for Alex?" John glared at the people sitting at the other end of the counter. People he once considered his neighbors and friends. "And what's wrong with the rest of you? Why would we drag the lake? My son is alive, and don't you forget it."

Hank put his arm around his friend's shoulder. "John, you know this whole town is behind you. Every one of us is willing to do whatever it takes to bring Alex home safely."

The room was stone silent.

"My grandson is the same age as Alex, and I still can't imagine what you're going through," Hank continued. "I haven't slept in my own bed since the 911 call came through that Alex was missing, and as soon as I finish this quick cup of coffee, I'm taking off again."

John Decker's shoulders slumped as he hung his head and exhaled heavily. "I know you haven't stopped looking for my son since he went missing, Hank, and the wife and I appreciate it. If these people think you ought to be checking out that lake area, then I reckon they could be onto something."

"Unless you have a better idea, I think you ought to jump on this one, Hank. This town needs answers. We all need to get out there and keep looking for Alex till we find him," Oliver Cook argued as he wiped the crumbs off the counter.

The people at the counter nodded in agreement and waited for Hank to answer.

He could see there was no changing their minds. The next thing Hank knew, the locals at the counter were in their cars on the way to search the Stony Creek beach area, and he was lining up a team of divers to drag the water for Alex Decker's body.

Their ground search was futile. By late afternoon a large crowd of people stood motionless on the shore, watching the silhouette of a small motorboat move across the new man-made lake and anchor near the dam. Three men in their scuba gear fell backwards into the water. The crowd waited the divers' return, their eyes never leaving the boat.

It was Oliver Cook who first saw movement on the water. One diver was making his way back into the boat, soon followed by a second. Although the divers' backs were to the shore, there was no doubt they were pulling something into the boat.

Before the sun set behind the hills that day, Alex Decker's lifeless body was lying on the banks of Stony Creek. As Hank worked his way through the somber circle of people, he could hear them whispering, "Poor Alex Decker... drowned... How could this have happened? He was such a good swimmer."

Hank took one look at the boy and knew it was no drowning. Alex Decker's neck was broken. *What happened that brought his life to such a senseless end?* Hank wondered. *And how did he end up way out here by the swimming hole without his bike?* The police chief glanced up at the old railroad bridge suspended high above the icy river. Did Alex fall from the bridge to the water below? Or did someone push him?

He knelt down beside the body and searched the clothing, hoping to find a clue. There was nothing. As he began to stand, he noticed Alex's left hand clutched in a tight fist. The crowd watched silently as Hank pried open the boy's fingers. In Alex's hand lay a gold Double Eagle twenty-dollar coin, the only piece of evidence in the case that Hank never solved.

Alex Decker had gone missing — and now possibly his own grandson. *What happened to Alex Decker is not going to happen to Tommy. I won't let it.* Hank picked up the phone and called Bill Paigenot, Esterville's new Chief of Police.

CHAPTER SEVENTEEN

Gertrude Rockelstadt

Orange light from the late afternoon sun flickered through the broken panes of glass, breaking the darkness into haunting shapes and shadows. The repeated banging of a worn-out shutter intensified the panic swelling inside of him. One boy was dead, a second one kidnapped, and he still hadn't found the Double Eagle gold coins.

Victor shivered as the cold fall air blew through the broken, kitchen window of the abandoned house. He buttoned his collar, trying to fend off the cold, as he thought about how easy it had been to steal the coins.

His plan had been simple, and the old woman was the perfect mark. He took care of her and became like family to her. She trusted him. He could have stolen more, but it wasn't necessary. The rare coins were worth more money than one person could possibly spend, and he would be gone from her house before she learned the small chest of coins was missing.

He spent days preparing to leave. He combed the house, making sure no trace of him was left behind. The few belongings he did have were packed in a worn-out duffel bag stashed under his bed.

The black van was filled with gas and awaited his escape. He hated that van. It was covered with rust, and the back bumper hung by wires from the frame. The interior was just as worn out and dilapidated. He deserved better. The old junker reminded him of his meager existence every time he drove it, and he swore he would buy a Tesla the second he sold the coins. Then people would see how important he was.

Victor spent weeks convincing the old lady he needed a day off, using family problems as an excuse, before she finally agreed to Wednesday. He planned on leaving Tuesday night, giving him almost thirty-six hours to travel before she realized he was not coming back.

Tuesday seemed to last forever. Tension consumed his body, waking him up early that morning. Every noise he heard was magnified. Branches brushing against the windows sounded like fingernails scraping on a chalkboard. Her shrilly old voice screeching orders sounded like some prehistoric bird attacking its prey.

"Victor, get in here! Victor, fix the storm window! Victor, shovel the snow! Victor, take out the trash…"

If he heard her shriek his name one more time, he thought he'd kill her; but he marveled at his patience. He kept telling himself, 'This is the last day… you can make it… just make it through today.'

She finally went to bed at eight o'clock. He waited still another hour before entering the study where she kept the coins. Quietly, he opened the desk drawer and removed the chest. He laughed as he read the inscription on the lid:

O wicked, lustful greed
Avoid temptation, mark my heed
Lifting this lid will take its toll
The Angel of Death shall steal your soul

He stifled another laugh. "Gertie, you stupid old bitty. Do you really think this silly riddle will protect your treasure?"

He remembered spying on the old lady through the crack in the study door. An auctioneer was slowly examining each coin before dropping it back into the metal box. He told her about the rare 1933 'Double Eagle' coin that sold for a million dollars at an auction the night before. "That sale set a new record, Mrs. Rockelstadt. These coins are at least as valuable."

And now they were his. He dropped the chest in his duffel bag and left through the back door.

Leaving in the middle of the night was not one of his better ideas. The snow was falling when he got up that morning, and it continued all day. By the time he was ready to leave that evening, six inches of snow covered the ground. The winding mountain roads were icy, and the North wind was wicked, making visibility terrible.

Weather forecasters had predicted a major blizzard. He had survived blizzards. These conditions made even those snowstorms seem mild. He had been driving for hours, but the snow continued to engulf the van like a raging avalanche.

The clouds of snow cleared only long enough for Victor to see vehicles scattered in the ditch along the roadway. Buses, SUVs, and even a squad car joined the smaller cars in one snow bank after another. He didn't like his chances for surviving the night.

The multi-colored lights on the dashboard seemed to flicker to the beat of the music. Amanda Lockwood was singing one of his favorite songs on the radio. Victor loved listening to her play guitar. Her voice flowed through the van; he could feel her arms wrap around him, warming him from the inside out.

He used to think she wrote her songs especially for him, each line describing his lonely existence, but not anymore. The bad times were over. The coins he lusted for were his. His luck was changing, and this time for the better. He smiled as the music ended, releasing the tension in his body, but a radio newscast brought him back to reality: 'Due to deteriorating weather conditions, the highway patrol is closing all major freeways from the Ohio border to Harrisburg.'

His plan had been to drive all night: put as many miles as he could between him and the old bag. Still, he couldn't afford a run-in with the police. Unable to see the road signs in the whiteout conditions, it was hard to tell for sure where he was. When his headlights illuminated the sign, 'Esterville: Population 5,220', he decided it was time for him to get off the freeway. It didn't matter where Esterville was. It was his first stop on the way to being a rich man.

He would rent a room for the night and be back on the road the next day. Late spring snow always melted quickly in Pennsylvania. The roads would be better tomorrow. He had the coins, and that was all that mattered. The song was over; he turned the radio off and kept singing, wishing Amanda was here to share his good fortune.

The back roads to Esterville were even worse than the four-lane highway. A semi-truck thundered by his van. The driver couldn't have been going more than twenty, but it seemed three times that speed to Victor. A whirlwind of snow enveloped the van, eliminating any trace of the road. The tires began to slide. His knuckles were white as he tried to steer the van in the right direction. Managing at the last moment to pull the van back on the road, Victor let out an exasperated sigh.

The next time the wind subsided, the faint yellow lights of Esterville began to glimmer off in the distance. His body slumped with relief. He knew he would make it now, even if he had to walk. He parked the van in front of the Esterville Hotel and turned off the ignition. His plan was in motion.

Victor was up at the crack of dawn, and people were already shoveling the sidewalks. Snow had drifted over park benches and almost covered many of the first-floor windows. The roads still weren't plowed. It was easy for him to see he wasn't going anywhere for quite a while.

Victor decided he could use the time to get a bite to eat. He crossed the street to Ruffin's Muffins, hoping the roads would be cleared by the time he was finished eating breakfast. Waiting to be seated, he saw a stack of *Esterville Gazette*s lying by the cash register. He paid ninety-five cents for a copy and sat down at the counter to read the paper.

A bad case of nerves made Victor comb the paper front to back, looking for an article about Gertie's missing treasure. He knew it was too soon for her to have discovered it was gone. She didn't expect him back at work until tomorrow, and there was no reason for the old lady to check on her gold coins. Still, he wanted to make sure.

Well, no news about the old bag today, Victor smirked. *And I already have hundreds of miles between us*. He finished reading the paper and laid it on the counter. Casually taking his last sip of coffee, he graced the waitress with a twenty-five cent tip and left the restaurant whistling his favorite Amanda Lockwood song.

He was only planning to stay in Esterville overnight, but when he saw the quaint little town in the daylight, he realized it was the ideal place for him to hide. Tucked away in the hills of Pennsylvania, its obscurity provided the cover he needed. It was the perfect hideout; at least until he knew if the police were looking for him and the missing coins.

Each day he combed the *Esterville Gazette*, looking for news about the stolen treasure. He timed his meals at

Ruffin's Muffins so he could watch the news on their thirty-inch TV. Days passed without any reports of the stolen coins. Was it possible that she still had no idea her precious treasure was missing?

It wasn't until Sunday that he finally saw the old lady's name in the *Gazette*, and not at all where he expected it would be.

Victor had been reading the obituary columns for years. At first it was just something to do: one more reason to pour himself another cup of coffee. Eventually, it became a habit. He read every entry to see how many survivors each deceased had left behind. He envied the people with big families. He hadn't seen his own sister in years, and for all he knew she was dead. Over the years he had come to realize that he would be one of those people listed with no surviving family.

Now, as he read today's obituaries, there was Gertrude's name big as life. Second column, third person from the top:

Gertrude Rockelstadt, age 86,
of Johnstown, Pennsylvania
passed away
Thursday, March 3rd
at 11:00 a.m.
from a massive coronary.
No survivors.

Was it possible? Victor stared at the words, unable to believe what he had read. The only other person who knew about the coins died before she ever knew he stole them. It was too good to be true.

There's only one eighty-six-year-old Gertie Rockelstadt of Johnstown, Pennsylvania. No mistake about that, Victor thought. And there she was in the obituaries, and not a word about the missing coins. It was more than Victor could have ever hoped for.

Now, after years of dead-end jobs, and drifting from town to town, he had finally got his big break. He steals a treasure worth more than he could count, and the lady he steals it from dies before she ever knew he took it. And no survivors! He wanted to leap on the counter and start dancing, but somehow he remained calm. Leaving his standard twenty-five cent tip, Victor paid the bill and left Ruffin's Muffins.

That was months ago. Now he sat in an abandoned house. One kid was dead and another kid locked in an upstairs bedroom, refusing to tell him where the treasure was. *I should be in Vegas by now. Instead, my life is spinning out of control.* The anger inside of him was raging and the familiar lyrics of his favorite Amanda Lockwood tune were clanging in his head:

*My luck is slippin' through my fingers
And I can't make it right
Life's in reckless ruins
I won't last the night...*

Victor stood up, picked up the old wooden chair he was sitting on, and threw it across the room. He kicked open the back door and ran to his van. *My luck isn't 'slippin' through my fingers'. Time to head back down to the carnival and finish my conversation with Pete. And this time I'm going to 'make it right'.*

CHAPTER EIGHTEEN

The Zipper

"We have wasted enough time, Baxter." Maxwell looked at his phone. "It's already three o'clock. Let's check out some more animals."

No response.

Maxwell yelled at Baxter again. "I'm done standing around. How about the horse barn?"

Still no answer. Taking a few steps closer, Maxwell realized Baxter and Marco were staring blankly in the same direction, transfixed like statues and barely breathing.

Paige finally walked over and nudged Marco. "What are you guys staring at, Marco?"

With his body as stiff as a board and his eyes frozen straight ahead, Marco's whisper was barely audible. "The Zipper…"

Towering over the entire Midway loomed an enormous oblong metal boom holding twelve two-person cars, each enclosed by steel mesh.

Without waiting for Marco to finish, Baxter charged into the conversation. "This ride hurls you twenty feet up in the air and whirls you round and round and upside down until you think you're going to be sick. And just when it starts slowing down and you think you might survive, it starts all over again, propelling you through the air like a rocket. It sucks you in, chews you up, and spits you out; and you're never the same again."

Maxwell shook his head. "And here I thought you were a victim of bad genes, Baxter. Little did I know your brain was scrambled by The Zipper."

Any other time, Baxter would have had a comeback for Maxwell's remark, but this time his snide comment went unnoticed.

The formidable Zipper was obviously taller than any structure in Esterville, and the mere sight of the metal giant had Baxter and Marco mesmerized. Paige held her breath to keep from laughing. She had never seen anyone scared stiff before, and her two over-sized friends looked pretty silly.

"It's reduced all of us to the size of a bug," Marco choked.

Baxter slowly took one step back after another, tilting his neck, straining to see the top of the metal beast. "The Zipper is so tall I can't even see the top car, Paige."

Paige was constantly amazed at the sheltered life her friends led in the small Pennsylvania town. She saw buildings twice that big every day in Arizona, but the three-story clock tower in the town square was the tallest structure in Esterville. She couldn't wait to tell Sam about Marco and Baxter's reaction to The Zipper.

Maxwell, on the other hand, was unfazed. "If the two of you understood the physics behind these rides, you would realize The Zipper is not half as frightening as it appears to be. It is really very safe."

Marco and Baxter's eyes grew wider yet. Their heads slowly turned from The Zipper as they re-focused their relentless stare upon poor Maxwell. From the look on their faces, Maxwell realized he should have kept his mouth shut.

"Have you ever dared ride The Zipper, Maxwell?" Marco muttered from his trance-like state.

"Well, no. I never have."

"Then let's have some respect for the Beast, Maxwell."

Paige shook her head. "You two can be so dramatic. I need to see this for myself. Nothing can be that scary."

Paige and Maxwell headed toward The Zipper. She turned around to see if the other two were behind her. Neither of the boys had moved.

"Are you guys coming, or do we have to check out The Zipper by ourselves?"

Baxter grabbed onto Marco's shirt. "Paige is right. It's probably not even hooked up to electricity yet. We should be safe."

Paige rolled her eyes. "Oh, I can't believe you guys. Let's go, Maxwell. I'm not scared."

Patton barked and The Zipper's spell was momentarily broken. Slowly, the four of them started walking toward the ominous metal creature. The Zipper grew taller and looked more colossal the closer they got.

Without warning, a large figure emerged from the menacing shadows cast by The Zipper. "What are you kids doing? It's dangerous here right now, and people are trying to get their work done." The voice was as loud as the metal Beast's roar when it awoke to hurl its victims through the air.

In front of them stood the only man massive enough to guard the daunting machine. The beard on his face was as black and unkempt as the shoulder-length hair on his head. His torn T-shirt was stained with the grease he used to nourish the steel monster. "You're gonna get hurt hanging around here."

"Boy, he's not kidding, and he's the one that's going to hurt us," Marco whispered.

"He's bigger than one of those guys carved on Mount Rushmore," Baxter cringed.

"This park is off limits till we open tonight! If you kids don't get out of here right now, I'm going to call security and have them toss you out," the stranger roared.

The Zipper was overwhelming, but the Zipper Master was unbearable. The man's enormous black shadow covered Baxter's entire body, and the sound of his deep, raspy voice exploded in his ears. With adrenaline racing through his body, Baxter spun around and ran for the fence, the other three only steps behind him.

Patton took off in the shuffle and ran smack into Baxter's leg. Baxter lost his footing and tumbled headfirst into the loose fence board. The board flew up. Baxter rolled through the opening, landing face down in the dirt.

Finally finding the strength to pull his head up off the ground, Baxter realized his nose was only inches from a pair of black and red Nike Airs. As he continued to lift his head, he saw the Nikes were connected to the legs of none other than Randy Bartlett, the Brainless Wonder.

I am definitely having a rough time with this fence today, Baxter thought. *And from the look of these shoes, it's not going to get any better.*

Randy was laughing his obnoxious laugh. It was really more of a low-pitched cackle that sounded like a broken foghorn. It had worn on Baxter's nerves since the day they met. He found the sound especially irritating lying face down in the dirt.

For a brief second the cackling stopped, and was replaced by the only thing Baxter found even more nauseating: Randy's obnoxious voice. "Wow, Baxter, that's one of your best moves yet. Will you teach me how to roll around in the dirt like that?"

Now all of the Brainless Wonders were laughing the same disgusting cackle. Baxter groped for one of his witty comebacks, but somehow lying in the dirt left him speechless.

Marco had been watching the whole event through a hole in the fence. "You want to look, Paige?"

"I don't need to look. I'd recognize that whiny voice anywhere," Paige whispered.

Marco shook his head. "Could our timing get any worse? We have King Kong breathing down our necks on one side of the fence and Randy Bartlett and the Brainless Wonders on the other."

Maxwell shrugged his shoulders. He found the situation absolutely stimulating; it was one of those rare opportunities for a real-life debate. This was one talent that came as natural to him as breathing. And today, with his new haircut and mod clothes, Maxwell oozed with confidence. "Randy isn't a problem. I can take care of him."

Maxwell charged under the fence. As he stood up, he realized his nose barely reached the chest of Randy Bartlett, who was easily fifty pounds heavier and two heads taller.

"Well, well, well, Maxwell Vanderbilt. I hardly recognized you without your Afro. Looks like you shrank five inches," Randy snickered.

Maxwell didn't blink an eye. Manipulating Randy was going to be a piece of cake. "'Fro o' no 'Fro, Homeboy, it's yo' lucky day." Maxwell's newly found swag was flowing, and he was working his rapper impersonation to a T. "If yo' go right now, yo' can get yo'self some free cotton candy, Bro. The guy over by The Zipper is giving it away. If he's not there, just go behind The Zipper and look for him. He said we can call him 'Greaser'."

"Free cotton candy! You've got to be kidding, Maxwell. Thanks for the tip. I'm starving. Tell Baxter we'll save him some if he ever stops rolling around on the ground." Randy let out one more of his nauseating chuckles.

"Pleasure's mine, Dude." Holding eye contact with Randy, a small smirk crossed Maxwell's lips.

As the Brainless Wonders scrambled under the fence, Baxter crawled to his feet. "Wait till Sam hears about this. That guy at The Zipper was like Big Foot's cousin. He's going to eat the Brainless Wonders alive."

"Good move, Maxwell," Paige cheered as she patted Maxwell on the back. "And you looked so handsome doing it!"

Maxwell puffed up his chest. "When your opponents are as brainless as Randy Bartlett, you can manipulate them into doing anything."

The rest of them started laughing. They were going to make sure Sam got a play-by-play account of the whole afternoon. As they walked to their bikes, Patton darted into the bushes. The branches began to shake; leaves and twigs were flying left and right. The Great Schnauzer's ferocious growl emanated from the vibrating foliage. Minutes passed. Finally, the endless thrashing stopped and Patton emerged victoriously from battle.

"What's he got in his mouth?" Marco asked.

Baxter took a step back from the growling animal. "Don't ask me. I'm not getting near that dog. He's mad. All he's missing right now is some white foam drooling from his mouth."

After riding to the fairgrounds with Patton sitting in her basket, Paige knew Mr. Ruffin's Schnauzer wasn't going to hurt any of them. "Come here, Patton. What do you have there, boy? Bring it here," Paige coaxed as she clapped her hands together.

Patton slowly moved toward Paige, a shiny object hanging from his mouth and a low gurgling sound in his throat. Paige carefully patted his head and then his nose. "It's okay, boy. Drop it."

Patton unclenched his jaw and dropped his newly discovered treasure on the ground. There in the dirt lay a mangled pair of yellow glasses. Marco bent over and picked them up. "It looks like a pair of those protective goggles my dad wears in his wood shop."

"They appear to be a little more refined than that, Marco," Maxwell analyzed.

Baxter grabbed the glasses out of Marco's hands. "Nah. These are ski goggles. My mom used to have a pair just like them." Baxter put the goggles on his face. With a pair of imaginary skis on his feet and matching ski poles in his hands, Baxter began twisting his hips, planting his feet first to the left and then to the right as if he was swooshing down a ski slope.

"Hey, I'm rockin' it now. How do I look?" Baxter asked.

Patton cocked his head and barked. The rest of them just laughed.

"You're not getting these back, Patton. They wouldn't fit you anyway, and Halloween is just around the corner."

With the newly found ski goggles firmly planted on his face, Baxter hopped on his bike and hollered, "Let's move it out!"

Still laughing, they climbed on their bikes. Patton leaped into Paige's basket, front paws on the rim. The entire group headed back up Stony Creek Hill and straight to Sam's house. They couldn't wait to tell him everything he had missed.

CHAPTER NINETEEN

Another Double Eagle

How could Tommy be missing? Sam closed his eyes, trying to escape what was happening, but his mother's words echoed in his head: "This would be a good chance for you to spend some time with Tommy. You know how he looks up to you…"

What had he done? A feeling of panic rushed through his body. He wanted to interrupt his grandfather to say he was sorry for leaving Tommy alone, but the words wouldn't come. Sam opened his eyes and tried to concentrate on his grandfather's phone conversation with Chief of Police Paigenot.

"Sam thinks it's been about forty minutes since he saw Tommy. A lot can happen to a little kid in that amount of time. I'd appreciate if you would alert the patrol cars that we're looking for him, and have them watch for him, too. There's no evidence of abduction right now, so let's hope he just wandered off…"

Sam watched Hank pace back and forth as he talked on his phone with Bill Paigenot. The sound of his kind, steady voice triggered mixed emotions in Sam. He felt a real loss when his dad died, but his relationship with his grandfather Hank helped fill that void. Moving back to Esterville had given both of them the time they needed to get re-acquainted. He trusted his grandpa would find Tommy. Hank would make sure of it.

Mary Paigenot, on the other hand, was not so sure as she listened to the tension build in Hank's voice. Unable to wait any longer for him to finish his conversation, she left the kitchen to search the house one more time.

She could hear the desperation in her own voice as she repeatedly called out, "Tommy! Where are you?"

Each room was as empty as the last. Frantically, she climbed the stairs, looking for something that would lead her to Tommy. In no time she found herself in Tommy's bedroom. The late afternoon sun flooded a room cluttered with toys and books. Pieces of his robots lay everywhere, but Tommy was nowhere to be found.

There has to be a clue to Tommy's whereabouts somewhere in this mess, Mary thought. *Being married to a policeman for twenty years should count for something.* She had no idea how many crimes Bill had solved over the years, but it was his attention to the unnoticed, incidental clues that often solved the case. He always said, "People lie, but the evidence doesn't."

Something isn't right here. There's a clue in this room somewhere, and I'm going to find it.

She began to search through the clutter, methodically inspecting every inch of space. Finally reaching the toy chest, she started picking up Tommy's toys and putting them in the chest. A glimmer of light flickering from a small metal object lodged under the edge of the chest caught her eye. Mary dug and pulled at the object until she pried it loose.

Lying in her trembling hand was a rustic twenty-dollar gold coin, unlike any money she had ever seen. Areas of the coin had been worn away, making it difficult to read the inscription or the date, but the eagle stamped on the coin was clear and added to its unique nature.

This looks like something that should be in a museum, not under a child's toy box, Mary thought. *What would a little five-year-old boy be doing with something so valuable?* She snatched up the coin and hurried back downstairs to show Hank.

The moment she entered the kitchen, Hank began talking to her. "Bill said he would issue an APB. He wants us to focus our search on the neighborhood." From the hopeless look on Sam's face, Hank knew he better try to keep the situation positive. "It's not going to be too hard for someone to spot a five-year-old boy walking around in a red winter jacket and yellow goggles, Sam. Tommy will be home in time for dinner."

Sam gave his grandfather a half-hearted smile. "Grandpa, it's going to be dark soon. Tommy hates the dark…" The sound of Sam's voice drifted off. He could still hear himself arguing with Tommy: "Get lost… I don't have time for you." His own words kept ringing over and over in his head. If only he could take back those words.

Mary sat down next to Sam, and laid the old coin on the table. "What do you make of this, Hank?"

One look at the gold piece and Hank's face turned ashen white. He had seen something very similar to it once before. "Mary, where did you find this?"

"Under Tommy's toy box. Doesn't it seem odd that there would be something so valuable in a five-year-old boy's room?"

Hank grabbed the coin from the table. "This coin is almost identical to the one I found in Alex Decker's hand when we pulled him from the lake. We never did find out what he was doing with it. How on earth could Tommy have one too? Sam, have you ever seen this coin before?"

Sam's mind was racing, trying to remember. "I did see Tommy with something like that a while back. It was the day before school started. He and mom had just come home from the grocery store. Tommy was saying something about Alex Decker, but I didn't understand what he was talking about."

Alex Decker. Hank could hardly listen to Sam say the name.

"Now that I think about it, I might have seen the coin in his hand, but at the time I just thought it was one of those Super Medallions he's collecting from the Pizza Villa downtown."

Hank walked over to the kitchen table and put his hand on Sam's shoulder. "Is there anything else you can remember, Sam?"

"Well, what he said was weird, Grandpa. He said Alex Decker gave him that coin."

Hank sunk into his chair. Was it possible that the unsolved case of Alex Decker was connected to Tommy's disappearance? Had his own grandson been pulled into the nightmare that surrounded Alex's death?

Hank held his composure, keeping his voice firm and steady. "Sam, that's not possible. Alex died before you moved back to Esterville. He couldn't have given the coin to your little brother."

"That's why it was so weird, Grandpa. If the Deckers sold the house to mom because their son died, there's no way Alex could have given Tommy the coin. But if Alex didn't give it to him, then where did Tommy get it?"

Sam thought about the day he saw Tommy with the gold coin. *How could I have ignored my little brother like that?* "I guess I didn't pay much attention to what he was saying. It's hard to know when Tommy's pretending and when he isn't. I just figured he was making up that stuff about Alex Decker giving him the coin."

Hank shook his head. How did Tommy end up with a coin just like the one Alex Decker had? And where did he get it? Hank failed to find Alex Decker in time; he wasn't going to lose Tommy.

"Grandpa, don't you think we should call Mom and let her know Tommy's missing?"

"Not yet, Sam. Let's give it a little more time to see if he just wandered off. He hasn't even been gone an hour; no need to worry your mom yet. We'll have your brother home in no time." Hank began to organize their search for Tommy when noise erupted from the backyard.

"Tommy!" Sam yelled.

The three of them ran to the door, only to find Paige and her companions parking their bikes by the back porch. Paige looked at Sam and then at her mother. Something was definitely wrong. "Sam, what's up? And Mom, what are you doing over here?"

Mrs. Paigenot opened the screen door and walked onto the porch. "Sam's little brother Tommy is missing. Your dad has the squad cars looking for him, and we're starting to search the neighborhood. You kids could be a great help to us. Sam's grandfather will tell you what he would like you to do."

"How long has Tommy been gone, Mom?"

"Less than an hour, but every minute counts. Listen to Hank. He will get you and your friends organized. We need to search as much of an area as we can before it gets dark."

Sam and Paige exchanged glances. Sam furrowed his brow, and intensified his stare. The shake of his head was barely noticeable. He was trying to tell her something. Sam was mouthing the word Guse's.

Paige finally nodded back; she got his message. He was trying to let Paige know that his grandfather still didn't know he left the house to meet his friends at Guse's. She turned away to hear what Hank was saying.

"More than likely we'll find Tommy at one of the neighbors' houses. Work in pairs. Two of you can cover the houses toward Stony Creek Road. The other two can head toward Division Street. Knock on every door. Explain you're looking for Tommy. Give them his description and my phone number, so they can call me if they find him. Check the alleys, backyards, and playgrounds. Somebody has to have seen something. Sam, you stay around the house in case Tommy comes home."

Sam nodded to his grandfather before he started describing Tommy to his friends. "The last time I saw Tommy, he was dressed up like Supremo Grande, that cartoon robot. He had on a blue stocking cap, a red winter jacket and black boots…" Sam's voice trailed off. Overwhelmed by the situation, he drew from every bit of strength he had to finish his brother's description. "Oh, and…uh… Tommy was wearing glasses on his face." He hung his head and spoke, more to himself than to his friends, "How could he have gone very far wearing all those clothes?"

Hank patted Sam on the back. "Don't worry, Sam; we're going to find your little brother. Does everybody know where they're going? Let's meet back here at five. One of us should know something by then." Hank took the car keys from his pocket and headed for his Chevy truck. *What's the connection between Tommy and Alex Decker?* he asked himself. *If I had solved the Decker case, maybe Tommy wouldn't be missing now.*

Baxter was thinking over what he had just heard while he finished twisting his new-found goggles onto the handlebars of his bike. *Tommy must have disappeared while Sam was down at Guse's.* His face lit up like a light bulb. "Hey, Sam, did this happen while you were...?"

Yanking on Baxter's sleeve, Paige interrupted him mid-sentence. "Come on, Baxter, get on your bike. You and I can work together. It's going to get dark soon; we're wasting time."

"Give me a second here, Paige; I'm trying to talk to Sam." Baxter tried to pull his arm away, but Paige held tight. With Paige standing right between the two boys, it was impossible for Baxter to finish talking to Sam.

"All right, Paige, you win. You can let go of my arm now." Baxter climbed on his bike and started riding away from the porch.

Waiting till she thought they were far enough from the house, Paige decided she could tell Baxter what she learned. "Tommy was missing when Sam got home from Guse's. I don't think his grandfather knows that Sam left Tommy alone to meet us. His grandfather still thinks Sam has been home all day."

"Wow. No wonder Sam looks so down. We gotta find Tommy, or Sam will never forgive himself." Baxter climbed on his bike, giving the yellow goggles an extra twist around the handlebar to make sure they wouldn't fall off.

Already on their bikes, Marco and Maxwell rolled over to talk to their friends. "Which way are you two going?"

"Paige and I'll take Stony Creek Road. We'll see you back here in an hour. Come on, Paige, let's go find Tommy."

Paige and Baxter pedaled down Horace Avenue and onto Stony Creek Road. Patton, The Great Schnauzer, was close behind.

CHAPTER TWENTY

A Gold 'Demallion'

After stopping at the first four houses, there was still no sign of Tommy.

"Somebody should have seen Tommy by now, Baxter. I'm scared."

"You think you're scared, Paige? It's been six months since Alex Decker died, and I still sleep with the light on." Baxter wiped the sweat off his face and looked over his shoulder again. It was the third time since they left Sam's house that he checked to see if someone was following him.

"Baxter, how come you guys never told me about Alex Decker?"

"People around here don't like talking about his death. I guess things like that aren't supposed to happen in small towns. They closed school for a whole week when he was missing, and there wasn't a kid allowed out of their house unless they were with an adult." Baxter tried to clear the lump in his throat, so he could continue. "Alex and I were the same age. Everybody liked Alex."

The serious tone of Baxter's voice sent shivers down Paige's spine. It was hard to see her over-grown friend so scared. "Esterville is a small town, Baxter. I can't believe they never found out what happened to Alex Decker."

"We always thought Sam's grandfather would find the guy, but he never did. Alex was kidnapped in front of the bakery. It took them three days to find his body. Kids at school said Alex was clutching a gold demallion in his hand when they found him. I just figured they were making it up."

"That's medallion, Baxter, medallion."

"That's what I said, demallion."

Paige rolled her eyes. "Now I see why Sam's Grandpa looked so worried. The kidnapper could still be around here. What if he has Tommy?"

"We have to find Sam's little brother. That's all there is to it. Here's the next house. Maybe they'll know something."

Paige rang the doorbell, and Nate Davison, the tall, gangly guy in her fifth-hour science class, opened the front door. He never gave anyone a straight answer, and Paige was hoping he would be a little more cooperative when she talked to him this afternoon.

"Hi, Nate. Baxter and I are looking for Sam's little brother Tommy. He's five years old and has blond, curly hair. He's wearing a red jacket, a blue stocking cap, black boots and some glasses. Have you seen a little kid around here who looks like that?" Paige felt funny asking if he had seen a little kid dressed up in all those clothes, but Nate didn't seem to think anything of it.

"No, I haven't seen any little kids around here. How long has he been missing?"

"We think he's been gone an hour or so. It's getting late, and we want to find him before it gets dark." Paige tried smiling at Nate, but he was staring right through her.

"You know my friend, Alex Decker, went missing last spring, and Sam's grandfather found his body at the bottom of the lake."

Paige gasped at the boy's response. She looked at Baxter, hoping he could move the conversation in a different direction.

Baxter gave her the nod. "Yeah, what happened to Alex still freaks me out. I heard his neck was broken when they found him."

Paige grimaced at Baxter's thoughtlessness. Paige knew she could be more sensitive than that, and she didn't even know Alex Decker. Elbowing Baxter in the side, Paige said, "What Baxter means to say is that's awful, Nate. I bet you really miss Alex."

Even Baxter was feeling uncomfortable now. He started twisting the elastic band of his visor around his finger, hoping he would think of something to say.

"Yeah, we were best friends. I was the one who talked him into going downtown. I left Alex waiting for me outside of the bakery, and I never saw him again." Nate's voice trailed off as he walked Paige and Baxter to their bikes. Looking down to hide the tears in his eyes, he noticed the yellow goggles hanging on the handlebars of Baxter's bike.

"Where did you get those goggles, Baxter?"

"I found them down at the fairgrounds today. Aren't they cool?"

"They are cool. Alex had a pair just like that. They were the only pair like that I'd ever seen till now. It's getting dark; I suppose you guys better get going. Hope you find Sam's little brother."

Paige and Baxter hopped on their bikes and continued their search, stopping at the last three houses on the block, but no one had seen Tommy.

"Baxter, we're at least a mile from Sam's house. There's no way that a little five-year-old kid wandered this far away."

"Yeah, and it's almost five o'clock. We're supposed to be back at Sam's house in a few minutes." Baxter shook the thoughts of Alex Decker from his mind. "Hopefully, one of those guys has found Tommy."

As they turned onto Horace Avenue, Marco and Maxwell were already parking their bikes under the hemlock tree in Sam's yard. Anxious to hear what their friends had discovered, they raced toward the house. With no little boy in sight, they knew the situation was becoming more serious by the minute.

CHAPTER TWENTY-ONE

Cracked Goggles

"Any luck?" Baxter asked.

Maxwell shook his head. "Not one person could help us ascertain Tommy's whereabouts."

"No luck here either," Paige responded. "We stopped at Nate Davison's house, and he told me all about Alex Decker. If Alex's kidnapper is still in Esterville, he could have kidnapped Tommy."

Marco dropped his bike on the ground and moved closer to his friends before he began to speak. "You're talking about someone who is wanted for kidnapping and murder, Paige. It would be crazy for a person like that to hang around the town where he committed the crime. That guy is long gone."

"Unless the killer lives in Esterville," Maxwell speculated.

Visions of Alex Decker's lifeless body were still fresh in Baxter's mind. "Let's hope you're right, Marco. They pulled Alex Decker from the bottom of the lake after he'd been missing."

Sam came out of the house in the middle of their conversation. With no sign of Tommy and the serious looks on their faces, Sam knew it wasn't good. He looked from one person to the next. Each one of his friends was staring at the ground, shaking their head. "Don't give up yet, you guys. We just started looking," Sam coaxed. "We'll find him."

Baxter didn't want to hear Sam's pep talk. "Sam, we were just talking about what happened to Alex Decker. Maybe it's time we let the adults handle this."

Paige was in full agreement with Baxter. She joined in right away. "What if Tommy was kidnapped? We're just kids and it's getting dark. We can't take on a kidnapper. We need to let the police find Tommy!"

"I can't just sit and do nothing either. It was awful waiting here by myself for you guys to get back. My kid brother is missing. I have to keep looking. If we pull together, I know the five of us can find Tommy."

Maxwell was nodding in agreement. "You're right, Sam. This group can do anything they put their minds to, and right now every minute counts. We need all the people we can get to look for Tommy. We have to keep searching for him while it's still daylight."

Marco was nodding his head in agreement. "I'm with you, Maxwell. We'll find your little brother, Sam. I can feel it."

"I knew you guys wouldn't let me down."

At that point, Hank pulled into the driveway. Anxious to see if he had found Tommy, Sam headed for the truck, but Baxter's bike fell over, blocking his way. The yellow goggles dropped off Baxter's handlebars and onto the ground in front of Sam.

Sam picked up the goggles. "Where did these come from, Baxter?" Sam gasped.

Unsure why Sam was so interested in his new yellow goggles, Baxter was slow to respond. "Ah, Ruffin's dog Patton dug them out of the bushes at the fairgrounds today. You want to try them on, Sam?"

"You couldn't have found them at the fairgrounds today. These are the glasses Tommy had on the last time I saw him. I can tell by the red trim around the frame and the crack in the glass. Tommy's were cracked in this exact same spot. He had to keep moving them over to the left side of his face, so he could see around this crack."

By this time, Hank had walked over to see what the kids were talking about.

"Grandpa, Baxter found these goggles when they were down at the fairgrounds today. But I saw them on Tommy when he was in my room earlier this afternoon." By now, Sam was talking so fast that his grandfather couldn't understand a word he was saying.

"Slow down, Sam. How do you know these are the same glasses Tommy had?"

"See this crack, Grandpa? It was in front of his left eye and he kept pulling the goggles over to the left side of his face like this, so he could see around the crack." Sam put the goggles on to show his grandfather what he meant. "And see this red trim? See how all the paint is flaking off?

I was looking at that red metal when Tommy had them on, wondering just how old these ski goggles must be." Sam handed Hank the goggles and waited for him to speak.

"These aren't ski goggles, Sam, they're old railroad goggles. Where would Tommy get something like that?"

"I don't know. I just thought they were a pair of mom's old ski goggles. I don't have a clue where Tommy could have gotten a pair of old railroad glasses, but he was wearing this pair this afternoon."

Paige remembered Nate Davison saying the goggles also looked familiar. "Mr. Rogers, we stopped at Nate Davison's house. When he saw Baxter with those goggles, he said his friend, Alex Decker, had a pair just like them."

Hank's face dropped. The similarities were overwhelming. First the gold coin and now the goggles. He carefully studied the goggles as he mulled over what he now knew about the two cases: *The coin from Tommy's room is identical to the one we found in Alex Decker's hand... Alex had a pair of goggles just like the ones the kids found at the fairgrounds... and Tommy was wearing them today... There's no way a five-year-old boy could have walked to the carnival by himself. Something more serious has happened, and every second that passes will make it more difficult to find Tommy.* Hank pulled his phone from his pocket.

Sam was still waiting for an answer. "Grandpa, what does all this mean? How could Baxter find Tommy's goggles at the fairgrounds? And how could Alex Decker have had a pair just like them?"

"That's what we have to figure out, Sam. Let's go inside. Maybe Mary will make you kids some hot chocolate while we wait for Chief Paigenot to get here. And it's time I called your mother to let her know Tommy's missing."

It seemed like only minutes before Chief of Police Paigenot arrived at the house.

Hank handed Bill the goggles as he spoke. "The kids found this pair of goggles at the fairgrounds this afternoon, and Sam is certain they are the same ones Tommy was wearing today. We need to start searching the fairgrounds, Bill, before the trail to Tommy grows cold."

Bill Paigenot nodded his head. "Absolutely, and let's get these goggles down to the lab; check them for fingerprints to see if they are Tommy's. I'll call the station and have someone pick up the goggles and this coin."

Hank agreed. "A lot of people's prints are probably on both of these items; we'll need something of Tommy's to send along so they can match the prints."

Mary knew they needed to make the most of each second. "Bill, I'll run the goggles downtown. I can be there in a few minutes." Before Bill could answer, Mary grabbed one of Tommy's toys to match the little boy's fingerprints to the prints on the new evidence and left the house.

Bill turned to Hank. "I'm heading down to the fairgrounds. See what leads I can come up with down there."

Hank was not about to sit idly by while the Chief of Police searched for his grandson. "I know this town better than anyone. I'm coming with you, Bill."

By the look on Hank's face, Bill Paigenot knew there would be no arguing with him. "Let's get going then. We're wasting time."

Sam and his friends leaped up and started for the door.

"Not so fast, Sam. Where do you think you're going?"

"With you, Grandpa."

"Oh no you're not. You and your friends are staying right here. Someone needs to be here in case Tommy comes home. We'll let you know if anything turns up at our end."

"But Grandpa, we have to go with you. Baxter can show you where they found the goggles."

Chief of Police Paigenot was not about to conduct a search for a missing child in the company of his daughter and her friends. "Baxter has already explained to us where he found the goggles. If we need more information than that, we'll let you know, Sam."

The two men headed for the car, and Sam and his friends were left standing in the middle of the kitchen, silently staring at one another.

Sam finally broke the silence. "It's getting pretty obvious that Tommy didn't just wander off somewhere, and I'm responsible. I have to find him, and I'm starting right now by going to the fairgrounds." Sam's voice trailed off as he headed for the back door. "Are you guys coming or not?"

Not this again, Marco thought. "Sam, you have to try listening to your grandfather. This has gotten way bigger than something kids can handle."

Sam shook his head. "I'm the one responsible for Tommy's disappearance. How can I stay here and do nothing?"

Clinging to the hope that Tommy might still show up, Baxter turned and walked to the kitchen window, searching the yard for the little boy and waiting for his friends to make a decision.

Maxwell had already analyzed Sam's latest plan, and knew he wasn't making a good decision. "A pattern is starting to develop here, Sam. Look what happened the last time you didn't do what you were told to do. Maybe we should just stay home like your grandfather said and let the adults handle this."

Sam didn't back down. "I can't stay here and do nothing, Maxwell. The longer we wait, the less chance we have of finding Tommy. Every minute counts. We need to go right now if we're ever going to find my little brother."

Maxwell rubbed his short hair. "We have to consider the new data, Sam. It is becoming increasingly apparent that Tommy didn't just wander off. Finding the goggles at the fairgrounds today is a good indication that something else has happened; someone else is involved."

Marco was nodding his head up and down. "Maxwell's right, Sam. You didn't live in Esterville when Alex Decker disappeared. It's been six months, and I still can't get to sleep at night. There's no way we can take on a kidnapper and maybe even a murderer. The grown-ups need to handle this."

Sam refused to listen. "I've already lost my dad, Marco; I'm not going to lose my brother too."

Silence fell upon the room.

Paige tried to imagine the guilt Sam was feeling. His brother was missing, and Sam thought he was to blame. She walked across the kitchen and stood by Sam. "Maxwell, you're the one who said this group could do anything we put our minds to. I, for one, agree with you. And right now, 'anything we put our minds to' means helping Sam find Tommy."

Sam knew the power Paige had over Maxwell. Everyone said Maxwell's IQ dropped twenty points the second Paige walked in the room. Sam was hoping that hadn't changed.

"Well, uh," Maxwell stammered as he looked into Paige's big blue eyes. He could feel his body temperature rising as he tried to continue. "We are all in firm agreement that we are friends no matter what." Beads of sweat were forming on his forehead as he watched Paige gently push a strand of hair from her face. "And uh... There is no doubt that best friends must help each other when they're in trouble," Maxwell sputtered as a drop of sweat rolled down his nose.

Paige smiled at Maxwell.

Her teeth are so white, and her eyes sparkle, Maxwell thought. His glasses had now slipped down his sweaty nose and were dangling on the tip. Maxwell pushed them back in place. "It certainly doesn't take a rocket scientist to comprehend that Sam's little brother is definitely in trouble…" Maxwell's confidence was returning, his head clearing. "Which brings me to the obvious conclusion that it's time for all of us to head down to the fairgrounds and find Tommy."

After considering their options, Marco was in total agreement. "Let's go find that Gypsy kid we met this afternoon. I bet he knows the fairgrounds like the back of his hand. He could tell us if Tommy's been down there."

With no sign of Tommy, Baxter was ready for some action. "Yeah, we'll get Ajoey! He's the man. He'll help us find Tommy."

"Let's go. It's almost dark," Sam yelled as he ran for the door.

Maxwell knew there was comfort and courage in numbers, and soon they would need all the strength and courage they could muster. What lay ahead would test them as never before.

CHAPTER TWENTY-TWO

Black Waters

"These stupid carnivals never give ya enough space to park a decent size vehicle. I've been around this lot three times now, and I still can't find a stinkin' parking spot." Victor laid on the horn. There wasn't anything to honk at. He just wanted to make some noise.

He drove around the lot again and finally squeezed his van between a shiny red Mustang convertible and a black 2018 Ford Ranger. As he took the keys from the ignition, the van coughed and sputtered. It sounded like a death rattle every time he turned off the engine.

There were only inches left on either side of the van, but he opened the driver's door anyway: smack into the Mustang convertible. Victor looked down at the three-inch space and knew he was never getting out of the van. He rolled his eyes and slouched over the steering wheel, gripping it till he thought it would break.

Esterville couldn't have been a better place to lay low after I stole the coins, Victor thought. *How did it go so wrong?* He banged his head on the steering wheel, trying to clear his thoughts to remember where the heist went wrong.

"The old lady was my pawn," he snickered. "Even after Gertie died, I waited to make sure her estate was finalized, and no questions were being asked about the missing coins," Victor mumbled to himself. "I took my time before making my move: before selling the coins and heading to Vegas."

The box of coins weighed a ton; there was no way I could carry it around with me. Victor fell deeper into thought. *The van didn't lock, and even if it did, someone still could have broken in and stolen the coins.* He laughed when he thought about his hotel room. That wasn't safe either. *Nothing was ever where I left it when that snoop of a maid was done cleaning.*

He could still remember driving around aimlessly, desperately hoping to find the right place to hide his coins. Not far outside of Esterville the van started misfiring. He groaned and shook his head in disgust. "I'm gonna have to pull over and check the stinkin' carburetor again. How can I be sitting next to a million dollar treasure and still not have any money to buy a new set of wheels?"

He parked alongside the road to check the carburetor one more time. While the snow was already melting in town, it was still deep along the country road. The trees and brush were covered with a beautiful white glaze, and the forest glistened in the sunlight. The scenic view let him take his mind off his engine problems for a brief moment.

As he was about to stick his head under the hood, he stopped. Looking again through the woods, he saw an old house covered with vines. The newly fallen snow clung to the creeping vines, melding the house and the forest together. Shutters had fallen from the fortress and the front door hung open, luring its uninvited guest closer.

Here on the outskirts of town, miles from anybody, tucked away in an abandoned house, was the place he had been looking for to stow his precious coins.

By the time he reached the front porch, he was freezing and his feet were soaked. He ran through the door, hoping the house would provide warmth, but its dank hollow walls only made him colder.

The windows were boarded up, making it difficult for him to see in the dark, and the uneven floorboards creaking beneath his feet were wearing on his nerves. Frustrated, he stomped on the loose board under his foot, hoping to stop the irritating squeak.

Victor screamed as the far end of the board flew up and hit him in the knee, sending a shooting pain through his leg. In a fit of anger, he picked up the board and hurled it across the room. As he bent over to grab another loose board, Victor saw a crawl space beneath the floor, and his rage came to an abrupt halt. The space beneath the floor was the perfect place to hide the coins.

Victor jumped into the crawl space and began digging a hole in the dirt to bury the chest of coins. His fingers already ached from the cold, and digging became increasingly painful. He dug in the half-frozen ground until his fingers bled. He couldn't dig one more second; his bloody fingers throbbed. He placed the chest in the shallow hole and scraped as much loose dirt over it as he could, but the top of the chest was barely covered. "This is going to have to do for now," Victor groaned, rubbing his aching hands. He placed the broken boards back over the hole in the floor and left the house.

His coins were finally safe.

Weeks passed. The snow had melted; the days were getting warmer. Spring was in the air, and it was time to make his move to Las Vegas. But he still couldn't find the contact he needed to buy the coins.

He had just returned from checking out a coin shop in Harrisburg and decided to get something to eat. Victor parked the van in front of Ruffin's Muffins and was already thinking about what he should order for lunch.

At first he didn't even notice the Decker kid, but the coin Alex was flipping sparkled in the sunlight, catching Victor's eye. As he watched the boy flip the coin in the air, he saw the eagle stamped on the shiny gold piece, and his heart stopped. The kid was flipping a Double Eagle twenty-dollar gold coin. *How could a kid in Esterville have a Double Eagle just like mine? They are too rare for this to be a coincidence.*

Victor stared at the kid and wondered, *What are the chances some kid could have that same exact coin? The coins have been hidden under the floor of the old house for weeks. I just checked on them yesterday. How could some snot-nosed kid have found them?* Victor clenched his fists as the rage swelled inside of him.

Looking back on it, he knew he should have taken time to calm down, but he wasn't thinking straight. Victor rolled down the passenger window and yelled at the kid. "Where did you get that coin?" No answer. Frustrated, Victor barked at him again. "Where did you get that coin?" Still no answer. Worse yet, the boy started backing up his bike, getting ready to ride away.

No one is going to take those coins from me. Victor leaped out of his seat and yanked the sliding door of the van open. He pulled the kid off his bike and into the van. Victor towered over the boy. His voice was so loud it vibrated off the van's metal walls. "Tell me where ya got that coin."

Alex was gasping for air, his words stuck in his mouth. Victor shoved him to the floor. "I asked you where you got that coin, kid."

Still trying to catch his breath, Alex remained silent.

Victor tied Alex's wrist to the front seat, jumped behind the wheel and drove away. He needed time to think.

I'll scare that little runt into telling me what he knows about the coins, Victor thought. Parking the van along the side of the road, he grabbed Alex by the collar. "I'm going to ask you one last time where you got that coin. And you better answer me, or you are going to disappear and no one will ever hear from you again!" Victor pulled Alex to within inches of his face and waited for him to speak.

Alex gagged. It felt like hours before he found enough courage to talk, but he knew it was only seconds. "All right, Mister, I have the coins. I found them in the abandoned house. I didn't know they were yours. Kids are messing around in that house all the time. Someone was bound to find them."

Victor's head was throbbing. "I'm not messin' with you, kid. You show me where they are right now."

"Okay. I'll show you where I put them; just get your hands off me," Alex said in a trembling voice. But his head was clearing, and he was finally able to think. *There's still a chance I can escape. I still might be able to get away from this guy.*

The chest filled with coins was heavy and impossible to carry home on his bike the day he found it, so he filled his pockets with the coins and tucked the empty chest under one of the old railroad bridge trestles. *Hopefully that decision will save my life*, Alex thought.

He would take his abductor to the old railroad bridge where he left the empty chest. While the guy was getting the chest from under the trestle, Alex could make a run for it. He knew it would be risky, but it was his only chance.

Alex directed Victor past the abandoned house and down the dead-end road. Victor pulled over onto the side of the dirt road and parked the van by the abandoned railroad bridge. Alex sat in the van, trying to explain to Victor where on the bridge the chest was located, but Victor wasn't having any part of it. He lost his fortune once; he wasn't going to lose it again.

"You're not going to tell me where you stashed those coins; you're going to show me. Get your sorry butt out of this van right now, you little puke, and start walking," Victor ordered.

Alex opened the van door and headed toward the trestle where he had hidden the empty box. Victor, only a step behind, was shoving Alex, trying to make him move faster.

"Okay. Quit pushing. The box is right over there under the ties along the edge of the bridge." Alex pointed in that direction, hoping Victor would kneel down and look, giving Alex time to get away. "Just look underneath the bridge; you'll see it."

"Not on your life, kid. You get down there and get me that box. How stupid do you think I am? And don't do anything funny. I'm watching you."

Alex knelt down, pretending to reach under the bridge for the hidden chest. If he was going to get away, Alex knew he had to create a distraction.

"Let's go, kid, I don't have all day. Get that box up here, and do it now."

"I'm trying, but it's stuck. I can't…" Alex continued to act like he was prying the box loose. "Ouch! I cut myself. I'm bleeding." Alex grabbed his hand to fake an injury.

"Get out of the way, ya little wimp. Let me see what's down there."

As Victor bent down to look for the treasure, Alex jumped up to make his getaway. Victor grabbed for the boy. Alex pulled away, losing his balance. His ankle twisted and his knee buckled. His foot slipped off the edge of the bridge. Alex was falling backwards.

Victor jumped up to grab Alex's hand, but it was too late. Alex's arms were already flailing behind him as he tried to regain his balance, but the pain in his twisted ankle made it impossible.

Victor reached for Alex one last time. The boy opened his mouth to scream, but there was only a silent gasp of air. Their fingers brushed, and Alex fell.

Victor stared into the black torrent waters below, searching for Alex. He ran to the opposite side of the bridge, again scanning the rapid currents for the boy. All he could see were the white caps of the breaking waves. Alex was nowhere to be found. The coins were his life, but Victor never wanted anyone to die for them.

Victor raced off the bridge and down the hill toward Stony Creek to rescue Alex. Reaching the bank, he plunged into the icy waters where he last saw the boy. Instantly, the swift current knocked him over, carrying him downstream. The piercing cold water tossed and turned his paralyzed body, pulling Victor into the darkness below.

When his body surfaced, Victor was crashing against the rocky shore. Forcing his feet into narrow spaces between the boulders along the water's edge, Victor pushed with every ounce of strength he had, hoisting his body away from the torrent river and over the stump of a fallen tree. He lay inches from the lethal waters, his body shaking, and the blood freezing in his veins.

He brushed the ice from his lashes and searched the white caps for Alex one last time, but the boy was gone.

Victor's body throbbed; his chest pounded, as he gasped for air. He had to get back to the van while he could still walk.

The feeling in his hands was gone, so he wrapped his arms around each boulder and pulled, dragging himself to the next rock and the next, until he reached the top of the hill. He turned toward the van and stopped. After all this, he still didn't have the chest.

Victor couldn't give up now; too much had been sacrificed; he began doddering toward the treasure. He covered his face from the wind and blew into his hands, wishing his breath would warm his fingers. He tried to make his feet move faster, but the walk down the track was endless.

The moment he lifted the chest from underneath the trestle, he knew it was empty. He ripped open the lid and screamed until the last breath of air left his body. "All of this for nothing! A boy is dead, and my coins are gone..." The empty chest fell from his hands.

Frozen to the core, he turned his back on his hopes and dreams and hobbled to the van. The heat finally kicked in, making the pain in his thawing feet return, and the pain in his heart explode.

Now, six months later, Victor could still see the graven image of the boy reaching for help as he fell into the raging river. Six months in prison had not erased the scene from his mind.

Victor lifted his face from the steering wheel and shook his head, trying to forget that painful day. Squinting from the flashing carnival lights, he covered his eyes with his hands and rubbed his face. *What's done is done. I can't bring that kid back, but I can still find the coins. Pete can still give me the name of the fence who will buy the Double Eagles.*

Victor looked down at the narrow space between the van and the red Mustang and pulled his driver's door shut. He climbed out through the back doors of the van and laughed. "Who said if you can't open the doors, it's not a parking spot?"

He slammed the rear doors shut and started walking toward the carnival. Victor jumped as the van backfired one last time and the rear doors bounced open. "Don't start with me," Victor yelled at the van. He carefully pushed the doors back into place and walked through the carnival entrance.

"Pete said he always wanted to be a chef," Victor mumbled to himself as he walked toward the diner. "I still can't believe he found a job right here in Esterville."

One way or the other, Pete is going to give me the name and number of that guy, or else, Victor thought. Elbowing his way through the crowd, he picked up his pace. *I still have a chance. I'll find my coins... and I'll be rich.* He pushed open the door and walked into Pete's kitchen.

CHAPTER TWENTY-THREE

File That Under Never

Never before did Sam have such a clear mission. He flew through the streets as if someone was chasing him, almost forgetting that he was the one in pursuit. His eyes were searching for concealed obstacles as he raced at breakneck speed toward the distant glow of the carnival to save Tommy.

As Sam propelled his bike through the darkness, he thought about everything that had happened and tried to imagine what he was about to encounter. He tried to picture Alex Decker and wondered why anyone would kidnap him and how he ended up dying.

"I can't let the same thing happen to my kid brother."

"Did you say something, Sam?" Paige asked, pedaling as fast as she could, trying to keep up with him.

Sam had been concentrating so hard, he didn't realize he was thinking out loud. This was no time to tell Paige what was on his mind. "I said thanks for helping me look for Tommy. You guys are the best friends I could have."

Paige smiled. She felt the same way. Now within blocks of the fairground, she watched as the soft glow of the carnival lights gradually transformed into a brilliant illumination. She listened as the sound of music and people's voices filled the air.

As they reached the parking lot, Marco finally caught up to Sam. "We've been pedaling like crazy trying to catch up to you!" He could hardly catch his breath. "At this pace, we'll have Tommy home before your grandfather even gets down here!"

Thinking about what he should do first, Sam barely heard what Marco was saying. "Let's leave our bikes over by the poplar trees."

Within seconds, the cadre of friends was piling through the narrow opening in the carnival fence, their adrenaline pumping. Glittering lights against the dark sky had changed the dingy fairgrounds into a sparkling illusion. They gazed around at all the promising sights and treasures the carnival had to offer.

Merchants were selling their wares, while others were luring people in to play their games. "Step right up... everybody's a winner... hit the bullseye and win the prize of your choice... guess the right number and win your girlfriend a teddy... bear, that is," snickered a scraggly vendor with only a few hairs left on the top of his head.

A crowd of people gathered to watch a juggler loft ball after ball in the air as he rode a unicycle around the stage. His audience roared as he spun a plate on the end of a stick that was balanced on his finger. "Come one, come all to the biggest show on earth," he shouted.

"Uncaged wild animals, the stupendous Brogan Brothers' high-wire act, and Huxford the Human Cannonball are all about to begin in the Big Top. Buy your tickets here…"

Paige shivered as strangers shuffled by her. "Boy, this place looks different at night," Paige whispered to no one in particular. She didn't want the others to know, but she was afraid. Did they really expect to find Tommy in the middle of all these people? And what about the kidnapper? They didn't know the first thing about police work, no matter how many chiefs of police they were related to. "Let's go back," Paige blurted out. "Who are we kidding? We should have stayed home like your grandfather told us to do."

"Now that's a superb idea, Paige. This is a big mistake." Maxwell had reconsidered his decision to leave the house a dozen times already. "It's not too late. Let's go home."

Sam spun around, staring at Maxwell in amazement. "Forget that, Maxwell! We need to find that Gypsy kid you guys met. What's his name? Ajoey? Where would he be?"

Baxter agreed with Sam immediately. "Yeah. Ajoey the Gypsy will know if Tommy's been here."

Maxwell was still shaking his head and muttering to himself. He couldn't get past the idea that coming to the carnival was a very bad decision, potentially life-threatening. "We still have time to go home," he mumbled to himself.

Tired of waiting for Maxwell to tell them where they should look for the Gypsy, Sam asked him again, "Where do you think we can find Ajoey, Maxwell?"

"Once again, his name isn't Ajoey. It's Marcel. He said he was a joey, that's someone training to be a clown." Finding himself locked in Sam's cold stare, Maxwell knew instantly that he should have kept that piece of information to himself.

With Sam's relentless stare still upon him, Maxwell scratched his head, trying to decide where the most logical place to find Marcel would be. "The Zipper is to the right. We know what's down there! I would say we are more than likely to find Marcel in the Big Top getting ready to perform with the clowns."

Sam grabbed Maxwell's arm. "Then let's go find this Marcel kid. We're wasting time."

As Sam and Maxwell spun to their left, Maxwell ran smack into Randy Bartlett, the Brainless Wonder. Bouncing off Randy's chest, Maxwell's glasses went flying as he landed flat on his hind end. Randy yanked Maxwell off the ground by his arm and pulled him within an inch of his face.

His eyes were so scrunched they had all but disappeared. And his face had surpassed red. It was purple! Randy was ticked. "So Greaser has some free cotton candy for us, huh, Maxwell?"

The other Brainless Wonders were only a step behind Randy, and the three of them were just as mad. They were huddled so close together, Maxwell thought they could have easily passed for a three-headed man in the carnival. He didn't need Sherlock Holmes to tell him that he was in big trouble.

As Randy reached out to grab Maxwell's other arm, Sam forced himself between the two of them. "Randy, if you have an issue to take up with my friend, Maxwell, you're going to have to go through me first."

Sam was not as tall as Randy, and he could have used at least another twenty pounds to really make his point, but at this moment it didn't matter. Sam was ready to take on the whole world with one hand tied behind his back if it meant finding Tommy.

Marco and Baxter couldn't believe their eyes. They always knew Sam had spunk, but they never thought they would see him stand up to Randy Bartlett. They moved in closer, making sure Sam knew they were there to help. After his run-in with Randy that afternoon, Baxter would have loved the opportunity to get even with him.

"Get out of the way, Sam. My fight isn't with you," Randy ordered. "Your so-called friend here set us up for a confrontation with some giant over by The Zipper this afternoon. He's not getting away with that."

"You're a big boy, Bartlett. Looks like you survived." Sam shoved Randy away from Maxwell. Losing his balance, Randy fell over one of the black electrical cables running along the ground, landing flat on his back. Instantly, Sam pounced on him, pinning his arms to the ground.

The Great Schnauzer Patton charged within inches of Randy's face. A fierce growl gurgled in his throat, and drool dripped from his mouth.

"I'm going to tell you this one time, Bartlett, and then I'm going to get up and walk away. And so are you. Maxwell is our friend. And that means you and your buddies are going to leave Maxwell alone. Stay away from him — and us for that matter! You don't scare us, and we don't have time for you or your whining."

Randy's face was still scrunched up like a sponge, but he didn't respond. Sam knew he had made his point.

Jack Porter, another Brainless Wonder, had bigger issues than Greaser or cotton candy on his mind. "Come on, Randy. You know what the coach told you about fighting. If he finds out you've been at it again, you'll never make the team."

Sam barely released the pressure on Randy's right arm to see what he would do. Randy didn't retaliate, for the time being anyway. Sam got up and held his ground, making Randy roll over on his side to stand.

Randy's best friend, Jimmy Smith, was getting tired of waiting for Randy. He was ready to have some fun. "Let's go, Randy. We'll take care of these little seventh graders on the basketball court."

Randy looked Paige up and down. "What are you hanging around with these losers for, Paige? You should come with us. We'll show you how to have some real fun."

Paige laughed. She couldn't stand Randy Bartlett. He was the most arrogant guy she had ever met. "You can file that answer under NEVER, Randy."

Randy's friends had already started to walk away. He turned to catch up with them. Then he looked back over his shoulder. "I'm not done with you, Sam. You better watch yourself."

Sam didn't move a muscle. "I'll be waiting for you, Bartlett. On or off the court!"

By now, Marco and Baxter were pounding Sam on the back. "Way to go, Sam," Marco howled.

"Way to kick butt!" Baxter cheered. "That was the coolest thing you have ever done."

Maxwell had finally caught his breath and was putting his inhaler back in his pocket. He tried to thank Sam, but his friend was already running toward the Big Top.

"Come on, you guys. We can't waste any more time," Sam shouted. "We gotta find Marcel Ajoey."

Maxwell thought about explaining one more time the Gypsy boy's name was just Marcel, but he knew it didn't matter to Sam.

Too much was happening. It was hard for Baxter to stay focused on finding Tommy when he was standing in the middle of all this excitement. "Look at that guy," Baxter exclaimed.

Their attention was immediately turned to a small crowd of astonished spectators watching a performer lying on a bed of nails while sliding a flaming sword down his throat.

Marco was shocked. "That's gotta hurt!"

"Ew! That's gross," Paige grimaced.

Maxwell assured them that while lying on a bed of nails appeared to be very painful, it didn't really hurt due to the even distribution of weight. "The performer's weight, although substantial, is spread out evenly over all of the nails, thereby avoiding impalement."

"But how can he swallow a sword? Look at that flaming blade? His stomach must be on fire!" Baxter cried.

Sam was not distracted. He ran past the sword swallower toward the Big Top. He was standing in front of Madame Myshka's fortune-telling tent before he realized his friends were not behind him. He couldn't wait any longer; he had to start looking for Tommy somewhere. What better place to begin than talking to someone who claimed to know the past, present, and future?

CHAPTER TWENTY-FOUR

When Your Life Goes Up In Smoke

Victor ducked behind the counter as the frying pan flew past his head.

"Now get out of my kitchen, or I'll call the police." This time the cook picked up a large black kettle and flung it at Victor. Victor ducked to the right, dodging the pan as it crashed into the wall behind him.

"You can't threaten me!" Victor retorted.

"You're in a world of trouble, and you are too stupid to know it. I'm not having any part of it," the cook raged. "I lay in that prison bunk night after night, listening to you brag how smoothly the robbery had gone. How you left the house with coins worth millions of dollars, and the old bag died before she or anyone else knew you had stolen them. So where are these coins? Huh, Vic?"

Victor was up for a good fight. He laughed, infuriating the cook even more. The cook grabbed the coffee pot and hurled it at Victor. The lid flew off, splattering coffee across the kitchen. Victor bobbed out of the way one more time as the pot hit the closet door behind him.

Wiping coffee grounds from his face, Victor walked toward his adversary. Now within inches of the cook's face, Victor's whole expression changed. His brows furrowed, his eyes darkened, and an angry scowl moved across his face.

"Listen up, Pete. You told me you'd get someone to buy these coins from me, and you're not going to back out of that promise now. I'm not leaving here without a name and a phone number."

"That was months ago when we were in prison. I told you Fred would buy those coins because I thought you had them. You got nothin'! Except one dead boy. A dead boy, Vic," the cook repeated. "And you were stupid enough to drag a second kid into this. And even dumber to drag him down here this afternoon. Worst of all, you got him holed up in some abandoned house, and there's still no sign of this so-called treasure. You are never going to get yourself out of this mess."

Victor backed off. "That kid is the only one who knows where Decker hid my Double Eagles; and don't worry, he's gonna tell me where they are, Pete. I'll have the coins for Fred by tonight."

"Okay, Victor. If you wanna know, I called Fred and told him all about you and your so-called treasure. And he laughed, Vic! Said he wouldn't get involved with anything as screwed up as you and those coins. So I don't care if you ever find them. You're out of control, and you're going to end up back in prison for the rest of your life, and I'm not going with you. Not for nothing. Not for you, and not for your treasure. Now get the heck out of here and take your problems with you."

Victor grabbed the cook by his shirt and yanked him closer. "I have lived through one miserable mess after another my whole life. These coins are my only chance, but they're worthless unless Fred will buy them. So get Fred on your phone now! Let him know I will have the coins to him tonight."

The cook didn't budge. "If you were stupid enough to get picked up for another DWI, then it's just a matter of time before you get hauled in for kidnapping and murder. And neither Fred nor I am having any part of it."

Victor's lip curled as he leered at Pete. "But I never would have met you if I hadn't gone to prison for that DWI. Isn't that right, Pete? And I still wouldn't have anyone to buy the coins. Would I? But you fixed that. Thanks to you, I got Fred."

"It took me weeks to land this job. And as pathetic as it is, I'm not going to let you screw it up."

Their confrontation came to an abrupt halt as they listened to the sound of men's voices outside the kitchen door. Pete recognized one of them as Louie, the assistant cook. It wasn't until he heard Louie address one of the strangers as 'Chief of Police' that Pete's panic went into overdrive.

"Did you hear that? Louie's talking to the Chief of Police. They can't see you with me," Pete stammered. "You're an ex-con. Get in that closet over there, and don't make a noise!"

Victor scrambled into the closet. Pete quickly picked up the pans that he had thrown at his cellmate. There was no time to wipe up the coffee. Trying to collect himself, he licked his fingers and smoothed his thin, greasy hair back into place. Within seconds, Pete, the ex-con, transformed into Chef Pierre!

"Chief of Police Paigenot, our cook's name isn't Pete; his name is Pierre," Louie, the assistant cook, tried to explain. "He moved to Esterville from France. The stories he tells about Paris are fascinating."

"Where can I find this Pierre? I would still like to talk with him." Chief of Police Paigenot straightened his tie as he waited for an answer.

Louie escorted the Chief and Hank Rogers through the kitchen door. "Chef Pierre is right here in the kitchen, and if you have no further questions for me, I am on my way to pick up a few last-minute groceries before the crowds begin to arrive."

Pete waited for Louie to leave before he began to speak. "Bonjour, gen-tel-men! To what do I owe zhees pleas-aire?"

When Pete got out of prison, he gave himself a new name, a new career, and even a new French accent. Years ago, Pete had spent many evenings learning French from a beautiful woman in New Orleans. If he was going to keep his new identity, he was about to need every French word she taught him.

But while Chef Pierre was trying to impress his guests with his French accent, Hank was checking out the spattered coffee dripping from the utensils in the kitchen. "Have a little accident in here, Chef?"

"Oui. Ex-cuse zhee mess. You know you have to watch zhee pot so eet nev-air boils o-vair. Silly me. I was not wat-ching zhee pot!"

Pete's French act was already wearing on Hank's nerves. During his last few weeks as Esterville's Chief of Police, he had seen a fax on Pete Peterson. He had a dozen aliases and a rap sheet a mile long. This impostor was fitting the description from head to foot.

Bill Paigenot ran his fingers across the wet counter and turned the palm of his coffee-stained hand toward Pete as if to say he wasn't buying his story. "I'm Esterville's new Chief of Police. I have a few questions I would like to ask you."

Attempting to enhance his meager performance, the French chef picked up a large wooden spoon and started stirring the pot of soup. "Ooh la la! La po-lees! My Eng-lees ease not zhee best, but I w-h-e-e-e-l try to help you."

Pete maintained his calm, cool appearance. Sipping a spoonful of soup, he added a dash of salt. "U-m-m-m-m. A secret fam-i-lee rec-i-pee!"

"Let's cut the bull, Chef," Hank ordered. "We're looking for my grandson, and we think you might know where he is."

Hank pulled out a picture of Tommy and showed it to Pete. "We're looking for the little boy in this picture. We have reason to believe that he was at the fairgrounds today."

The cook took one look at the picture, and knew it must be the kid Victor had brought down to the carnival earlier that afternoon. He turned beet red and patted his forehead with a towel. He should have guessed a bumbling loser like Victor would have kidnapped a cop's grandson. His knees buckled. Trying to keep from collapsing, he braced himself against the counter.

"Zhees is a ver-ee nice look-ing boy," Pete sputtered as he scraped the chopped onions into the soup. Hoping his French accent sounded authentic, Pete forged ahead with the show. "Votre grenouille a mange mon dejeuner, gen-tel-men."

Pete thought his latest French babble translated into something like, 'Your frog ate my lunch', but he didn't care. At this point he was desperately stringing together any French words he could think of, in an effort to keep his act going.

Pete's last hope was that the two cops didn't speak French either, or his gig was up. He watched the two men's reactions, checking to see if they understood what he said.

By now, Chief of Police Paigenot had lost all patience. He squared his hat and stepped toward Pierre. "Look here, Pierre or Pete, or whatever you're calling yourself this week, Hank asked you if you've seen the little boy in the picture. Now either you've seen this kid or you haven't. We need a simple yes or no. Which is it?"

Chef Pierre glanced over at the closet to make sure there was no sign of Victor. "No, no. I have not seen zhees child. If I do, I will call zhee po-lees right a-way, no?" He grabbed his apron and started to dry his hands. He was dying to wipe the sweat from his forehead again, but he didn't dare.

Hank put Tommy's picture back in his wallet, never taking his eyes off Pierre. "There's a little kid missing, and we don't have time for this ridiculous act of yours. We know you're Pete Peterson, and you just got out of prison. If you don't want to end up back in prison, Pete, you better tell us everything you know right now."

"No, no! I have nev-air seen zhees boy. I have not left zhees kit-chen since yes-tair-day. You should have asked my assistant Lou-ee before he left. He would have told you that I have be-e-e-en here con-stant-lee sla-ving over zhees hot stove."

Hank studied the chef, who was vigorously shaking his head up and down, trying to assure the two men he was telling the truth.

In one last ditch effort to convince his guests that he had not left the kitchen, the cook casually swung his hand toward a small cot in the far corner of the kitchen. "You see, I e-van sle-e-e-p here in zhee night. Cooking for all zhees people takes men-knee hou-airs."

It was obvious they weren't getting anywhere with Chef Pierre. His phony act just kept getting worse, and it was making Hank sick. He wasn't going to waste one more second listening to it. "My grandkid's missing, and if I find out you're involved, I'm coming back here, Pierre. And believe me, you're going to wish we never met."

Chef Pierre's entire body stiffened. He tried smiling, but couldn't. His lips were stuck to his teeth.

The men turned and walked out of the diner. "He may not have seen Tommy, but there's definitely something fishy about this guy," Hank mumbled under his breath.

Bill rolled his eyes. "You're not kidding. He's phonier than a three-dollar bill. He doesn't have a clue how to speak French. He said something in French about my frog eating his lunch. We're far from done with that guy."

Pierre tried to squeeze out one final bonjour, but the word never left his mouth. Sweat rolled down his face as he ran over to the closet and opened the door.

Victor pushed the chef aside and climbed out of the closet. "Have you lost your mind completely? What kind of stupid charade was that?"

Still shaking, Pierre choked trying to answer the question. "It's the kind of charade you put on when the cops are swarming around looking for a boy that an insane ex-con kidnapped. Now take your problems, and go find someone who cares, Victor!"

Victor laughed. "You don't think you were fooling them, do you? That act was the most ridiculous thing I have ever heard. There's not a soul on earth who would have believed that performance."

"I never would have had to give that performance if it weren't for you. And the police never would have been here to begin with if you hadn't kidnapped the cop's grandson. Only you would do something that stupid. And to top it all off, you bring the kid down here this afternoon like the two of you were on vacation. Who knows who saw you with that kid? You're nothing but trouble. I wouldn't help you no matter how many gold coins you had."

Victor grabbed Pete and shoved him against the wall. "If you had set up that meeting with Fred when I was down here this afternoon, the kid would be home by now and I would be long gone. I'm not leaving this time till you pick up your phone and call him."

Pete pushed Victor away. "A meeting for what? You don't have the coins. How can you sell something you don't have? All you have is another kidnapped kid. And who knows what's going to happen to that poor kid."

"I told you: I'm going to the kid's house tonight and get the coins. It's the only place they can be. As soon as I have them, I'm out of here. Then I'll let them know where they can find the little punk. If he'd told me where those coins were this afternoon, he wouldn't be missing now."

Pete couldn't imagine how Victor thought he was going to sneak into the kid's house for a third time and get the coins. He could only picture another one of Victor's bumbling disasters. "You're lucky you got out of that house this afternoon without anyone seeing you. Now for the last time, leave me out of this. You screw up everything you do. I don't want any part of you, the murder, or this kidnapping."

Victor tried to think, but his frustration was building. "If you're not with me, Pete, you're against me. It can't be both ways. You know too much."

He sprang toward Pete, hitting him in the jaw with a left hook. Pete tried to retaliate, but his opponent was too quick. Victor grabbed him again and punched him in the stomach. Pete went flying against a pot of boiling grease, burning his arm. Pete shrieked. The pan fell off the stove and the grease spread across the floor.

Trying to escape Victor's wrath, Pete stumbled toward the back door. He tried to regain his balance, but the room was spinning. Out of nowhere came Victor's final blow to Pete's jaw, knocking him through the emergency exit and to the ground. He was out like a light.

A black shadow darkened Victor's face. Striking a match, Victor threw it into the spilled grease. He jumped back as flames erupted and shot across the room toward the cook.

Victor stared at Pete's lifeless body. "You would have ended up telling the police everything you know, Pete. And I just can't let that happen. I've gone through too much."

Picking up a towel, he cleaned off his hands and threw it into the fire. "Been nice knowing you, Pete," Victor cackled as he left the kitchen.

The grease fire swept its way through the kitchen, racing toward the propane tank that fueled the diner. A massive explosion erupted. The earth quaked beneath Victor's feet; his ears rang from the blast and the smell of the gas burned in his nostrils. He looked over his shoulder as the flames from the fire shot high into the evening sky.

Poor Chef Pierre finally starts a new career, and then he dies in a tragic fire. What a shame, Victor thought. *I always wondered what it would look like when your life went up in smoke*, Victor snickered. *Ya should have stuck with me, Pete. You would have ended up on Easy Street, rollin' in the dough.*

Flames roared into the night air. Within seconds, the fire had consumed the diner and spread to the Big Top filled with people. Terrifying screams from the innocent victims echoed through the carnival as the orange and red inferno stretched higher into the sky, lighting Victor's way to the van.

CHAPTER TWENTY-FIVE

The Crystal Ball

A black and yellow sign hung over the tent:

Madame Papuza Myshka
Fortune Telling and Celestial Readings
Cleanse your Body, Mind, and Spirit

Sam could not resist looking inside the Gypsy lady's tent. An old woman garbed in a long-flowing purple skirt was sitting in the center of a smoke-filled haze. Layers of multi-colored satin scarves hung around her neck. A glowing brooch in the middle of her turban completed her foreboding appearance, almost hypnotizing Sam.

Tarot cards were spread out across the table and a crystal ball sat within her reach. Her one-eyed, brown, stub-tailed dog lay at her feet. It was growling just loud enough to keep Sam at bay as he entered Madame Myshka's lair.

"Come closer, young man," she said in a hoarse whisper, making her sound more like an old man than a woman. She curled her long, skinny finger toward Sam as if she possessed the power to draw him nearer.

Madame Myshka rose from behind the table and studied her young guest as he approached her. She was a master at analyzing people, constantly searching for the secrets people tried to hide.

Barely five feet tall, she stood on her toes and leaned forward, allowing her to peer into Sam's eyes as she spoke. "You are in search of something of great importance."

Her breath smelled of garlic and her fingers were stained with a brownish-yellow color from the smoke of her thin cigars. Sam wanted to leave, but was drawn closer by the vortex of her will. He felt the fortune teller's eyes penetrate his tough façade. Shivers ran through his body as he cringed, trying to resist her control.

"You come seeking, but you bring great trouble with you." Her stare intensified as she shook the edges of her long silk skirt, evoking the old Gypsy custom to scare away evil spirits.

"I don't need to be analyzed. I need answers," Sam insisted.

She slumped into her wicker chair and picked up her thin cigar. The smoke curled around her head as the gigantic feather in her turban drooped in front of her, making it difficult for Sam to see her face.

"Sit," she commanded. Never breaking her stare, she stacked the Tarot cards in front of Sam. The weathered face of the old Gypsy woman held him spellbound.

By now the rest of his friends were gathered around Sam. Through her life, Madame Myshka had seen it all and knew the difference between childish curiosity and fear. Her eyes moved from face to face, and she instantly knew these were five very troubled kids in great danger.

"We're looking for my brother. He might have been kidnapped," Sam explained.

"You may have come to the right place. There are many here that are not so disfigured of the body as of the soul. Beware this evil you seek does not discover you first."

Sam sat up straight in the chair and leaned toward the table. "We're not afraid."

She coughed, trying to clear her raspy voice. "Your little brother is relying on you. You must be careful. It is a fool who laughs in the face of danger. These cards will reveal your past and explore the present. Most of all, they will tell your future. Shuffle the cards and cut them."

Sam continued talking as he shuffled the cards. "You need to tell us where we can find Marcel. We think he might know if Tommy's been here."

Ignoring Sam's words, she picked up the first Tarot card and laid it in front of him. She gazed at Sam and then at the card. The first card was the Nine of Swords. It pictured a man in great sorrow, holding his head in his hands. Nine swords hung above him.

"Ahhhhhhhhh," sighed the old lady. "This card symbolizes your past. It represents the pain we bring upon ourselves. It shows the grief that is found deep inside of us where our doubts and fears dwell. You have experienced great despair and are unable to let it go."

The Gypsy woman instinctively reached for the second Tarot card, but stopped. The lifeless crystal ball sitting in front of her exploded with color, shimmering in hues of red and orange.

The angry colors shooting from her own crystal ball startled her. She had been telling fortunes her whole life, and had never seen such bright lights flash before her. She brushed the feather from her face. "One boy has already died. Your brother is in great danger." Madame Myshka picked up her thin cigar and drew it to her lips. "This boy who has passed stands among us now. I can feel his presence."

Paige grabbed Maxwell's arm and huddled closer. The Gypsy's psychic powers scared her. She searched the tent, looking for the boy Madame Myshka spoke of, but only her friends were banded around her.

Trying to ignore the signs of trouble, the old lady turned over the next card.

Their eyes focused on a picture of a man trying to carry ten heavy poles, representing life's burdens. The figure was clutching them so closely he was unable to see what lay ahead of him. The card was the Ten of Wands.

A low gasp from the woman's lips was all they could hear. "You are presently laden with heavy guilt. The weight of this shame is almost more than you can bear. Be strong of heart, for you will be tested by fire. Each step you gain will be a struggle."

Madame Myshka turned over the third and final card, the King of Wands. Falling back into her chair, she stared at Sam in wonderment. "You possess great wisdom, young one. You hold immense powers. It has been many years since a member of the Court of Fire has been in my presence."

As the Gypsy woman reached for Sam's palm, there was another sudden burst of radiant colors in the crystal ball. This time it was accompanied by a vibrating KA-BOOOM.

The terrific explosion rocked the small tent, knocking all four of Sam's friends off their feet.

Trying to break his fall, Baxter grabbed the side of the tent. The 'medium certificate' from The National Spiritualists Alliance hanging proudly above the Gypsy woman came crashing down on top of her, and she tumbled to the ground.

Madame Myshka pulled herself back up to the table as the one-eyed dog ran whimpering under her skirts. Grabbing her cane to lean on, the Gypsy woman listed to her left and gaped under the doorway. Madame Myshka screamed. "The greater powers are not sending me a message. My crystal ball is reflecting the summit of the Big Top going up in flames!"

"The Big Top is on fire!" Madame Myshka jumped out of her chair, wildly shaking her skirts. A look of horror covered her face. "I knew you kids were trouble! You've been chasing danger and now it's found you. Leave my tent right now," she snarled.

"You have to tell us where we can find Marcel," Sam shouted.

"Did you not hear me?" Madame Myshka yelled as she slammed her cane on the table. "The Big Top is burning! It's going up in flames!"

The Gypsy woman wildly shook her skirts as the tent began filling with smoke. Her look of horror quickly changed to an angry scowl. "And leave my Roma boy alone!"

They scrambled to their feet and ran from the tent into a mob of frenzied people, pushing and shoving their way out of the burning fairgrounds. People were screaming as they stampeded from the Big Top. A red-haired man rolled his wife on the ground, trying to put out her burning jacket. The Ringmaster ran from the Big Top with the tails of his tuxedo ablaze.

Red and yellow flames shot high into the black night as the fire engulfed the mammoth Big Top. The roar of the burning tent was deafening, and the sirens from the fire trucks off in the distance gave little hope.

Maxwell's eyes watered from the heavy smoke, and the intense heat scorched his wire-rimmed glasses, making them almost too hot to wear. He took them off and rubbed his eyes with his shirt sleeve, but the soot-stained sleeve only made his vision worse.

"We have to get out of here, Paige. Baxter and Marco are already ahead of us. If we're going to survive, we have to hurry." Grabbing onto Paige's arm, Maxwell quickened his pace, maneuvering through the crowd the best he could.

By now, white ashes from the burning canvas were falling from the air. The popcorn wagon outside the Big Top was reduced to a smoldering frame. Maxwell pulled Paige closer, trying to protect her from the chaos that surrounded them.

Marco and Baxter stood by the front gate, hoping their friends would appear. People were coming out of the fairgrounds in droves, but there was no sign of their friends.

Baxter began pacing back and forth, scanning the crowds. He couldn't wait another second. "Something bad has happened. I know it. We have to go back in and find them." Baxter turned and headed for the entrance.

Marco grabbed his arm. "No way! We're not going back inside. We'll get trampled. Just give them a few more minutes, Baxter. They'll get out. You'll see."

Finally, Maxwell appeared with Paige clinging to his arm. His soot-covered face was dripping with sweat, and the bridge of his hot glasses barely hung onto the tip of his nose.

Marco and Baxter began yelling and waving their hands. "Over here, Maxwell. Over here! Paige, we're over here by the ticket booth."

Paige and Maxwell ran toward them. Overwhelmed with relief, the four of them huddled together, hanging on to one another as if they would never let go.

Paige's eyes filled with tears. "You guys are all right. We were so scared."

"We all made it," Baxter sighed.

"Baxter wanted to go back in there and find you guys, but I knew you'd make it out," Marco sighed with relief.

"People are overcome with fear; they are out of control! You might not have made it out a second time," Maxwell sighed as he took his glasses off and wiped the sweat from his eyebrows.

"A guy as smart as you couldn't…" Marco stopped mid-sentence. His eyes grew as large as silver dollars and his mouth fell wide open. "Where's Sam?"

Maxwell's smile faded into a look of horror. "We thought he was out here with you guys."

Marco hung his head. "We thought he was with you…"

They waited until the crowds of people had slowed to a mere trickle, but there was still no sign of Sam. Was he trapped inside? Or had he stayed on purpose, hoping he would learn something about Tommy? Sam's friends charged back into the still-flaming inferno. They had to find their friend. No matter what.

CHAPTER TWENTY-SIX

It's Not Easy Catching an Elephant

The fire destroyed Sam's chances of tracking Tommy. Frenzied people shoved and pushed against him, making it almost impossible to move. It didn't take a crystal ball to tell Sam that Tommy's life hung in the balance, and any hope of rescuing him was fading.

I'm not giving up. Not now. Not ever! Sam thought as he continued squeezing his way through the mob of frightened people. *Maybe my friends were right; maybe the Gypsy boy does know something. And at this moment he's my only hope.*

Sam pressed on toward the burning Big Top. People were yelling at him, screaming to turn around. Some grabbed at his sleeve, trying physically to change his direction, but he was determined to keep going. Adults towered over him, making it difficult for him to see where he was going, but the flames of the Big Top shooting high into the air guided his way.

As Sam reached The Big Top, he could see the explosion from the kitchen had blown the canvas wall of the main tent wide open, revealing an old man in the midst of the dense smoke frantically trying to restrain one of the circus elephants. Frightened from the catastrophe, a one-tusked, mammoth beast was reeling out of control.

It swayed its head left and right, trying to move around the old man and escape the fire. Finally, with one sweep of its trunk, the huge animal knocked its trainer to the ground, nearly trampling him as it raged past.

One of the clowns who had been working to get the crazed animal under control quickly ran to help the injured man. Even in his baggy costume, the clown appeared to be in good shape and moved quickly to help the man. The clown's speed and agility made him seem much younger than the injured man. Sam hoped he had finally found the Gypsy boy.

Another circus hand ran over and lifted the old man off to the side, while the clown jumped up and continued trying to calm the wild beast. Screeching moans resounded from the ferocious elephant as it reeled further out of control.

"Stop, Ganesha, stop!" The clown's commands were useless. The animal refused to obey.

In a last-ditch effort to restrain the beast, the clown grabbed onto the rope tied around the animal's hind leg, and hung onto it with both hands. Every turn and sway of the wild mammal yanked the clown off his feet in a new direction. His head snapped in one direction while his body jerked in another. Clouds of dust exploded as the clown bounced up and down behind the elephant on the sawdust floor.

Without warning, flaming timbers from the ceiling crashed within inches of the raging bull. Ganesha hurled his long trunk into the air and let out a deafening bellow. The frightened animal spun one complete turn and headed straight for Sam.

The beast's erratic change of direction flung the clown into the air. Determined not to let go of the rope, the clown flew even higher, barely clearing a burning pile of wreckage.

With the wild beast raging toward him and annihilation only seconds away, Sam threw himself under the bleachers and prayed for protection.

Ganesha thundered by, crashing into a towering tent pole and breaking it in half. The top of the huge pole came crashing down on the metal grandstand that sheltered Sam. Violently ricocheting off the metal bleachers, the post spiraled toward the center ring, sparing Sam.

Ganesha showed no signs of slowing down, and the clown had had enough. Letting go of the rope, he dropped within inches of Sam. The bull elephant raced full charge through the hole in the canvas wall and past the burning rubble of the diner.

A painful "Ugggghhhhhhhhhhhhh" was the only sound Sam could hear from the clown's motionless body.

Sam lunged forward to help the clown. "Are you okay?"

The clown lifted his head to see who was talking to him. Unable to recognize the person speaking, he dropped his head back on the ground and let out another long "Uggggghhhhhhhhh."

The clown tried to crawl to his feet, but his legs were too weak. He dropped to his knees and rubbed off the white makeup rolling down his forehead and into his eyes. The remaining bright blue paint around his eyes was streaked, and the last of his big red smile was slowly dripping down his chin.

"You better rest here for a minute. That was quite a ride you just had," Sam said sympathetically.

"I don't have time to rest. I have to get Ganesha back before he hurts someone." The clown struggled to stand again, but fell to the ground.

Overwhelmed with his own problems, Sam grabbed the clown by the wrist. "You can't go yet." Sam spoke faster as the fear of never finding his brother ran through his body. "Is your name Ajoey? Are you the person my friends met this afternoon? There were three guys and a blonde girl."

"Ah, the blonde girl. She was very beautiful." His face lit up just thinking of Paige. "I tried to tell your friends this afternoon that my name is not Ajoey. It's Marcel. I AM A JOEY. That's someone training to be a clown. My grandmother is Madame Myshka the Fortune Teller."

"My name is Sam. I'm looking for my little brother. My friends thought you might have seen him around here this afternoon."

"Lots of kids wander off at the circus. Don't worry about him. He'll show up."

"It's not like that. He's only five years old and he's been gone for hours. My friends found a pair of goggles when they were down here this afternoon, and he was wearing them the last time I saw him. We're worried that he was kidnapped. Maybe by one of you Gypsies!"

Marcel gasped in disbelief. "My grandmother said prejudice against Gypsies was horrible in Northern Romania where she grew up. I didn't expect to find it here in Esterville. The Gypsies did not kidnap your brother."

Sam couldn't believe he had accused the Gypsies of kidnapping Tommy, but he was mad. Another hour had passed and he still had no idea where his brother was. "I'm sorry, Marcel. I don't think the Gypsies kidnapped my brother, but I don't know what happened to him. My friends and I were hoping that you've seen him."

"Tell me what your little brother looks like."

"Tommy has blond curly hair. The last time I saw him he was wearing a blue hat, a red jacket, black boots and yellow goggles on his face."

Marcel shook his head. "I haven't seen anyone like that around here today. It's kind of warm to be wearing all those clothes, so he would be pretty hard to miss, even around here."

As Sam began to speak, Marcel snapped his fingers. "Wait! Now that I think about it, I did overhear some guy talking to the new cook about a little kid."

"What was it? What did he say?"

"He said that he was taking the kid out to some old abandoned house till he figured out what to do with him."

"I'll bet that's the Miller house on Stony Creek Road," Sam blurted.

"I can't remember anything else he said about the kid. The cook was really hyper, though. He said that guy with the kid had just gotten out of prison, and he was going to end up back in prison for sure."

Marcel's news was his first sign of hope. Sam jumped to his feet. "I have to get home and tell my grandfather. This could be the breakthrough we've been looking for. Thanks, Marcel." Sam lifted Marcel to his feet. "Are you okay?"

"I think I'm all right now. I better get going too; it's not easy catching an elephant." Marcel smiled at Sam as he took off, running after the beast, now just a fading gray blur on the far side of the fairgrounds.

Sam had wasted too much time already. He left the tent, sprinting in the opposite direction. He had to get home and tell his grandfather what he had learned. If it was Tommy that Marcel heard the men talking about, his kid brother needed him now more than ever, and Sam was not about to let him down.

CHAPTER TWENTY-SEVEN

From Bad to Worse

Sirens screamed into the night. Flashing lights silently pulsated against the smoky haze, faintly lighting their way. As they passed the fire engines, they came to a group of paramedics carrying a badly burned man away from what remained of the diner.

Paige glanced down at the burn victim on the stretcher. She grimaced as she turned her head away, relieved it wasn't Sam. "How are we ever going to find Sam? He could be in one of these ambulances for all we know."

Marco was far from ready to think that something bad had happened to his friend. "Don't panic, Paige. Sam was fine the last time we saw him. He knows how to take care of himself."

Maxwell was analyzing the fire damage. "The last place we saw Sam was over by Madame Myshka's. The fact that her tent never caught on fire is some indication that Sam is still okay."

Paige agreed with Maxwell. "Sam was looking for Marcel. He probably went over to the Big Top to find him."

"With all these ambulances and fire engines around here, how are we ever supposed to get to the Big Top?" Marco groaned.

Baxter nodded in agreement. "Yeah, we can't walk through these smoldering ashes. The soles of my new Adidas will melt." Baxter checked the tread on the bottom of his new shoes to make sure they were still okay.

Maxwell pointed to a metal table still standing by the ticket booth. "Let's work our way over there. That will get us to the Big Top." Paige took Maxwell's hand and started walking toward the main tent.

As Marco fell in line to follow Maxwell, Baxter grabbed his arm and pulled him behind a large, white garbage Dumpster.

Marco pushed Baxter away. "What do you think you're doing? Try and stay focused, Baxter!"

Ignoring Marco's question, Baxter started yelling to his other friends, who were still walking to the main tent. "Maxwell! Paige, get over here. Now!"

Marco was more confused than ever. "What's going on, Baxter? Will you get a grip?"

"There's Paige's dad over there by the diner," Baxter whispered. "I can't tell if he saw us or not. If we don't get Paige and Maxwell back here, they're going to walk right into him." Baxter's whisper was so strained that Marco could barely understand what he was saying.

Baxter repeatedly pointed his index finger toward the remains of the diner until Marco saw Bill Paigenot standing about twenty feet from them, talking to one of the paramedics.

Marco took one look at the Chief of Police and jumped two feet sideways, landing behind Baxter. "We gotta get Maxwell and Paige over here right now."

Baxter leaped out from behind the Dumpster one more time and latched onto Maxwell's sleeve. Yanking with all his might, Baxter pulled his friend behind the Dumpster and out of sight.

Taking a breath from his inhaler and adjusting his glasses at the same time, Maxwell looked at Baxter, trying to figure out what his friend was doing. "Have you completely lost your mind, Baxter?" Maxwell drew in another breath of air before he continued talking. "We need you to stay on task. Sam could be in serious trouble."

Baxter didn't hear a word Maxwell said. He was too busy trying to get Paige's attention. Marco nudged Maxwell in the side and started pointing at Paige's dad. Maxwell only needed one look before he ducked behind Marco and out of Chief Paigenot's sight.

Baxter tried yelling Paige's name one more time in another one of his loud, hoarse whispers, but she didn't hear him. "I have to go get her. Her dad can't find her down here. She's supposed to be at Sam's house waiting for her dad to return."

Baxter glanced over at Bill Paigenot, who was still involved in a serious conversation with one of the paramedics. This was Baxter's chance. He darted out from behind the Dumpster and ran behind the ambulance. Paige was almost within his reach.

Baxter waited. When he saw Bill Paigenot start writing on a notepad he had taken from his back pocket, Baxter leaped from behind the ambulance. Grabbing Paige with both arms, he pulled her back behind the vehicle. Losing their balance, they rolled to the ground.

Before Paige even recovered from the fall, she turned to Baxter and punched him in the side. "Baxter, I have about had it with you tonight. Don't you think we have enough problems trying to find Sam without you playing one of your silly games?"

Paige started to get up off the ground, but Baxter pulled her back down. "That hurt. You should be thanking me, Paige, not hitting me."

Baxter nodded his head toward the smoldering diner, and Paige gasped. "My dad! He'll kill me if he sees me down here. I won't ever be allowed out of the house again."

Paige thought about how hard she tried to live up to her dad's expectations. She could already hear him saying, "Bad decisions make for bad consequences." He would never understand why she had gone to the carnival.

She barely understood it herself. She just knew her friend was in trouble, and when she saw how worried Sam was about his little brother, she knew she had to help him.

Paige crawled behind Baxter. Peering over his shoulder, Paige checked to make sure her dad hadn't seen them. "What are we going to do now, Baxter? If this ambulance takes off, we'll be standing here in plain sight. Our cover will be blown for sure."

"Paige, can you see Marco and Maxwell over there, hiding behind the Dumpster? We're just going to have to wait for our chance and get over there with them." Baxter knew how ridiculous he must have sounded. He was telling Paige to be patient, when he didn't have a patient bone in his body. And Paige knew it.

Bill Paigenot and the paramedic began walking to the back of the ambulance, forcing Paige and Baxter to scramble around to the far side of the vehicle. The paramedic opened the back door of the ambulance. When Chief Paigenot leaned in to check on the burn victim, Baxter grabbed Paige's hand and ran for cover.

Rounding the corner of the Dumpster, Baxter tripped over Maxwell's foot and landed on top of Marco. "That was a close one," Baxter sighed.

Marco groaned as he pushed Baxter off of him for a second time. "We're not safe yet," Marco whispered. "We can't sit behind this Dumpster all night. It's already past seven. We have to find Sam."

Maxwell was shaking his head. "This is what happens when we don't listen to the grown-ups. I knew we should have stayed at Sam's house like his grandfather told us to do."

Marco rolled his eyes. "Save your lectures for later, Maxwell. Right now we've gotta get out of here."

As the four of them tried to figure out what to do, a methodical pounding shook the ground, shaking Maxwell's glasses down to the tip of his nose.

"Now what? Like we don't have enough problems?" Baxter peered around the corner of the Dumpster. To his amazement, 'Ajoey' was walking his elephant straight toward him. Baxter waited until 'Ajoey' was right in front of the ambulance.

"Here's our chance!" Baxter grabbed Paige, nearly yanking her off the ground. "Let's go."

He leaped from behind the Dumpster and started walking beside the Gypsy boy and his elephant Ganesha. Marco and Maxwell followed close behind. The elephant created the perfect screen between them and Chief Paigenot.

"Hey, Ajoey, remember me?" Baxter patted the elephant's wrinkled belly as he talked.

"Sure. I just met another one of your friends a while ago. What's his name?"

"Sam?" Maxwell responded.

"Yeah; he was pretty worried about finding his kid brother."

"Exactly what time did you see him, and where did he go?"

The look alone on Marcel's face was enough to show Maxwell how ridiculous he thought his question was. "We've been a little busy around here with the fire and all. I haven't had time to check my watch."

Maxwell couldn't stand when people were unable to provide him with accurate information. "It's seven o' clock right now. Approximately how long ago did you see him?"

"I've probably been chasing Ganesha for at least a half an hour, so I suppose it was like... six-thirty." He walked the lumbering elephant around a pile of smoldering rubble and tied it to a post outside what remained of the Big Top.

Maxwell continued his interrogation. "Where did Sam say he was going?"

"I'm not sure. He was asking if I'd seen his little brother. I told him I overheard one of the cooks talking to a guy who said he was holding some little kid in an abandoned house." Marcel was having trouble concentrating on Maxwell's questions. Now that his elephant problems were under control, his attention had once again shifted to the beautiful blonde-haired girl.

Paige was oblivious to everything except what her father was doing. She leaned around the elephant to check on her dad, making sure he wasn't coming in her direction.

"Holding a kid in an abandoned house?" Maxwell's face turned pale with shock. "What did Sam say when he heard that?"

"I can't remember what he said." Marcel's voice trailed off. He had lost total interest in the conversation with Maxwell and was trying to get Paige's attention. After missing his chance with the beautiful blonde girl earlier that afternoon, he was going to make sure he made up for it now. "Maybe you would like to stop by tomorrow, and we can take a ride on my elephant," Marcel offered as he smiled at Paige, who was still too busy watching for her father to notice him.

Maxwell dragged the palms of his hands down the sides of his face. "Can't anyone around here stay focused?" *I feel like I'm back in elementary school*, Maxwell thought. He shook Marcel's arm, trying to get him to respond. "Think. What did he do? Can't you remember anything Sam said?"

"Oh, he just jumped up and said he had to get going. That's about all I can think of right now." Marcel walked over to Paige to see what she was looking at so intently.

Maxwell groaned with disgust. He turned to Marco, hoping there was still one person left able to carry on a normal conversation with him. "Sam must have decided the cook was talking about Tommy."

Marco knew that was trouble. "I bet Sam went out to the abandoned house after his brother. We can't let him go out there by himself."

"Be more specific, Marco. Out where? What abandoned house is he talking about? Where do you think Sam went?"

"The only abandoned house I can think of around here is the old Miller place. You know, the one by the railroad tracks on Stony Creek Road. It's not far from here. We have to go out there and see if that's where Sam went."

"That does it!" Maxwell had had enough. "Things here are going from bad to worse, Marco. It is bad enough that we can't find Tommy. But it is beyond comprehension that we have lost Sam. There probably is a kidnapper — and worse yet, a murderer — on the loose, and for all we know Sam could be dead."

"But if...," Marco tried to interrupt, but Maxwell was having no part of it. He was on a rant.

"Now we are standing here in the middle of a pile of burning rubble. Not to mention that we're sneaking around like criminals, hiding from Paige's dad. And you want us to go out to some old abandoned house in the middle of the night where we could encounter who knows what. A crazed kidnapper! A killer! I don't think so. I'm going over and get Paige's dad right now and tell him what's going on here. We need some help."

As Maxwell turned to make his exit, Baxter ran in front of him. "You're not going anywhere. Chief Paigenot would lose it if he found out that his daughter left Sam's house after he told her to stay there. And he would ground her for life if he knew she was down here. I know you wouldn't want to see that happen."

Maxwell thought about what Baxter said. He knew his friend was right about Paige. Her dad expected her to do what she was told. He couldn't ask Chief of Police Paigenot for help without getting Paige in serious trouble. But going out to an abandoned house in the middle of the night was definitely not a good idea either. "It's not just going to the abandoned house that is the problem. What if Marcel is right, and the kidnapper is holding Tommy there? How could the four of us possibly protect ourselves against a kidnapper?"

"We're not going out there to look for the kidnapper," Marco retorted. "Right now we're just trying to find Sam. If he's there, we'll bring him home. If we find any more than that, we'll call Hank and Chief Paigenot, and let the grown-ups handle it."

The situation was bad, and Maxwell was running out of options. They still hadn't found Tommy, and now they had lost Sam. He watched as Paige's dad climbed back in the squad car and picked up the walkie-talkie. His last chance to make a sensible decision was slipping away.

CHAPTER TWENTY-EIGHT

Not Again

He ran into the house. A sickening silence filled the room. Sam was alone. He had raced home from the carnival, expecting to find his grandfather waiting for him. Hank was always there when he needed him. And Sam needed him now. He couldn't go to the abandoned house alone.

Far in the distance, a howling dog broke the silence. Sam peered through the window, hoping the dog's cry was a sign of Hank's return. But the thin gray clouds crossing the crescent moon only darkened unfamiliar shadows in the empty yard and heightened the panic that stirred within him.

Sam thought about his friends, hoping they had escaped the carnival fire unharmed; but the gnawing fear ripping at his insides kept him focused on his brother. It seemed like forever since he had seen Tommy. He tried to stay positive, but he wondered if he was ever going to see him again. If only he could re-live this afternoon. He would have made better decisions. He never would have left the house after his mother told him to stay home.

Sam choked back the tears. Alone in the house, he realized how helpless he was. He needed his Grandpa now more than ever. He thought about the week his dad died. It was one of the few times Hank had come to visit them in Minneapolis. After the funeral, Sam found Hank sitting in the guest room, holding a pocketknife in his hand.

"I've used this knife a lot," Hank said. "Got it from my dad, and I was planning on giving it to your dad, but I guess I never got around to it. I always thought there would be time for that."

Sam understood exactly what his grandfather meant. There should still be time for ball games and fishing trips and all the things he wanted to do with his dad, but none of that would ever happen now. There were times he missed his dad so much he thought his heart would literally break, and he could see his grandfather missed him, too. Hank was trying to be strong, Sam thought, but it's not easy.

They spent the afternoon looking at picture albums and sat for a long time without saying a word. Finally, Sam decided to try some of his mom's advice on his grandfather. "My mom says that when one door closes, another door opens, Grandpa. Another door will open for you."

"Your mom is a very wise person, Sam." Hank wrapped his arm around Sam's shoulders and gave him a bear hug. "Looks like that door opened for you and me this afternoon, Sam. I think it's time for you to have this pocketknife." Hank placed the knife in Sam's hand and closed the boy's fingers around it. Not another word was spoken about the knife, but Sam never forgot that day.

Now Tommy was missing, and the same sick feeling of losing someone special was back. Wiping away the tears, Sam turned away from the window. "I lost my dad; I'm not going to lose my brother too," Sam vowed.

For a brief second the tomb-like silence was broken. A faint noise rustled above him. He held his breath, and stopped to listen. Was there a chance that Tommy had returned home? He listened again, but there was only silence. Was the house creaking, or did he really hear something?

He had to find out. Sam ran through the house. Taking the steps two and three at a time, he was up the stairs in seconds. He raced down the hall and turned into Tommy's room.

Before he could turn on the light, a large hand reached out from the darkness and grabbed Sam around the neck, almost cutting off his air supply. He tried to yell, but another hand covered his mouth. Sam pulled on the hands, trying to free himself, but the pressure around his throat only grew tighter.

A raspy voice whispered in Sam's ear, "Don't move a muscle, kid. I don't want to have to hurt you."

Trying to do what he was told, Sam let his body go limp, hoping the person would loosen his grip and give him a chance to breathe.

The pressure around Sam's neck loosened. His chest heaved as he gasped for air; his words were almost inaudible. "You're the one who took my brother."

"Your little brother has something of mine, and I'm here to get it. As soon as I have it, I'll leave. Nobody has to get hurt."

"Where's Tommy?"

"Not so fast, kid," the gruff voice hissed. "First, I'm going to get what I came for, and then I'll tell you where your brother is."

"What could my little five-year-old brother have that you want?" Sam tried to remain as still as possible, hoping the man would loosen his grip even more.

"I'm looking for some gold coins. I saw the Decker kid with one, and your brother had one, too. So they must be in this house somewhere."

Sam thought about the gold coin he saw in Tommy's hand and the one that Mary Paigenot found. Did Tommy stumble across coins Alex Decker had hidden in the house? Sam shook his head. It was just too unbelievable. "My little brother doesn't have any gold coins. He never even knew Alex Decker."

"The fact that he didn't know the Decker kid proves I'm right. Your brother and the Decker kid both had one of these coins. I saw them with my own eyes. What other place would those two boys have in common besides this house? Those coins have to be here somewhere."

"I don't know about Alex Decker, but you're wrong about my brother. Tommy doesn't know where your gold coins are."

"Those coins are in this house, and I'm going to find them."

"Well, then let me go and I'll help you look. I don't care about the coins. I just want my brother back."

"There's no way I'm letting you go. The Decker kid pulled that one, and I'm not falling for it again." Victor was tired of talking. His head throbbed, his vision was blurred. He ran a hand through his hair and tried to think. "Get in that closet over there, and do it now," Victor snarled.

Sam's chance to save Tommy was over if he got himself locked in the closet. "You're crazy if you think I'm getting in there."

Victor started pushing Sam across the room. "You're going to end up in the same place as your brother if you don't do what I tell you to do. Now get in the closet."

Victor pushed Sam again. This time, Sam lunged forward. Grabbing onto the bedpost, Sam rolled onto the mattress and scrambled across the single bed. Jumping to his feet, Sam waited for Victor to make his move.

"You're not going to make this easy, are ya, kid?" Victor jumped onto the bed after Sam. His foot twisted as he sunk into the mattress. Victor lost his balance.

Sam darted through the door and headed down the hall. Victor rolled off the bed and ran after him. Within an arm's reach, Victor grabbed for him. Sam could feel the stranger's fingers brush across his back. He could hear the man's erratic breathing; almost feel it on his neck. The stranger was gaining on him.

There wasn't time for Sam to make it down the stairs to the front door, but he had to escape this maniac. Sam dodged into his bedroom. The window was still open. Sam scrambled across the room, crawled out of the window and onto the trellis.

Victor lunged after him. Grabbing Sam's shirt, he began to drag him back inside.

As Sam jerked away from Victor, the lattice beneath his feet began to shatter. Still fighting to free himself from Victor, Sam groped for a solid board that would support his weight, but each piece of wood he landed on broke into even more shattered pieces than the last. The thin wooden lattice crumbled one piece after another till there was nothing left for him to hang on to; nothing to help him regain his footing.

Sam began to fall. He hit the ground and his neck snapped back. He looked up at the window and heard his attacker groan, "Not again…"

CHAPTER TWENTY-NINE

Copy That

The familiar static of Hank's two-way radio interrupted his concentration as Bill Paigenot's voice came over the air. "7110 to 7102."

Standard procedure would have required Hank to turn in the radio when he retired, but Bill asked him to keep it. Hank knew Esterville like the back of his hand, and Bill wanted to be able to contact him in an emergency.

Tonight was definitely an emergency, and Hank was as grateful as Chief of Police Paigenot for the communication. Hank pushed the button on his two-way radio. "7102 to 7110. What's your status, Bill? Any sign of Tommy?"

Bill's voice came over the radio. "All first responders at the carnival were given a description of Tommy and told to look for him while we evacuated this place and he's not here, Hank."

"There must be a clue somewhere that will lead us to my grandkid." Defeat hung on every word Hank spoke. "Are you going to be able to get away, Bill? I could use your help."

"The fairground is still a real mess. The ambulances are having a hard time getting the burn victims to the ER, and the traffic leaving is backed up, so it's going to be slow getting out of here. But we might have a break, Hank, and I want to get you up to speed on some new information. We've been talking to the French cook again, and it sounds like the fire started in the kitchen; he's pretty badly burned. Hard to make much sense of what he's saying, but he keeps rambling on about who kidnapped Tommy."

"I knew that scoundrel was hiding something. What did he say?"

"He's talking about some guy named Victor Venema. Ever heard of him?"

"No, I haven't. What about Victor Venema?"

"He's rambling on about Venema going to Decker's old house to look for gold coins. After seeing the gold coin Mary found in Tommy's room, he might be telling the truth."

"If that cook is telling the truth about Venema going to Rose's house, our kids are in real danger." Hank's hands tightened around the steering wheel as he spoke.

"Exactly. We need to get over to the house right away and see what's going on, Hank."

"Already tried calling my grandson, but he's not answering. I'm on my way there now to check it out."

"Copy that. One more thing, Hank. We were right about Chef Pierre. He's as American as apple pie. Seems to have completely lost his French accent since the fire. I'll bet my bottom dollar this guy is Pete Peterson. I have someone checking on him right now."

Hank was already thinking about the gold coin that Mary Paigenot found in Tommy's room and pushed the button on the radio one more time. "I don't know if you knew this, Bill, but Alex Decker had a twenty-dollar gold coin clutched in his hand when we recovered his body from the lake. Looked just like the one Mary found in Tommy's bedroom. I never did learn where he got it. If what the cook says is true and Venema is after those coins, it's the evidence we need to connect him to the Decker case."

"If Victor Venema was responsible for the death of Alex Decker, then we are dealing with more than just a kidnapper. And if he's at Rose's house, all the kids are in serious trouble. Watch yourself, Hank. Those kids are going to need you."

"Copy that, Bill. I've been waiting for this guy a long time."

"I'm on my way, Hank, but getting past all this traffic is going to take a while. I'll be there as soon as I can. Over and out."

Hank punched the gas pedal; his tires squealed as he turned onto Horace Avenue. The house sat undisturbed as he searched for the smallest sign of reassurance that Sam and his friends were unharmed. *Please let the kids be safe*, Hank prayed as he pulled into the driveway.

He took the keys from the ignition and unlocked the glove compartment. Hank pushed aside the county maps and grabbed his .45. Stuffing it in his coat pocket, he ran toward the house.

CHAPTER THIRTY

A Step into the Unknown

The front wheel hit a rock, and the bike flew into the air. Marco flipped over the handlebars and landed in a pile of brush. His agonizing groan stopped the entire caravan as Baxter ran to help him.

"Are you okay, Marco?"

Patton had already come to his rescue and was standing over Marco, wagging his tail and licking his face.

"I'm fine," Marco assured his friends as he brushed broken twigs and leaves from his clothes. "Just get this dog away from me."

Baxter pushed The Great Schnauzer away. "I couldn't see for sure, but it looked like you did a complete one-eighty."

Marco groaned.

Maxwell pulled the last of the debris from his motor and wiped his hands on his new shirt. "Whose idea was it to go through these woods anyway?"

Marco pushed Patton away one more time and crawled to his feet. "We had to take the back road, Maxwell. That traffic on Stony Creek is terrible at night, especially after the fire. One of us would have gotten hit by a car for sure."

Baxter nodded in agreement. "This shortcut is a lot faster anyway." Baxter picked out the last of the leaves stuck in his chain and leaned his bike against a tree. "Traffic or not, we saved at least fifteen minutes coming this way, Maxwell. That counts for a lot."

Paige nodded her head in agreement. "Marco's right, Maxwell. If we had taken the highway out here, we would have had to go the whole way back through town before we ever got onto Stony Creek Road. We'd still be pedaling up that big hill."

"Well, we lost the path a long time ago. Leaves and sticks keep getting caught in my motor," Maxwell moaned. "We're going to have to walk the rest of the way."

Paige agreed. "I can't see where I'm going, and we can't keep lifting our bikes over these dead trees."

Marco picked up his bike and leaned it against Baxter's. "Let's leave our bikes here and get them on the way back. It's not much farther. We can make it the rest of the way on foot."

Forcing his way through the tangled brush, Baxter took the lead and headed toward the abandoned house.

Only the moonlight escaping from behind the clouds helped to light their way. A fallen oak blocked the clearing where the ancient wooden fortress stood, lost in time and neglect. Shifting shadows moved across its walls like loyal sentinels guarding their castle from unknown intruders.

Baxter gasped as cawing crows circled overhead, warning them to turn around. Trying to steady his breathing, he whispered, "No signs of Sam here. I think we need to go…"

Paige clung tighter to Maxwell as the crows collected on a branch of the fallen oak. "Something tells me we're not supposed to be here."

Marco didn't want his friends to know, but he agreed. He felt like he was in the middle of some awful nightmare. If he didn't keep moving forward, he was going to turn and run, for sure. "We have to concentrate on finding Sam. That's why we're out here." His voice was shaking and his legs were weak, but he had to stay strong for Sam's sake. He cleared his throat and lowered his voice, hoping he would sound more confident. "It's just an old house. No one has lived here for years. What could we possibly have to worry about? Let's just look around for Sam; then we'll go."

Baxter was not to be outdone by his friend. "Well, I guess if you aren't scared, Marco, then neither am I. Let's keep going. We gotta find Sam."

With Paige hanging onto his sleeve, Maxwell could feel the slightest bit of courage beginning to surface. "I can see there's no point in trying to talk any sense into either of you," Maxwell grumbled. "So don't let us stop you two. Lead the way. Paige and I are right behind you."

They listened for the slightest noise. All their senses heightened, hoping to detect any sign of danger. Wide-eyed and cotton-mouthed, too scared to talk, they made their way to the back of the foreboding mansion.

Maxwell still found himself trying to reason with Baxter and Marco. "There are no more signs of Sam or Tommy back here than there were in the front of the house. How many times must we conclude that our friend and his brother are not here?"

Ignoring Maxwell's question, Baxter tried to pull himself up to the kitchen window and look inside. "Maybe Sam's already inside the house." He held on to the window ledge as long as he could, before finally dropping to the ground. "I'm not tall enough to see in there. Marco, you're going to have to get down on your hands and knees so I can stand on your back. It's the only way I'll be able to look in the window."

Marco glared at Baxter. "That's what you think, Baxter. You'll break my back if I let you stand on it."

"Paige and Maxwell aren't strong enough to hold me. Let's go, Marco. How else am I supposed to see if Sam's in there?"

"You're bigger than I am. You get down on the ground, Baxter. I'll stand on your back," Marco retorted.

Baxter got down on his hands and knees, letting Marco climb on his back to peer through the window. Marco groaned at the sight of a rat running between the broken pieces of furniture scattered across the floor. Cobwebs filled the dimly lit room, and blocked his view of what awaited them. His courage was slipping away. "There's no one in here that I can see. I guess we can go home." Marco jumped to the ground, hoping the rest of them agreed.

"We can't leave yet," Baxter insisted as he crawled to his feet. "We gotta go inside and make sure Sam and Tommy aren't in there; then we'll go. Let's try the back door."

"Oh no," Maxwell protested. "That is the final straw. We're here for one reason: to find Sam. We haven't seen him, and it's safe to assume he's not standing inside some dark, abandoned house by himself. We agreed we would let the adults look for Tommy. It's time for us to go home."

Marco had used up what remained of his courage. He knew Maxwell was making a lot of sense. Coming out here at night wasn't a good decision. It was time to go home. "Maxwell is right. We're supposed to be at Sam's house right now, waiting for his grandpa. This is getting way out of control. We've been gone too long already."

Baxter rolled his eyes. "Marco, would you make up your mind. You're the one who talked us into coming out here in the first place. After all this, we're going to make sure Sam and his little brother aren't here. We're not leaving till we check everywhere, including upstairs and the basement."

Marco tried to persuade Baxter one more time. "Coming out here sounded like a good idea when we were at the carnival. But now we're standing in the back of an old abandoned house in the middle of some dark, creepy forest, Baxter, and I'm not so sure. Anything we find inside that house is going to be more than four kids can handle. I say we get out of here while we have the chance."

Someone is finally showing good judgement, Maxwell thought. "Marco's right, Baxter. Marcel said he thought Tommy could be here. If he's right, that means the kidnapper could be here, too. Can't you see how dangerous this situation is? How can four kids take on a kidnapper, and maybe even a killer? We could be in great danger. You have to realize that, Baxter."

Not waiting for Baxter to answer, Paige broke her silence. "I'm more scared than all three of you put together, but I agree with Baxter. We told Sam we would help him find Tommy. Now we've lost Sam, too. We're his friends. We can't go home until we know for sure that he and Tommy aren't here."

"Way to give it to 'em, Paige." Baxter patted Paige on the back. "And Maxwell, you're the one who said Ajoey thought Sam was coming out here," Baxter continued. "He also said Tommy might be here too, so we can't give up now. We didn't come all the way out here to turn around and go home. We have got to go inside and look for Tommy and Sam." Baxter turned to Marco. "Are you and Maxwell coming with Paige and me, or not?"

Marco took a long, deep breath. "I guess it was my idea for us to come out here," he stammered, as he watched Baxter's patience grow shorter by the second. "I can't leave you and Paige out here alone. And Maxwell, you can't go back to town by yourself. It looks like the four of us are stuck going in this house together."

The three of them looked at Maxwell and waited for him to speak.

Maxwell saw the moment of reason slip away once again. "Well, I'm not going to be the one who keeps us from finding Sam and his brother." Maxwell puffed up his chest and squared his shoulders. "If you guys are going in there, then so am I. Just remind me to get some new friends in the morning. Ones that like to stay home at night and watch the History Channel," he muttered to himself as he climbed the back steps.

The door swung open on a single hinge. Stale, dank air filled their lungs; boards creaked beneath their feet as they inched their way through the kitchen. Each step, more uncertain than the last, carried them deeper into the darkness.

CHAPTER THIRTY-ONE

The Click of a Safety

Crawling on his hands and knees, Victor worked his way back out of the closet. "Ouch!" A sharp pain shot up his leg as his knee landed on another metal soldier. He picked it up and threw it out of his way.

The problem was, Victor was crawling out of the little boy's closet backwards. He knew it would be easier if he took the time to turn around, but he was hot. He needed some fresh air.

He had no idea what time it was. He had wasted at least a half hour searching the attic to find absolutely nothing. *Now here I am crawling around in his closet, and there's still no sign of the coins.* Victor pushed another soldier aside. "Rotten little good-for-nothing kids. I haven't met one I like yet," he grumbled to himself.

Victor brushed aside another battery-operated truck when his right foot slammed into what felt like the trunk of a huge tree. Trying to feel his way around the obstacle, his left foot landed against another object just as big. Before he could turn around to see what was in his way, he was yanked off the floor and hurled against the bedroom wall.

When he finally opened his eyes, Victor was staring into the face of a giant filled with uncontrollable rage. The man now had him pinned against the wall with one hand, Victor's feet barely touching the ground.

Even in the dark, Victor knew he had seen this face before. The opportunity to remember where was interrupted when he was slammed against the wall again and then pulled to within inches of the stranger's face. "Who are you and what are you doing in this house?" the stranger growled.

Victor tried fighting back, but there was no use. The man was enormous, and his grip only grew tighter. He gasped for air as he tried to think of what he could say that would convince the man to back off. "How can I tell you anything when you've got me shoved against the wall? Let go, man," Victor choked.

"I'll let you go when you tell me what's going on. There were five kids downstairs when I left here, and now they're gone. Who are you, and where are those kids?" Hank spun Victor around, wrenching his arm behind his back and smashing his face against the wall. "I'm just getting going here, scumbag. Now start talking because if you don't, the pain is going to get a lot worse."

"Come on, mister. You're breaking my arm."

Hank twisted Victor's arm tighter. Victor groaned, his chest heaving up and down. "All right! But I've only seen one kid here. He left a while ago through the window in the other bedroom." Victor wasn't about to tell this guy that kid fell out of the window.

Hank applied more pressure, pushing the intruder's face harder against the wall. "Even if I did believe you, it still doesn't tell me what you're doing here."

Victor fought to free himself, but he couldn't. Hank held him tight against the wall. "I'm waiting for an answer, slimeball."

Victor tried one last time to loosen Hank's grip, but his arm was locked in place. He wasn't going anywhere. "Okay. I'm a relative of the Deckers, and I think they left something of mine here when they moved. I'm not here to cause any trouble. I just want to get what's mine and leave."

"Not cause any trouble! You're already up to your eyeballs in trouble." Hank took the gun out of his pocket and shoved the barrel in Victor's back. "You're not one of the Deckers' relatives. Your name is Victor Venema, and you're here looking for gold coins. I'm guessing you're the one who kidnapped my grandson earlier this afternoon." Hank spun Victor around and grabbed him by the shirt. "Where is my grandkid? What did you do with him?" Cocking back the hammer of his .45 and holding it to Victor's temple, Hank waited for an answer.

The cold metal shoved against his head and the click of Hank's safety told Victor his time was up. *How does he know who I am? And how can he know about the coins?* Now, looking down the barrel of a .45 revolver, Victor's mind raced for something to say that would make this guy believe his story. But the words didn't come. The gig was up; his body slumped; the game was over.

"All right, don't shoot. The kid is in the abandoned house on Stony Creek Road."

"You piece of dirt." Hank grabbed him by the shirt again, pulling him even closer to his face. "If you've hurt Tommy, you're a dead man."

Victor's eyes bulged. "He's fine," Victor groaned as he gasped for air. "He's locked in one of the rooms upstairs. Livin' like a king. I just gave him something to eat before I came over here."

"He better be all right. Now tell me where those other kids are."

"I still don't know what other kids you're talking about. I've only seen one kid here tonight. It was the little kid's brother, and I told ya before, he's gone."

"Yeah, and that kid supposedly left through a bedroom window. Right." Hank tightened his chokehold, hoping to pry more information out of Victor.

Hank had to believe that Tommy was all right. It was the only thing that kept him from losing complete control. He thought about the Decker case: the senseless murder of a young boy; the pain it caused his parents; and the fear it cast on the people of Esterville. Had he finally found the person responsible?

Victor remained silent. He had said too much already. One kid was dead and he had kidnapped another one. As soon as this lunatic learned a third boy fell out the window, he would be thrown in the slammer for the rest of his life.

"You're wasting precious time that I don't have." Hank pushed Victor toward the door. "Let's go. We're checking out your story, and for your sake you better be telling the truth." Hank force-marched his prisoner down the hall. "Which window are you talking about?"

"The one in this room right here." Victor stopped in front of Sam's bedroom.

Hank turned on the light. There was no sign of Sam or his friends. He shoved the gun in Victor's back, forcing him across the room. Victor held his breath as he watched Hank look out the window.

"No one's down there."

Victor saw the kid drop from the second story window with his own eyes. He had to be there. No one could walk away from a fall like that. He looked out the window for himself. The kid was gone. Victor stifled a long sigh of relief. "Well, of course he's not down there now. It's been at least an hour since he left. He's long gone."

Hank glared at Victor. "And I think you're a lying scumbag."

Still in disbelief, Victor stuck his head out the window one more time. "I'm not lying. Check out the trellis. Can't you see it's broken? That happened on his way down."

Hank looked out the window for a second time. He could see the shattered pieces of wood lying on the ground. There was a chance Victor was telling the truth, but it still didn't tell him where Sam and his friends had gone. For the moment he was just going to have to pray they were safe.

"Okay. That story is going to have to do for now." He grabbed Victor and pushed him down the hall. "You and I are going to the old Miller house and get my grandkid. If you want to live to see tomorrow, you better hope I find him safe and sound."

Hank thought of Alex Decker's tragic death. He shook his head and prayed, *Not Tommy. One senseless death is more than we can bear. Please, God, not Tommy, too.*

CHAPTER THIRTY-TWO

The Closet Door

The moonlight faded as they began their trek down a long dark hallway. Each one clung to the faint silhouette in front of them, hoping to find the strength to continue.

By now, Maxwell could barely see his own hand in front of his face, but he had to keep going. He knew they weren't leaving until they searched the entire house. He pulled his inhaler out of his pocket, taking a deep breath as he approached the stairs. "I suppose we better check upstairs too," Maxwell mumbled.

Paige heard what Maxwell said, but could hardly bring herself to respond. She wanted to leave, but too afraid to go by herself, she knew she couldn't. She had to find Sam and his little brother. "I suppose we better," she finally whispered almost to herself.

Maxwell grabbed onto the banister and led his friends up the winding staircase. For the first time that Maxwell could remember, he was not trying to analyze the situation. *The less I know about this place the better. Maybe I'll just let my instincts take over for now*, he decided.

The darkness had robbed them of their sight, and every wooden plank they stepped on sent its own unwanted noise echoing through the house. Maxwell tried to keep the boards under his feet from creaking, but his legs felt like lead weights. It took all of his strength and courage to climb another worn-out step, knowing it could possibly alert the kidnapper they were here.

Baxter tugged on Marco's sweatshirt. "Did you hear that? Listen."

Marco stopped. "Wait, you guys. Baxter thinks he heard something."

They held their breath. Trying to hear above their own heartbeats, they listened for another sound. A faint noise broke the silence. No one moved. The sound haunted them again, still too soft for them to tell what it was.

"It sounds like it's coming from behind that door." Marco's voice was barely loud enough for them to hear.

Patton ran to the door and sniffed. The sound emanated from behind the door a third time. The Schnauzer pounced down on his front paws and cocked his head.

Maxwell turned to his friends and murmured, "Now what are we supposed to do?"

Baxter spoke in a hushed tone. "Let's move a little closer; see if we can figure out what's making the noise." He took the lead and another step toward the door.

Marco followed behind him, nudging Baxter closer. Baxter put his ear against the door and listened. Another sound, barely audible over the pounding of Baxter's heart beating in his chest, held him motionless.

Marco poked his friend in the back. "Go on, Baxter. Open the door."

Baxter gulped for air. He wiped his sweaty hand on his pants, turned the knob, and pushed. Nothing happened. He tried again, but the door wouldn't open. "It must be locked. Maxwell, see if you can get this open with your penknife."

"Oh no. I'm not opening that door. Who knows what's on the other side," Maxwell protested. By this time, Baxter could have been the green Hulk there to protect him, and Maxwell's confidence still would have failed him. "It's not necessary for us to go in there. Half the windows in this place are broken; it's probably just a squirrel… or a bird… or a…" Maxwell's voice trailed off into a faint whisper.

"Whatever. The kidnapper's sure not in there," Marco argued. "Why would he have locked himself inside a dark room? And he sure wouldn't be in there making wimpy noises like that. Come on, Maxwell. Unlock the door."

Maxwell took the knife out of his pocket and carefully jiggled it between the door jamb and the metal lock. With very little effort, he heard it click. "There you go, Baxter. It's all yours."

Baxter didn't move.

"Go on, Baxter. You're the one who wants to open the door," Maxwell grumbled as he took one big step to the left, making sure Baxter had plenty of room to turn the knob.

Baxter pushed the door open a crack and looked inside the room.

"There's something... on the floor," Baxter whispered. "Like a coat or a blanket..." He took another step and leaned farther into the room. "Otherwise it's empty."

The closet door on the far side of the room creaked open, revealing an even darker abyss.

The four of them froze.

Baxter's breathing was shallow and his hands were shaking. Turning to make sure his friends were still behind him, he grabbed onto Marco and pulled him closer.

Without warning, a dark figure leaped out of the closet, knocking Baxter off his feet. Instinct alone compelled Baxter to fight back, but the sheer strength of his assailant held him to the ground. Marco and Maxwell ran to Baxter's defense. Each grabbing an arm, they dragged the attacker off their friend.

Baxter sprang to his feet to help his friends and gasped as he looked into the face of his adversary. "Sam!" Baxter grabbed his friend and smothered him with a huge bear hug. "I was beginning to think we might not ever see you again."

"It's good to see you guys, too. Hope I didn't hurt you, Baxter. I thought you were the kidnapper. I already ran into him once tonight at my house." Sam turned toward the closet. "Tommy, it's okay. Come on out."

Tommy emerged from the black shadows and latched onto Sam's side. Paige knelt down and hugged the little boy. "Tommy, we've been looking all over for you. Are you okay?"

Sam ruffled Tommy's hair. "He's a little shaken up, but I think he's going to be fine. Aren't ya, Tommy?"

Rubbing the tears from his cheek, Tommy nodded. "I'm o-kay."

"This will warm you up," Paige said as she helped the little boy on with his coat she found lying on the floor.

Marco took the phone out of his pocket and handed it to Sam. "Call your grandpa right now and tell him we found Tommy."

Sam brushed the screen saver aside, tapped the phone icon, and entered Hank's number. "Oh no." Sam shook his head in disbelief. "There's no reception."

Marco groaned. "Esterville never did have great service; what are the chances we'd have it out here in the middle of nowhere?"

"That tower is pretty close to the fairgrounds. Maybe the fire is interfering with it," Maxwell added.

"Now what are we going to do?" Marco asked.

Baxter rolled his eyes. "Looks like we're on our own till we get closer to town."

Paige was still thinking about what Sam had just said. "What's this about the kidnapper being at your house? Why would he be at your house when Tommy's here?"

"Tommy's kidnapping has something to do with stolen gold coins. The kidnapper thinks they're hidden in our house, and that Tommy knows where they are."

Maxwell pushed his glasses up on his nose and rubbed his chin. "That's the most ridiculous thing I've heard tonight. How does he think a five-year-old kid would know anything about stolen gold coins?"

Sam shrugged his shoulders. "He said he saw Tommy at the grocery store with one of the coins, and decided Alex Decker must have hidden the coins in our house somewhere. He was at my house tonight looking for them, and was probably trying to find them this afternoon when he kidnapped Tommy."

Now, Maxwell was looking at the situation like one of his math problems. "So he left Tommy here, thinking he had a better chance to find them if he could look around the house by himself tonight."

Paige pulled the little boy close to her. "Tommy, do you know where the coins are?"

Tears ran down Tommy's cheeks. "No." His voice was a mere whisper as he fell against Paige's shoulder. "I told him I don't know where they are anymore."

"Speaking of the kidnapper, we've got to get out of here right now, before he comes back." Maxwell started walking toward the door. "Let's get going."

"Maxwell is right. One round tonight with that guy is enough for me. Let's go." Sam picked up his little brother and started his trek home. In the cold dank house, Sam still had a feeling of warmth. Even after the fire, his friends never gave up looking for him or his brother. Now they were together again, and Tommy would be home in no time.

CHAPTER THIRTY-THREE

A Loose Screw

Hank shoved Victor into the pickup and grabbed a pair of old handcuffs out of the glove compartment. Chief Paigenot laughed when Hank told him he thought he'd keep a pair of cuffs "just in case". Now he was glad to have them.

He locked Victor to the armrest and slammed the door shut.

"Watch it, will ya," Victor grumbled. "I am a human being, ya know. Ya don't need to treat me like some animal." He yanked on the metal cuff, trying to loosen it, as he watched Hank walk around the front of the pickup. *He doesn't really think this piece of junk is going to hold me, does he?*

Victor tugged on the handcuff one more time. He could feel the metal digging into his skin. He pushed the cuff down on his wrist to loosen the pressure and rubbed his bruised skin.

Hank climbed into the driver's seat and peeled onto Horace Avenue, banging Victor's head against the back window of the truck as he punched the accelerator. "You better pray my grandkid is all right, or you're sucking in your last breath of fresh air."

"I told ya, the kid's fine. I'd never hurt anyone intentionally," Victor mumbled as he rubbed his head. He thought he could actually feel his brain pulsating. *If this guy would just shut up a minute*, he thought, *maybe I could figure out how to get myself out of this mess.*

"That's the problem with people like you. You never take responsibility for anything." Hank had the gas pedal pressed to the floor. He was going sixty, and getting more livid by the second as he yelled over the roar of the engine. "Your kind always ends up hurting innocent people, and it's never your fault. The fortunate part is you end up leaving a trail of evidence a mile long. Any idiot could track you down."

The last thing Victor needed was a lecture from this old coot. The pounding in his brain felt like a herd of buffalo running through his head. He squinted, trying to make the pain stop. "The idiot in charge of the Decker case sure didn't find a trail of evidence a mile long." Victor cringed the second the words came out of his mouth. He couldn't believe he said that out loud. *Don't bring up the Decker case again, you fool*, he scolded himself. *Just take a big breath and try to stay calm.*

Hank couldn't believe his ears. Was this guy actually going to spill his guts about Alex Decker? "The Decker case, huh? So what do you know about the Decker case?"

Victor tried to cover up his foolish remark. "Well, who doesn't know about the Decker case? It was in the news for months. There's not a person around who doesn't know those 'idiots', to use your word, never solved that case." He carefully moved his hand up and down the armrest while he talked, searching for somewhere to slide the handcuff through. *I can escape from here*, he thought. *This old pickup is a piece of rusted-out junk.*

Hank hit an open stretch of road and began passing a long line of cars. The traffic didn't interrupt his train of thought. "Yeah, well one of those idiots in charge of the Decker case has you handcuffed right now, and he's going to make sure you're brought to justice."

The conversation was starting to wear on Victor's nerves. He couldn't resist the opportunity to taunt the old coot; maybe it would shut him up for a while. "You're that ex-cop who picked me up hitchhiking last week. You had me right under your nose then, and you didn't have a clue who I was."

Victor snickered as he kept fiddling with the armrest, groping for a way to free himself. He brushed across a loose screw and started picking at it. *Months wasted on nothing. Why didn't I walk away from all this while I still had the chance*, he wondered. *Talk about a trail of evidence. When they find out what I've done, they'll, lock me up, and this time I'll never get out. It can't end this way. Not after everything I've been through.*

"If I had my way, I'd throw you off the Stony Creek Bridge right now. Let you see for yourself what you did to that poor Decker boy," Hank snarled.

"You're not pinning that on me. That was an accident. No way I killed Decker. I tried to save him."

Hank cringed. "I can't believe you're saying that with a straight face. It's always an open and shut case with scum like you."

The screw in the armrest was loosening.

With the bulk of traffic behind him, Hank took a second to look at his prisoner. Even in the black of night his face was now as clear as day. The drifter he picked up hitchhiking on Stony Creek Road a week ago was once again sitting beside him. Was Hank slipping? He had spent his life memorizing faces. How was it that he hadn't remembered the face of this hitchhiker? And now, as fate would have it, the face of the man he had spent months hunting in the Decker case.

His thirty-year career and almost perfect record was permanently scarred by the death of Alex Decker. People he had known his entire life turned their backs on him, unwilling to accept the fact their Chief of Police couldn't save Alex. Couldn't bring his kidnapper to justice. He hoped that getting away from the job would help him forget, but it didn't.

His failure to solve the Decker case tormented him into his retirement. The sleepless nights were endless. Countless hours were wasted working and re-working the evidence, trying to find the missing clues. And now, almost by accident, his search was over. The man he was looking for was sitting next to him.

"Don't think for a minute that I don't have a clue who you are. You're a piece of scum that kidnaps little kids, and I can only imagine what you do to them. So sit there and shut up. I can't stand to look at you, let alone listen to anything you have to say."

Victor stared at his own reflection in the passenger window. He hardly recognized the face. Hunched over, the man he saw was unshaven and unkempt. His eyes were hollow. It was the face of a thief, a kidnapper, and a murderer. *How did this happen?* he wondered. *I never meant for the Decker boy to die, and I never wanted to kidnap this man's grandkid. There are some people who were never meant to be happy, and it looks like I turned out to be one of those people.*

Hank picked up the two-way radio. "Bill, are you there?"

"Copy. I should be at your house any minute now."

"I caught Venema upstairs in Tommy's room. Says he's holding my grandson out at the Miller place. I'm on my way to get Tommy right now. Meet me there, will you?"

"Where is this place? I've heard about it, but never been there."

"It's out on Stony Creek Road, about five miles north of town, near the freeway entrance. You won't find it on your GPS. No one's lived there for years."

"If I remember, there's a lot of wooded area out there; right, Hank?"

"Yeah. The place covers almost twenty acres."

"Copy. I'm on my way there right now. I'll radio you once I'm outside of town. Then you can tell me where to meet you."

"One last thing, Bill. The kids weren't at the house when I got there tonight, so hurry. Once we know Tommy's all right, we need to find out what happened to the rest of them. You can have the pleasure of taking Venema down to the station and booking him for kidnapping Tommy, the murder of Alex Decker, and who knows what else."

Bill was stunned. "He's confessed to the murder of Alex Decker?"

Hank glared at his passenger. "He says it was an accident, but I'm not buying it."

"We'll get to the bottom of it when we get him down to the station."

Hank pictured the lifeless body of Alex Decker laying on the shore of Stony Creek and answered, "I'd like to be there when you interrogate him."

"Wouldn't have it any other way, Hank. "Over and out."

The engine of the old Chevy pickup rumbled as Hank passed the last car in the long line of traffic. He prayed his trusty old Chevy would make it through the night. *Six kids' lives are at stake*, Hank thought. *How is that possible?* "You don't prey on little kids and get away with it," Hank growled to himself as much as to the con sitting next to him. "Not innocent little kids."

CHAPTER THIRTY-FOUR

Eyes of a Monster

Sam led the way as he carried Tommy down the dark staircase. The little boy trembled in his arms. "Sam, I want to go home."

Sam held him tighter. "That's where we're going, Tommy. You'll be home before you know it. Everything's going to be okay."

Sam wanted to go home, too. In the solitude of the night, he thanked God for finding Tommy and thought about the bad choices he had made that day. He would have to live with the awful things that happened because of those choices.

He cringed as he thought about sneaking out of his bedroom window, and his selfish decision to leave Tommy alone. Had his family really meant so little to him? Losing his brother taught him just how much he loved his family. It was a painful way to learn that lesson, but it was one he would never forget.

The darkness made it difficult to see where they were going. Marco was only a step behind Sam and wanted his friend to move faster, but carrying Tommy slowed him down.

Once we make it down the steps, we can pick up the pace, Marco thought. He patted Sam on the back. "I can take Tommy for a while. It might be easier if we took turns carrying him."

"Thanks, Marco. He's okay right now. I'll let you know if I need a break."

"Cut the chatter up there, would you," Baxter whispered from behind. "We're not out of trouble yet. We have to get out of here before whoever took Tommy comes back."

"Not out of trouble yet? That's an understatement!" Maxwell muttered to himself. His mind was in overdrive, trying to mastermind the safest plan of escape. *Every minute counts. Leave through the back door; take Tommy home on the scooter; get in touch with Paige's dad, let him know we found Tommy; and never come out here in the dark again...*

Paige turned around and looked at Maxwell. She couldn't tell if he was talking to her or to himself, but in the midst of the darkness her friend's voice was a comfort.

She thought about Sam, the fire, and the strange chain of events that had brought her to this dark, obscure place. She had felt such a sense of relief when they found Tommy, but it was the moment she knew Sam was safe that told her that he was more than just a friend.

The sound of Tommy crying broke her concentration. She had to remain focused for his sake. The little boy had been through too much already. "We're going to get out of here. We'll be okay," she kept repeating, trying to convince herself as much as the rest of them that they would get home safely.

Sam led them through the back door and into the forest. Navigating through the dark woods was impossible. The last bit of moonlight had faded, and so had their hope of finding their way. The deeper into the woods they went, the more lost they became.

Maxwell stopped. "We've walked by these same dead trees three times now. We have to get our bearings before we go any farther."

Before Sam could answer him, a dim light flickered in the distance. He held his breath as he watched it grow increasingly brighter. "Looks like someone is coming," Sam whispered as a set of headlights emerged from the blackness. Even through the woods, the lights illuminated their silhouettes in the dark forest. They had to find cover.

Marco ducked behind a fallen tree. "Quick! Over here."

The yellow headlights still loomed in the night like the eyes of a tiger stalking its prey. Peering over the tree, Sam watched to see what the driver would do. His friends huddled behind him as they listened to the hum of the car engine slow to a stop.

"He's back," Paige gasped. Her hands shook as she spoke. "What are we supposed to do now?"

"This is exactly why we never should have come out here by ourselves," Maxwell muttered to himself. "We're supposed to be protecting Tommy, and we can't even defend ourselves."

Marco grabbed Sam's sleeve. "Let's take off in the other direction before he sees us. We can make it if we go right now. He'll never see us in the dark."

Sam didn't move. "Wait, Marco. Not yet." Sam watched as the car door opened and the interior lights came on. At the same moment, red and yellow flashing lights on top of the vehicle began to rotate, illuminating the entire area. A man slid off the seat and started walking toward them.

Sam hugged Tommy. His shoulders slumped with relief. "It's a police car. Paige, your dad is here."

"We're safe." Paige let out a big sigh. "We can take Tommy home in Dad's squad car, and get our bikes in the morning."

"All right," Baxter sighed. "For a minute I thought we weren't going to make it out of here alive."

"That's about as close as I ever want to get to not 'making it out alive'," Maxwell added in pure relief.

Sam finally put his brother on the ground. "Tommy's getting heavy. Let's wait till your dad gets here. He can help us carry Tommy to the car."

As Paige stood up to greet her dad, she watched a blackened silhouette hobble through the trees. She took a second look and ducked back down behind the trunk of the tree. "I don't know who that is, but it's not my dad," she whispered.

"Who else would be out here in a police car, Paige?"

"I don't know, but look at that guy. He's hunched over, and he's dragging his left leg. My dad doesn't walk like that, and I've never seen anyone my dad works with walk like that either. Sam, I'm scared."

Sam strained to get another look at the man coming toward them. "Tommy, I have to let go of your hand for a second. Baxter is right here next to you. You can be brave, can't you?"

Tommy nodded his head and curled up next to Baxter.

Sam peered over the fallen tree and slumped back down to the ground. "I don't see him, Paige. Where'd he go?"

"He was just walking toward us, Sam. I saw him. Let me look again." This time, the red and yellow emergency lights flashing in the night were all that Paige could see. "I don't know where he went, but that's not a cop car either. That's an ambulance."

"An ambulance! What's an ambulance doing here?" As Maxwell stood up to check out the vehicle, a darkened figure emerged from the trees. Grabbing him by the shirt, the shadowed form yanked Maxwell toward him with one hand and held a gun to his back with the other.

"Where did you kids come from?" An animal-like moan emanated from the stranger.

Even in the darkness, the flashing lights revealed repulsive sores oozing on the attacker's face and arms. Single strands of his remaining hair fell onto his disfigured face. From behind the bludgeoned mask stared the eyes of a grotesque monster.

CHAPTER THIRTY-FIVE

A Cheap Fiddle

Tommy grabbed onto Sam and screamed. "It's him! It's him!"

Sam pulled his brother against his chest, hiding him from the sight of the man's disfigured face. "Tommy, you don't know this man."

"Yes, I do. It's his voice... his voice." Tommy buried his head deeper into his brother's chest, trying to block out the sound of the man speaking.

The intruder nodded. "The boy is right. He and I met at your house. Your little brother is the one who showed me where to find Victor's precious treasure."

He shoved his gun deeper into Maxwell's back while he reached into his pocket and hoisted a leather pouch into the air with his left hand. He laughed as he shook the jingling bag of coins in the air.

Sam took a step back. "So you have the coins the other man was looking for."

"And unfortunately for Victor Venema, he never will have his stolen treasure." Gagging sounds resonated from the intruder's throat as he continued to talk. "Poor fool. I played Vic like a cheap fiddle from the day we met in prison. He does all the dirty work, and I end up with his priceless treasure." His burnt lips curled into a wicked grin. "And if everything goes as planned, he's on his way back to prison, and I'm set for life."

Sam clutched Tommy in his arms. "So now you have the stupid treasure. Just let us go."

The cold wind stung his burned lips as he gasped for air, making his tormented groans even louder. Each word he spoke took more effort than he seemed to have. "That little boy, and unfortunately, now you kids are the only ones who know I have it. You can identify me; I can't let you go." The stranger stood silent for a brief moment, trying to picture his escape. "And who knows, now that I think about it, five little hostages would be a great way to keep the cops at bay till I'm clear of this town."

The bandages wrapped around his left hand unraveled as he shoved the bag of coins back in his pocket. The cold air made his raw skin burn. Pain shot through his body, bringing back the images of Victor leaving him for dead in the flaming kitchen and the sounds of the blast echoing in his ears.

He remembered crawling to his feet and stumbling from the kitchen door as he tried to escape the raging inferno. And then the explosion hit, blowing him farther from the burning kitchen, and probably saving his life. Drawn into the thoughts of his narrow escape, he sneered, "Even after all that, you came up short again, didn't ya,

Victor?" The name stuck in the cook's throat, making him choke.

In that lost moment of concentration, the cook's right hand fell to his side. Maxwell grabbed it and dug his fingernails into the open wounds. Pete shrieked with pain. Maxwell held on, burying his fingernails even deeper into the bleeding flesh. Sheer reflex from the pain made him jerk his hand away, losing control of his hostage.

Marco charged the stranger, driving his shoulder into his side and pushing him to the ground. The cook wrestled to his feet as he grabbed Maxwell and shoved his gun into Marco's side, but the rest of them began to scatter.

"Run, you guys. Run," Marco yelled.

Paige took off into the woods, but Baxter spun on his heels and ran for the road. "Let's go, Sam, here's our chance."

Sam tried to keep up with Baxter, but it was impossible for him to move with any speed carrying Tommy in his arms.

Baxter looked over his shoulder to check on his friend. The distance between them was growing. "Hurry up, Sam. We gotta get out of here."

Sam's arms felt like rubber, and Tommy was slipping. He couldn't carry him another step. He sat his little brother under the branches of a fallen tree and motioned to Baxter to keep going.

"Tommy's getting too heavy for me to carry any farther. Keep going, Baxter."

By this time, Baxter had already reached the bottom of the hill and was only feet from the dirt road. He ran back toward the foot of the hill, trying to find Sam, but the distance between them had become too great.

Sam moved closer to the crest of the hill, hoping that would help Baxter hear him yell, "Go, Baxter, go get help." He frantically waved his hands at his friend to keep going, but Baxter didn't move. As Sam took another step to close the gap, his foot caught on the root of an old birch tree; losing his balance, he fell forward. He grabbed for the branches of the dead tree, but his fall turned into a full roll that didn't stop until he reached the bottom of the hill, and what might as well have been miles from his little brother Tommy.

As Baxter ran to help Sam, gun fire resounded, illuminating the silhouette of Marco, Maxwell and now Tommy standing at the top of the hill. All three were locked in the hands of the deranged madman.

The cook held Maxwell around the neck with one hand, while he pointed the pistol at Marco's head with the other. Tommy clung to Maxwell's side. "If the rest of you take one more step, I'll blow this kid away. Now get back here."

Sam crawled to his knees, but Baxter held him down with both hands. "That guy is holding a gun to Marco's head, Sam. He means what he says. He'll kill him."

Sam nodded his head. "Check your phone. See if we have a signal yet."

Baxter swiped his phone and groaned. "One bar. We might as well be on Mars."

"We have to save them." Sam tried to get up again, but Baxter pulled him to the ground.

"There's nothing either of us can do. He has a gun. One of us has to go get help. It's our only chance."

"That has to be your job, Baxter, because I'm not leaving here without Tommy."

"Sam, you're twice as fast as I am. I could never bring anyone back here in time."

Sam shook his head. "I left Tommy alone once today and look what happened. It was a miracle that I found him. I'm not leaving him again."

Another shot rang in the air. "There's still at least one of you little brats out there. I'm gonna give you one more minute to get back here. After that, your little friends are dead. And I don't have to tell you they're scared out of their minds."

"Did you hear that, Sam? He said that at least one of us is out here. He doesn't know how many of us there are. He'll never know if you come back or not. You're the one who has to go, Sam. Your speed is our only hope."

"I'm not leaving here unless we all leave together, Baxter."

"If you don't go right now, none of us is ever going to leave this place alive. I'll take care of your brother. I promise. Now get going. Go get your grandpa or Paige's dad. We need them, now."

Baxter stood up and pulled Sam to his feet. "Hurry back, Sam." He patted his friend on the back and started his way up the hill. "Okay, mister, don't shoot. Here I come."

Once again, Sam was running through the dark of night. This time he was running away from his friends, and worse yet, away from Tommy. Gravel kicking up under his shoes was the only sound he heard. His legs were stiffening, and he was exhausted, but adrenaline kept him going.

He thought he had hit rock bottom an hour earlier, grasped in the stronghold of a full-grown man: a kidnapper and killer. But he escaped and found his little brother and his friends. He pictured himself rescuing Tommy and carrying him in his arms to safety, only to have him snatched away again by a deformed madman.

Fatigue wore on his emotions, making it difficult for him to think clearly. Doubt consumed him. *What if I can't make it back to town in time? What if something happens to them before I can bring help? Am I ever going to see my brother or my friends again?*

Tears ran down his cheeks. He chose to run when those who meant the most to him were in danger. "I'm nothing but a coward."

A blanket of shame fell upon Sam in his flight away from the abductor. The flashing lights of the ambulance had vanished. Enveloped in the cold darkness, Sam had to make the right decision. Not for himself, but for the people he cared about.

His heart sank. His friends were in serious trouble. He had found the courage once to save his brother. He had to find that courage again. There was no time to get Hank. He was their only chance. He stood at the end of the gravel road, watching the lights from the traffic on Stony Creek Road soar by him. *I have to do what's best for them this time*, he thought.

A blackbird swooped through the air, shaking the autumn leaves from an old oak tree. Sam looked up at the night sky. "God, give me the strength I need to save them," he prayed.

Sam turned and ran back down the dirt road and into the woods. Branches grabbed at him like bony fingers, trying to slow his pace. Shoving them away, he forced his way through the thicket, to his friends and the peril that awaited him.

CHAPTER THIRTY-SIX

The Big Dipper

He grabbed Paige from behind and wrestled her to the ground. His hand was over her mouth before she had a chance to scream. She pushed and kicked with every ounce of strength she had, but she couldn't get away.

"Stop it, Paige. Stop it," he whispered. "It's me, Sam."

"Sam?"

"Yeah, Paige. It's Sam. Try to be quiet. We can't let him hear us."

"You're okay, Sam! I thought he got you, too. Who is that guy, and what happened to him?"

"I don't know who he is, but he's not the kidnapper. The guy that mugged me at the house wasn't burned."

"Sam, what are we going to do? He has a gun."

He could feel her shaking. He held her tight. "Paige, we have to get help and rescue our friends; they're depending on us. We have to save them."

Paige was silent.

"I saw how strong you were the first day I met you on the basketball court, Paige. You can do this."

Paige shook her head in disbelief. "I was on my way to get my bike, but I still wasn't sure what to do. I was so worried I would never see you again," she whispered. "Now you're all right, and the kidnapper has Tommy and our friends."

Sam's heart stopped. *She was worried she would never see me again?*

"We ran back into the carnival, Sam, and tried to find you. The Big Top was still on fire, but we had to know that you were okay. Then we came out here looking for you. When you weren't here either, I thought I'd lost you for sure."

Lost me for sure? I never knew she felt that way about me. He wanted to wait, hoping she would say more, but he knew they had to keep moving and get help. He had to interrupt her. "Paige, I just got Tommy back; I can't lose him again. And Baxter's counting on me to bring help."

"You're right, Sam. We can't let that monster hurt them. I'll do whatever I can to help. We have to do something."

"I told Baxter I would go back to town and get your dad and my grandpa, but there's not enough time for me to do that. That guy is crazy. He could do something awful to them any second. Our friends are in big trouble, and the only way we can help them is if we split up."

Paige knew Sam was right. "All right. What should I do, Sam?"

They peered over the boulder that hid them from the mad man. Paige pointed toward the house. "We left our bikes over there."

"Is Maxwell's scooter there?"

Paige nodded.

"You're the one who has to get help, Paige. Take the scooter into town. Use the dirt road and you can be there in ten minutes. You'll have reception on your phone by then, so try to call your dad or my grandpa and bring them back here. I'm going back to the ambulance. I have to try to rescue those guys."

"Sam, you can't go back there by yourself. That man is evil. He's capable of anything."

"He is evil, and that's exactly why I have to go. I don't have a choice, Paige. I can't leave our friends or Tommy alone with him. They need me."

Paige heard the determination in Sam's voice and knew she wasn't going to change his mind. "All right, Sam, I'll take Maxwell's scooter into…" Paige stopped mid-sentence. "What about Maxwell's utility pouch? There must be something in there you can use to protect yourself."

"That's a great idea. Let's go." They ran through the woods, reaching the scooter in what felt like seconds.

Sam unbuckled the pouch from Maxwell's scooter and tucked it under his arm. "Be careful, Paige."

"You too, Sam." Paige threw her arms around him. "Don't let anything happen to you." Paige kissed Sam on the cheek and jumped on the scooter.

Sam could hear the purr of the hand-built engine as Paige drove away. A brief sense of confidence fell upon him as he thought about the utility pouch under his arm. There was no doubt Maxwell had it packed with something he could use. He admired his friend's keen intelligence now more than ever. "Thanks, Maxwell. I owe you one."

He looked up at the Big Dipper one more time and marveled how each star of the constellation shone so brightly in the black sky. Instinctively, he ran toward the two pointer stars that led him north and lit the way to his friends.

CHAPTER THIRTY-SEVEN

Over and Out

Even with the gas pedal pressed to the floor, the five-mile drive to the Miller house was taking forever. The knocking sound from the engine was getting louder, and the rust-bucket Chevy truck was losing speed rapidly. *Please let me get there*, Hank prayed. He banged his fist on the dashboard, trying to ease the tension running through his body, but it didn't help.

The five-mile trip for Victor was what he needed to finish loosening the screw on the armrest. He bit his lip to keep from laughing as the screw from the armrest dropped to the floor of the pickup, allowing him to free the handcuffs from the door.

Hank picked up his scanner. "Bill, are ya there?"

Bill's voice came across loud and clear. "10-4. I'm headed north on Stony Creek Road right now. Still about six miles from the Miller place."

Hank pressed the Talk button. "I'm on the west side of the property, Bill, but the engine is dying, and I still have a couple miles to go. I'm just hoping to make it into the driveway."

"I'm only a few minutes behind you, Hank, so hang in there."

"When you get to the fork in Stony Creek Road, Bill, stay right on the paved road. Then take the first left onto a gravel driveway. It's pretty overgrown with brush, so go slow, or you'll miss it."

"Got it, Hank."

"If you don't make that turn, you'll end up on the east side, walking through the woods out by the old railroad bridge. It will take you forever to get here."

"Copy that. Thanks for the heads-up, Hank."

"Bill, I'm coming up on the Miller place now, but the truck is on its last leg. I'm going to park it as soon as I turn in the driveway. You'll find Venema cuffed to the armrest. I'm on my way to the mansion. Over."

"Go find Tommy, Hank. I'll lock Venema in the back of the squad car when I get there and meet you at the house. We're not losing him again."

"I'll leave the lights on in the cab, so you won't miss the turn."

"Copy that. Over and out."

Within seconds, Hank turned into the property and the truck chugged to a stop. "Venema, you're going to stay chained to this truck like the dog that you are." Hank flung open the driver's door and started running toward the abandoned house.

"At least you could shut the door." Victor yelled, heckling the old man. "The light is blinding me."

As Victor watched Hank start his trek down the road, he opened the passenger door and slid off the seat into the darkness. *Another great escape*, Victor snickered as he ran into the woods. *No one can keep me down.*

Bill Paigenot arrived seconds later. With the squad car's beacon lights flashing brightly, he could see Hank running down the long driveway. Bill turned to the pickup and looked through the driver's door into the empty cab. The passenger door hung open, and the broken armrest lay in pieces on the floor.

Bill rushed around to the passenger side of the truck and then to the edge of the woods, searching for Victor, but he was gone.

CHAPTER THIRTY-EIGHT

S-S-S-T-T-T-O-O-O-P-P-P

Exhausted, Sam stopped behind one of the towering hemlock trees. He felt small and insignificant amidst the forest of huge giants. *How can I possibly save them?* He shivered as he watched his friends being force-marched to the back of the ambulance. "I just have to be patient," he whispered to himself. "The right time for me to help them will come, and hopefully I'll know when that is."

Even from a distance, Sam could see Maxwell's chest heave up and down as he tried to catch his breath. "Use your inhaler, Maxwell," Sam agonized. "Now's not the time to prove how tough you are."

Maxwell finally reached in his pocket for his inhaler.

"I told you to keep your hands out where I could see them," the stranger hissed as he shoved Maxwell with his bandaged hand. "Just keep moving and no funny stuff."

"I can't breathe," Maxwell choked.

Baxter stopped and waited for Maxwell. "He has asthma. If you don't let him use his inhaler, he's never going to make it to the ambulance." Baxter glared at the disfigured man, almost daring him to make a move.

Without another word, Baxter reached into Maxwell's pocket and found the inhaler.

Maxwell grabbed it from Baxter and gasped for air. Standing firm with his friends, Marco put his arm around Maxwell's shoulder and waited until the rhythm of Maxwell's breathing returned to normal.

"All right. Let's go. If you want to be the kid's nursemaids, do it on your own time. Not mine," the man ordered as he pushed Maxwell toward the back of the ambulance.

Baxter's gut reaction was to push the guy back, but he promised Sam he would take care of Tommy. The little boy's safety had to come first. They filed into the ambulance and the door slammed shut.

Sam jumped. Something nudged him from behind. As he turned, The Great Schnauzer jumped up and licked his face. "Patton!" Sam hugged the dog. "It's good to see you, boy. I can use all the help I can get." At that moment, the headlights of the ambulance came on and Sam watched as the vehicle turned left onto the dirt road.

The roar of the engine faded into the distance. They were moving north. *North?* Sam panicked. *North is a dead end. The only thing at that end of the gravel road is the railroad bridge, and it will never hold the weight of the ambulance.*

"Come on, Patton, we've got to go." Sam took off in a dead sprint through the woods, hoping the shortcut would bring him to the bridge in time.

The inside of the ambulance was silent. Baxter sat in his seat, thinking about the abuse he had taken throughout his life, some from the people who said they loved him. He spent years watching other kids with their dads. Just once he wished his dad would have showed up at a basketball game, or been around on the weekend so they could hang out together, but he was never home. Driving truck kept him away for weeks at a time.

He remembered sitting on the porch, waiting for his dad and hoping this time would be different. But it never was. It was always the same. After a long road trip, he would come dragging in the house too tired to spend time with his own son.

"You're lucky to have a roof over your head," he would yell as he got a beer out of the refrigerator. "I break my back all week long for this family. I need some time for myself. Now get out of here, and go play with your friends."

The rest was almost too painful for Baxter to think about. The verbal abuse and beatings went on until Baxter just avoided going home when his dad was there. Baxter shook his head. *Kids shouldn't have to put up with that*, he thought. "Don't worry, Tommy. Nothing's going to happen to you. I'm going to make sure of that."

Marco nudged Baxter in the side and whispered under his breath, "Where's this guy think he's taking us? We're heading toward Stony Creek Bridge. What's going to happen when he reaches the dead end?"

Baxter shrugged his shoulders and shook his head. "We'll all have a problem if he thinks he's crossing that bridge. It will never hold us."

"We gotta get him to stop this thing before we get there."

The evil eyes glared at Baxter in the rearview mirror. "Shut up back there, or you'll wish you did. I'll get rid of you right here and now!"

Baxter had spent years listening to his father yell meaningless orders. It didn't matter what his instructions were, they always ended with the same tired threat: "or you'll wish you did." But his dad seldom followed through with his threats; he was just too lazy to get out of his recliner.

This guy wasn't any different. *What could he do to me that someone hasn't already done?* Baxter thought. *What do I have to lose?* And with that thought in mind, Baxter's bantering began. "Do you have a clue where you're going, Mister?"

The driver laughed. Mixed with his cries of pain, he sounded almost inhuman. "When I need directions from one of you kids, I'll let you know." The rearview mirror framed the man's face. His eyebrows were singed, and the skin around his eyes was raw. Blisters covered the rest of his face.

Baxter cringed as he looked at the man in the mirror. He turned away as he spoke. "I think you do need some directions, 'cause we're headed down a dead end."

Marco and Maxwell sat silently. They had seen this side of Baxter countless times before, and once he started taunting someone there was no stopping him. His mouth had gotten them in more trouble than either of them cared to think about. But this time he was their only hope.

Pete glared at Baxter in the mirror. "Don't mess with me, kid, and don't forget who has the gun. Now sit there and shut up."

The orders rolled off Baxter's shoulders like he never heard them. "I'm not messin' with you, Mister. I'm telling you the truth. Aren't I, you guys? The Stony Creek Bridge is just up ahead, and it's been closed for years. It'll never hold this ambulance."

Marco and Maxwell vigorously shook their heads up and down in agreement.

"I have been planning this gig since I met Victor Venema in prison, and if you think I'm gonna let a couple of little runts ruin it for me now, you're crazy." He looked at the burns on his face in the rearview mirror and winced. "I've been through way too much to let that happen, so for the last time, do what I told ya and shut up."

"Well, okay, but even if this wasn't a dead end, how far do you think you can get with four kids and a stolen ambulance? You're in bad shape, Mister. You have to get to the hospital. What's more important than getting some medical attention?"

"There are dozens of things that are more important." Pete reached down and pulled up a fistful of gold coins. One by one, the coins fell through his fingers and back into a leather pouch. This time his evil laugh was broken by a gagging cough that ended in a long, agonizing groan.

Maxwell was overwhelmed with the stupidity of the situation. He was sitting in the back of an ambulance heading straight off the end of a bridge, so some creepy guy could keep a bag of gold coins. He couldn't stay silent any longer. "You have approximately two minutes to listen to what my friend is trying to tell you." Maxwell held his hand against his chest and wheezed, trying to catch his breath before he continued. "The Stony Creek Bridge was built in 1864 and was slated to be torn down ten years ago. But because of Esterville's self-concerning need to preserve their minute place in history, it's still standing. Barely."

Maxwell sucked in a breath of air from his inhaler. "And now, because of your complete ignorance, all eleven thousand five hundred pounds of this Life-Line Ambulance, along with its 7.5-liter turbo-charged diesel engine and automatic transmission, are going to end up in the bottom of Stony Creek. And if you don't stop this vehicle right now, you and those ridiculous coins will be down there with it!" His last words were barely spoken before Maxwell franticly put the plastic inhaler to his mouth and drew a desperately needed breath of air.

The driver, still unable to believe what he was hearing, looked over his shoulder at the boy gasping for air and searched for some indication that the kid was telling the truth.

"If you don't believe me, read those signs ahead," Maxwell panted. "That will prove we're telling the truth."

The headlights sped by a large, yellow, diamond-shaped sign that read: BRIDGE CLOSED. Only seconds later, they passed another small sign: FOOT TRAFFIC ONLY. For a brief moment there was hope that the ambulance was slowing down, but it kept racing forward.

Baxter took off his visor and threw it on the floor. Was this guy deaf or what? He looked at the burned face in the mirror one more time, and without a moment's hesitation, started yelling. "Have you heard a word my friend said? He wouldn't be wasting his last breath of air if he didn't think we were all about to die. If you don't stop this ambulance right now, we're going to end up in the bottom of the river, and you can kiss those stupid coins goodbye."

Pete held his revolver above his head and pulled the trigger. The blast shot a hole in the roof and shook the ambulance like a flash-bang grenade. Their ears rang and the smell of gunpowder filled their nostrils. "Go ahead. Keep it up, kid, 'cause the next one's for you."

Maxwell's hands shook as beads of sweat rolled down his forehead. Nudging Baxter's side, he pointed toward the oxygen tank next to him, knowing if that bullet had hit the tank, they all would have been blown off the face of the earth. Horrified at what was about to happen, Maxwell's face fell into the palms of his hands.

Baxter sank forward in his seat. He had done all he could. He searched the blank stare that had glazed over the eyes in the rearview mirror. The man's almost lifeless expression hadn't changed, and neither had their chances of survival. The driver hadn't listened to a word they said.

As his fear turned to hopelessness, he held on to Tommy, regretting the promise he had made his friend to take care of the little boy.

Out of the dark abyss emerged one last large, yellow and black metal sign: DEAD END. Without thinking, Baxter lunged forward. Grabbing the captor's shoulders with both hands, he screamed at the top of his lungs, "S-S-S-S-S-T-O-P-P-P-P!"

His blood-curdling yell hit Pete like a bolt of lightning, jolting him from his seat. Riveting pain ran through his body as his head cracked against the steering wheel, and then back against the seat. Instinctively, he stomped on the brakes until they squealed like a wild boar.

The four of them were hurled in all directions as the vehicle fell into an uncontrollable skid. The oxygen tank crashed against the door, snapping the valve upon impact. The seeping gas from the broken valve began to fill the ambulance. The vehicle continued to swerve out of control, its yellow headlights still unwilling to reveal its final resting place.

CHAPTER THIRTY-NINE

They Always Come Back

Hank kicked open the back door, slamming it against the wall. He maneuvered around the broken pieces of furniture as he tore through the dark kitchen. Hollering Tommy's name, he ran down the dark hallway and up the stairs. He broke open the first door. In the middle of the empty room lay Tommy's blue stocking hat. Hank called out Tommy's name again, but there was no response. Hank crumpled to his knees. "Not my own grandson... Please, not Tommy."

Reaching the top of the steps, Paigenot saw Hank kneeling in the middle of the empty room. *We can't have lost Tommy again*, Bill thought. He charged down the hall, calling the little boy's name. Shoulder-butting one door open after the other, he found each room as empty as the last.

Bill raced back down the hall. "Venema wasn't in the truck, Hank. He's on the loose again and he must have Tommy. Come on, Hank, think. He's only a step ahead of us. We can still get him. What did Victor say? What's his next move?"

Hank had learned more about Victor Venema that night than during the entire Decker investigation. "The coins. It's the gold coins, Bill. This isn't about Tommy. And it wasn't about Alex Decker. He's after the gold coins. Somehow, these kids just keep getting in his way. I say he headed back to the grandkids' house and took Tommy to show him where the coins are hidden. Tommy is his last chance to find the treasure."

The two men charged down the stairs and into the night. Hank's lungs burned as he raced through the cold night air. *I'm going to find Venema if it's the last thing I do. He's going to pay for everything he's done.*

Paigenot was the first to reach the clearing. "Hank, your pickup is gone."

"He must have found the extra set of keys under the mat. We can still catch him. That old clunker is on its last leg. He's lucky he got the thing moving." Hank was already climbing into the squad car. "That scoundrel has to be on his way back to the house. There's no way he'll leave Esterville without those coins."

Flicking on the squad car's emergency lights, Bill squealed onto Stony Creek Road and sped toward Esterville. The ride seemed endless. The two men sat side by side without saying a word. The unbroken silence only compounded their feeling of helplessness.

Bill Paigenot finally spoke. "Hank, the Decker case was six months ago. How does Victor Venema kidnapping Tommy tie in with Alex Decker?"

"Alex Decker died with a gold coin clutched in his hand. Mary found a similar coin in Tommy's room tonight. Venema is looking for these coins. He must have had them stashed somewhere, and somehow Alex Decker stumbled across them. From there the only thing I can figure is Alex had them hidden at his house, and Tommy found them."

"Why did Venema wait six months to come after the coins?"

"There could be a number of reasons. Maybe he decided to lay low after Alex's death, or for all we know a scum like him could have been locked up doing time somewhere. If we ran a check on him, I bet we'd learn a lot. Doesn't matter where he's been. People like him don't leave something as valuable as those coins behind. They always come back."

"So Victor Venema was at the house tonight looking for the coins?"

"Yup. Caught him in the grandson's bedroom, but the scoundrel still didn't have the coins."

"He probably never intended to kidnap Tommy or Alex, did he?"

"I don't think so. Both those kids just got in his way. I bet he broke into the house this afternoon to find the coins, and ran into Tommy. Once he thought Tommy could identify him, he had a whole new set of problems. You should have seen the look on Venema's face when I found him tonight. He was desperate. If he decides Tommy can't help him find the coins, I don't know what he'll do. Now facing kidnapping and murder charges, he's got nothing to lose, and that makes him capable of anything."

Bill picked up the scanner and radioed the precinct for extra help. He could only hope they still had a chance to capture Victor Venema, and he was going to do everything he could to make that happen.

CHAPTER FORTY

A Lifeline to Safety

Rock and dirt spewing from the back tires of the ambulance bombarded Sam as he hid along the dirt road. Trying to catch his breath, he waited for the wreckage to come to a stop.

He watched the red brake lights soar into the night. Sheer momentum propelled the ambulance through the darkness. A thunderous boom shook the bridge as it smashed through the metal barrier that blocked the worn-out bridge. The ambulance soared over a mound of rubble, bounced off the ground, and rocketed into the air.

Worn-out railroad ties shattered as the raging vehicle came crashing back down onto the bridge. Broken pieces of wood flew in every direction, the tracks vanishing behind the vehicle as it swerved across the bridge.

One of the bridge's main trestles broke loose, ricocheting against the side of the wooden bridge before plummeting to the river below. The force of the trestle hitting the bridge rocked the ambulance from one side of the tracks to the other. The ambulance slammed against the large wooden guardrail, forcing it to its final stop in the middle of the bridge.

The night camouflaged what was left of the bridge, making the vehicle look like it was suspended in midair. The red taillights flickered, as if trying to divulge the peril it had just survived.

Sam held his breath, waiting for its fatal plunge, but the ambulance sat silently high above the Stony Creek like a wild animal caught in its snare. He snuck to the edge of the bridge and stared across the black ravine that lay between him and his friends. "What am I supposed to do now?"

Sam looked at the last of the support beams still attached to the annihilated bridge and knew the answer to his own question. Unable to see the river below, the sound of the rapid currents crashing against the rocky banks cautioned him of the risk he was about to take.

The Great Schnauzer wagged his tail, telling Sam he was ready to go.

"No, you're staying here. I'm not even sure if I can make it out there."

Refusing the order, Patton stood fast in his ready position.

"I said no, Patton! This is my last chance to save those guys. I can't screw it up. You are going to stay right here."

Patton barked.

"If Paige was here, you would listen to her." For a second Sam thought about Paige riding back to town in the darkness, and hoped she was safe and bringing help. "Now lie down, boy. I have to go."

The Great Schnauzer finally conceded, and obeyed the command.

Sam took a long cable that Maxwell had coiled up in his utility pouch and anchored it to a tree. "This won't get me the whole way across, but it's long enough for me to find out if that beam is going to hold me."

Hooking the other end around his waist, he inched his way onto the wooden girder. Timidly joggling the beam beneath his foot, he tested its stability. He froze as a loud cre-e-e-a-k shot across the bridge, but the beam held. He took a deep breath and headed toward the ambulance.

The turbulent waters of the Stony Creek roared as they hit the rocks below. The wind swirled, tugging and pulling Sam in all directions. He clutched a wooden beam that ran alongside the bridge, trying to steady himself. *Don't look down, whatever you do*, he told himself.

He looked over his shoulder at Patton, who already seemed miles away. The end of the metal cable wrapped around his waist, linking him to safety, faded into the night. Suspended high in the air and consumed by the darkness, he knew he had to keep moving forward no matter what the risks. "Give me the strength to do this," he prayed. "I can't fail them now."

It seemed like only another second before he felt the end of the cable yanking at his waist. His hand shook as he unhooked the safety line. Wrapping one arm around the wooden beam, he dropped the metal cable.

Splinters ripped into his hands as he felt his way along the worn-out timber. He wiped the sweat from his brow and closed his eyes, trying to find his courage. "Don't give up now. You can do this. You're almost there," he whispered to himself. His breathing slowed as he continued his trek to save his friends.

Finally reaching the middle of the bridge, Sam crawled across the shattered ties and crouched behind the ambulance. The driver's door swung open.

The driver glared at his passengers in the rearview mirror. "I'm getting out to see if the bridge is gonna hold us. If you kids want to live to see tomorrow, stay right where you are, and don't move a muscle." Pete slid from the driver's seat and onto the bridge.

Sam waited until the man began walking across the ties, before he maneuvered around to the driver's side of the ambulance. Still huddled on the floor, the four of them gasped as Sam peered over the driver's seat.

"Sam! What are you doing here?" Baxter whispered.

"I don't have time to explain. This bridge is going to collapse any second. You guys gotta get out of here while you have the chance. If you climb out the rear door, hopefully he won't see you."

Sam quietly snuck around the vehicle and opened the back door to help his friends out of the ambulance. Mere inches from the side of the bridge, they stood motionless, looking at the destruction that had taken place only moments earlier.

Baxter was the last to climb out, holding Tommy in his arms. "I told you Sam would come back for you," Baxter whispered in the little boy's ear as Tommy grabbed his brother's hand.

It was almost over. There was just one last step before his brother was safe. "You guys have to crawl across that beam to get off this bridge. That's how I got out here. If you go one at a time, it should hold you."

Maxwell shook his head. "What do you mean, hold us? You're coming with us, Sam."

"I'll meet up with you in a little bit. As long as I have this, he'll let you guys alone." Sam held up the precious bag of coins that he found lying on the front seat. "Now get going."

Baxter released Tommy's fingers from Sam's hand. "Come on, little guy. We gotta get you to safety."

One by one, they crawled onto the ledge that led across the open water. Marco looked back at Sam. "Hurry, Sam, we can't lose you now."

Sam tried to smile. "Don't worry, Marco. You guys can't get rid of me that easily."

As his friends inched their way across the weathered beam, a gunshot exploded. The bullet ricocheted off the bridge only inches above Maxwell's head. "Stop right there, or I'll shoot every last one of you." Pete groaned as he tried to move toward the ambulance. The pain in his legs was crippling. He was out of strength. The gun was his only means left to stop them.

Another shot rang out. A second wood beam broke loose, crashing against the bridge as it fell. The impact knocked Maxwell to his knees. Grappling for the side of the bridge with both hands, he slowly pulled himself to his feet.

"Hurry. You guys can make it. I'll be right behind you." Sam watched his friends inch their way along the worn-out beam.

Stepping out from behind the ambulance, Sam waved the leather pouch full of coins in the air. "You're not going to shoot anyone, if you still want to get your hands on these. Fire that gun one more time, and I'm dropping your precious treasure into the Stony Creek."

"Where did you come from?" the man wailed as he waved his gun at Sam.

Sam didn't move. "Lay down your gun and start walking toward the far end of the bridge. When my friends have gotten across that beam, I'll put the bag down, and you can come and get it."

"It's taken months for me to get those coins from Victor; you're not stoppin' me now." Pete made his move toward the ambulance.

Instantly, Sam sprang to the edge of the bridge and dangled the treasure over the rapids. "I'm not kidding. One more step and you've lost your coins."

Pete stopped in his tracks. "Okay, kid, okay. Just move away from the edge of the bridge."

"Then put your gun down and get going. Start walking to the other side of the bridge right now, or I'm dropping them." Sam shook the bag in the air, making the coins jangle.

Pete's body ached. His raw skin burned. He had almost died for those coins. It would all be for nothing if he lost the treasure now. Tightening the grip on his pistol, he took a couple of steps back and stopped. *If I can get the kid to move away from the edge, maybe I can gain control. Until then I'll pretend to go along with his demands.*

For every step Pete took away from the ambulance, Sam took another step in the opposite direction and closer to the planks that led him to safety. He looked over his shoulder and saw his friends working their way across the bridge. He wanted to join them, but he had to make sure they got away. He fought his urge to run, and shook the leather bag high in the air. "Keep going, Mister. You can move faster than that. And I'm not telling you again to put the gun down."

Out of nowhere, yellow headlights flooded the bridge. Pete spun around. The blinding red and yellow emergency lights of Bill Paigenot's squad car exploded in the darkness. A unit of officers lined the entrance on the far end of the bridge, blocking Pete's escape.

He was trapped.

From the far side of the bridge, a loud voice echoed from behind the blazing lights. "Drop your gun and walk toward us. Do it now! It's over!"

Pete shielded his eyes and turned away from the glaring lights. "That's what you think, sucker. It's far from over." Dropping to his knees, he scrambled to the ambulance and climbed inside. He aimed the gun at the blinding lights and fired.

The .45-caliber slug ripped through the ambulance, igniting the seeping oxygen that had silently filled the cabin. The vehicle exploded into an enormous ball of flames as the entire bridge skyrocketed into the air, before collapsing into the cold, dark waters of the Stony Creek below.

The brilliant lights of the blast silhouetted the shadowy figures on either side of where the bridge once stood. There was no trace of the ambulance, Pete Peterson, or the young man who had risked his life to save his brother and his friends.

CHAPTER FORTY-ONE

A Shifty Devil's Double-cross

His ears were ringing, and his body ached. He squeezed his eyes shut till his teeth hurt, too afraid to open them. He lay without moving, wondering where he was and what had happened.

Then he remembered, and panic hit him like a bolt of lightning. "The explosion!" He covered his ears, wishing the ringing would stop. Another shot of terror raced through his body as visions of the blinding lights erupted.

A voice echoed from somewhere above him. "You're all right, Baxter. Open your eyes."

He covered his face with his hands, unwilling to look.

The voice was familiar, and the warmth of the hand on his shoulder comforting. His courage was returning. Baxter slowly let out a long sigh of relief as he opened his eyes and saw Hank's face come into focus.

Without thinking, Baxter jumped to his feet, spinning in all directions. "Where's Tommy?"

Hank put his arm around Baxter's shoulder. "Tommy's safe, Baxter. Thanks to you. He's with his mother right now."

Baxter turned toward the lights of the VW. Tommy was in the front seat, cradled in his mother's arms. Marco, Maxwell, and Paige were close by.

"Sam!" He turned to Hank. "Where's Sam?"

Hank shook his head. "The oxygen tanks in the ambulance must have been leaking. When the gun went off, the whole thing blew sky high. There's nothing left of the bridge or the ambulance. We still can't believe you kids got off the bridge in time." Hank hung his head. "Sam didn't make it."

"Sam didn't make it?" Baxter repeated. Tears ran down his cheeks as he fell limp to the ground. Hank sat down next to Baxter and pulled him close, trying to absorb the boy's pain.

"We would have all been in that ambulance when it exploded if it wasn't for Sam." Baxter choked on his tears. "He's the one who saved us. He was supposed to go back into town for help, but if he had, no one would have rescued us. Sam showed up just in time. He got us off the bridge before it blew up. We would all be dead right now if it wasn't for him."

Baxter's face fell into his hands as he thought about his friend's courage. *How could I let Sam stay on the bridge with that madman? Sam should have left with the rest of us, and I should have made sure he did.*

Overcome with grief, Baxter envisioned the determination on Sam's face as he rescued them from the annihilated bridge and the grasp of a crazed monster. He rubbed the tears from his eyes and looked closer at the image of his friend, as the sound of Sam's voice resonated from the vision.

"Do you think a guy could get some help around here?" Weak from the explosion, Sam collapsed face-down in the dirt.

"Sam!" Baxter ran to his friend and pulled him into the clearing. His face was blackened and his clothes ripped to shreds. He was soaked to the bone.

Hank wrapped his jean jacket around his grandson and held him tight, trying to stop the boy from shaking. "We thought you were dead, Sam. How could you possibly survive that explosion?"

"When the headlights lit up the bridge, that burned guy turned around to see where the lights were coming from. It was the chance I needed. I jumped onto the plank and scrambled to shore. The wire cable I used to cross the bridge had caught on one of the trestles. I barely had it wrapped around me when the explosion hit. The bridge blew right out from under me." Sam closed his eyes, still trying to catch his breath. "I'm not sure what happened after that. Next thing I remember is waking up on shore with the cable still around my waist." Sam's head fell onto Hank's chest. "Grandpa, is Tommy all right?"

"Your brother is safe, Sam. He's with your mother."

Tears filled Sam's eyes. "What about everyone else, Grandpa? Is Paige okay?"

"Relax, Sam. Everyone is safe."

Relief filled his body and tears fell down his cheeks. He had rescued his friends and saved his brother. Huddled in his grandfather's arms, Sam thought about Alex Decker, the boy whose tragic death began his journey, and wondered if the two of them would have been friends. In that moment a blond, freckle-faced boy standing behind the VW smiled a grin filled full of braces and waved to Sam as he turned to walk away.

Before Sam could respond, Hank pulled his grandson close to him. "We have to get you home, Sam, before you catch your death of cold." Hank carefully helped his grandson to his feet and started walking toward the VW.

"But Grandpa…" Sam stopped to look for the blond-haired boy again, but he was gone.

Baxter couldn't contain his excitement one more second. Wrapping his arms around Sam, he picked him up and yelped, "Ye-e-o-o-w! I can't believe you're okay, Sam!"

Baxter's one-of-a-kind yelps instantly caught Marco's attention, and he ran to join his two friends' celebration. With the three of them jumping up and down, The Great Schnauzer Patton was not going to be left out, and with one deep growl, he jumped into Sam's arms and began licking his face until slobber ran down Sam's chin.

Sam laughed and wiped his chin. "I can't believe I made it either. Grandpa, how did you find us?"

"Chief Paigenot and I were at the Miller place searching for Tommy. Luckily, we passed Paige on Stony Creek Road on our way back into town."

Sam groaned. "Grandpa, you were out here tonight and you didn't know we were here?"

"We were on the other side of the property, son. The woods are so thick we had no idea you were there." Hank shook his head in disbelief. "Less than a half mile between us, and we didn't have a clue what was happening to you kids."

Sam grabbed onto his grandfather's arm. "But you did find us, Grandpa. You were here when we needed you the most."

"We can thank Paige for that. She told us what happened and got us over to this side of the property. When we didn't pass the ambulance on our way here, we gambled on the chance that it was headed down the dirt road toward the bridge."

At that moment, Sam saw Paige talking with her mom. "Grandpa, I need a second and then I'll be ready to go home." Sam walked up behind Paige and took her hand in his, slowly turning Paige toward him.

"Sam! You're alive!" Paige wrapped her arms around Sam and kissed him. "I knew you would make it."

"Paige, I was so worried when you left to go into town. I can't believe you're okay."

Paige held Sam's hands as she told him what happened. "My dad dropped your grandfather and me off on this side of the bridge. Then dad crossed the river down at Miller Street and backtracked to the other side of the bridge, hoping to stop that guy from escaping. And you know what happened after that."

Sam smiled. There was a special bond between the two of them. He could feel it. "Thanks, Paige. I knew you would bring help."

Bill Paigenot's squad car pulled up beside his daughter and Sam. He turned off the engine and climbed out of his squad car with a big smile on his face. "Looks like everyone survived the explosion after all."

Hank ruffled Sam's hair. "When things settle down, these kids are going to have some explaining to do. Last thing I remember, they were supposed to be waiting for us at home in the kitchen."

Sam hung his head, wondering if his feelings of guilt would ever go away. So much had happened and he felt responsible for all of it.

Hank put his arm around Sam and pulled him close. "Life is full of choices, Sam. Hopefully, we all learn from those choices and make better ones the next time."

Paige looked at her dad. He had that 'glad you're not hurt but wait till we get home' look on his face. She tried smiling at him, but a cringe was the best she could do. She knew she had let him down. *It's not easy to make the right decision. Sometimes you have to follow your heart even when your head knows better*, she thought. She looked at Sam and smiled. It felt good to know they had rescued Tommy and everyone had survived the night.

Maxwell was already speaking to an ever-growing crowd of reporters. The lights from the first news media to arrive on the scene flooded the area. While holding his glasses in his left hand, Maxwell used his right hand to help emphasize how various pieces of evidence led them to the carnival and eventually to the Miller mansion; into the hands of the kidnapper and murderer; and especially to the bag of gold coins.

Paige heard Maxwell saying, "Sam Rogers, Tommy's older brother and our good friend, never gave up searching for his little brother. Even when the bridge exploded and we thought it was his dying moment, Sam never stopped putting the safety of his brother and friends first…"

Paige knew Maxwell was in his element. *None of us could give a more thorough, more honest account of what happened tonight than Maxwell Vanderbilt*, she thought.

"Just got a call on the radio," Bill reported. "They stopped Victor in your pickup outside of Pittsburgh."

"If they found Venema in Pittsburgh, then who was the guy in the ambulance?"

"When we gave the police up in Pittsburgh the kids' description of the guy driving the ambulance, Victor told them right away who it was: his good buddy, the cook, Pete Peterson, alias Chef Pierre."

"So the two of them were in cahoots together? Hard to find anyone more evil than those two."

"No, they weren't working together. Victor says Pete stole the coins out from under him. Sounds like he really lost it when he heard Pete had the missing treasure. Victor was convinced Pete was actually trying to turn his life around by becoming a chef."

"Venema looked all over for those coins, and here Pete Peterson had them the whole time." Hank smirked. "I would have liked to be there when he found out his good buddy two-timed him."

Bill nodded. "He sang like a bird. Said he stole them from an old lady up in Johnstown. She died before she ever knew Victor took them. Then he stashed them under the floor of the Miller house while he looked for someone to buy them. Somehow, Alex Decker stumbled across the coins and Victor's problems began."

"So Victor Venema did confess to Alex Decker's murder?"

"He says it was an accident; that the kid fell off the bridge. We'll have to get his story down before we can sort out the facts."

The Decker case was finally solved. Hank thought about Alex's senseless death and the pain that Victor Venema had caused the boy's family. "Where was Victor during the investigation?"

"He was doing six months for drunk driving. Got sent up before he could recover the coins. He came back to Esterville to find them as soon as he got out of prison, but Pete Peterson beat him to it."

"How does Pete Peterson fit into this?" Hank asked.

"The two of them were cellmates. Victor says he told him the whole story, hoping Pete would help him find a buyer for the coins once he got them back."

Hank pictured Victor crawling out of Tommy's closet empty-handed. "Only Victor never did get them back."

"Pete must have been one step ahead of his good buddy the whole way. Found the coins, and was going to skip town without Victor knowing he had them."

Hank put his arm around Sam's shoulders and started walking toward the VW. "Shifty devil double-crossed his own cellmate."

Sam shook his head. It had been a long night. "I still can't believe he killed Alex and kidnapped Tommy over some stupid coins, Grandpa."

"Money makes some people do evil things, Sam." Hank shook his head in disbelief. "Well, those coins are long gone now. No one's ever going to find them after that explosion."

"Maybe not, Grandpa." Sam pulled the leather pouch filled with coins out of the pocket of his baggy jeans. "I took this off the front seat of the ambulance. I used it to lure that guy away from the gang and to keep him from killing us."

Baxter's mouth dropped wide open. "Sam, you're rich! Is that awesome, or what? You can buy a new dirt bike, get those Nike Airs you've wanted, take us to the movies every night…"

"Not so fast, Baxter." Bill Paigenot took the pouch from Sam. "I'll take those down to headquarters and find out what happened to the rest of the estate. But you kids might be interested in knowing there is a reward for information leading to the arrest of the person who kidnapped and killed Alex Decker. We'll let you know what happens with that."

Marco grabbed Baxter's arm. "A reward, Bax! Can you believe it? Just think how much that will be! We can split it five ways!"

Bill and Hank looked at each other, shook their heads, and started laughing.

Sam thought about the coin he saw in Tommy's hand, and the one Mrs. Paigenot found in his room. "I wonder if there are still more gold coins at home, Grandpa." Sam reached through the window of the VW and grabbed his brother's hand. "Where did you find those coins, Squirt?"

"I told you. Al-ex Deck-er gave them to me."

Sam thought about the freckle-faced, blond-haired boy and wondered if what Tommy said was possible. Shaking his head in disbelief, Sam smiled at his little brother. "After all of this, and I still can't get a straight answer from you. Alex Decker is dead, Tommy. He couldn't have given you those coins."

"Oh yeah-h-h-h. Well, who do you think gave me the yel-low gog-gles, Sam?"

"You probably just found them in the attic somewhere, Squirt."

Tommy looked at his big brother and smiled. "Al-ex told me you would say that."

Printed in the USA
CPSIA information can be obtained
at www.ICGtesting.com
CBHW031304050724
11009CB00007B/626